Love's Unending Legacy

Books by Janette Oke

www.janetteoke.com

CANADIAN WEST

When Calls the Heart   When Breaks the Dawn
When Comes the Spring   When Hope Springs New

Beyond the Gathering Storm
When Tomorrow Comes

LOVE COMES SOFTLY

Love Comes Softly   Love's Unending Legacy
Love's Enduring Promise   Love's Unfolding Dream
Love's Long Journey   Love Takes Wing
Love's Abiding Joy   Love Finds a Home

A PRAIRIE LEGACY

The Tender Years   A Quiet Strength
A Searching Heart   Like Gold Refined

SEASONS OF THE HEART

Once Upon a Summer   Winter Is Not Forever
The Winds of Autumn   Spring's Gentle Promise

SONG OF ACADIA★

The Meeting Place   The Birthright
The Sacred Shore   The Distant Beacon
The Beloved Land

WOMEN OF THE WEST

The Calling of Emily Evans   A Bride for Donnigan
Julia's Last Hope   Heart of the Wilderness
Roses for Mama   Too Long a Stranger
A Woman Named Damaris   The Bluebird and the Sparrow
They Called Her Mrs. Doc   A Gown of Spanish Lace
The Measure of a Heart   Drums of Change

★with T. Davis Bunn

JANETTE OKE

Love's Unending Legacy

BETHANY HOUSE
MINNEAPOLIS, MINNESOTA

Love's Unending Legacy
Copyright © 1984, 2004
Janette Oke

Newly edited and revised

Cover design by Jennifer Parker

Published by Bethany House Publishers
11400 Hampshire Avenue South
Bloomington, Minnesota 55438

Bethany House Publishers is a division of
Baker Publishing Group, Grand Rapids, Michigan.

Printed in the United States of America

ISBN   978-0-7642-2852-0

Library of Congress Cataloging-in-Publication Data

Oke, Janette, 1935–
    Love's unending legacy / by Janette Oke.— Newly edited and rev.
      p. cm. — (Love comes softly ; bk. 5)
    ISBN 0-7642-2852-8 (pbk.)
      1. Davis family (Fictitious characters : Oke)—Fiction. 2. Accident victims—Fiction.
I. Title. II. Series: Oke, Janette, 1935–   . Love comes softly series ; bk. 5

    PR9199.3.038 L67   2004
    813'.54—dc22   2003023479

Dedicated with love
to my third sister, Amy June Wilson,
who, because of her gentle
disposition, made it possible for
me to have one sister with whom I didn't fight as a kid.
We have shared many good times—often
with the help of the old pump organ.

And to my talented brother-in-law,
John F. Wilson

JANETTE OKE was born in Champion, Alberta, to a Canadian prairie farmer and his wife, and she grew up in a large family full of laughter and love. She is a graduate of Mountain View Bible College in Alberta, where she met her husband, Edward, and they were married in May of 1957. After pastoring churches in Indiana and Canada, the Okes spent some years in Calgary, where Edward served in several positions on college faculties while Janette continued her writing. She has written over four dozen novels for adults and children, and her book sales total nearly thirty million copies.

The Okes have three sons and one daughter, all married, and are enjoying their dozen grandchildren. Edward and Janette are active in their local church and make their home near Didsbury, Alberta.

Visit Janette Oke's Web site at: *www.janetteoke.com*.

Contents

ONE

Homecoming

Marty's trembling hand pushed back a wisp of wayward hair from her warm, moist face as she peered once more out the window. Why was she shaking so? Was it because they had been bouncing hour after long hour in the seemingly slow-moving stagecoach, or was it her intense excitement at the prospect of once again being home? Marty made an effort to still her hand—and the tumult within her. Her slight movement must have caught Clark's eye. Though busy talking with a fellow passenger about the need for rain, he reached for Marty's hand, and she felt the pressure of his fingers, his unspoken message that he understood—not only her weariness, but her impatient longing to be home again, as well. She returned the squeeze, assuring him that she was all right in spite of her overwhelming desire for the trip to end. Clark gave her a quiet smile, then turned again to the man who was speaking. Marty leaned forward for the umpteenth time to get a better look out the small stagecoach window.

They were in familiar territory now. Marty recognized the landmarks, but they only served to make her more distressed with their slow progress. Oh, how she pined to be home again—to see the dear children whom she had not seen for so many months! Though her body was physically exhausted, her eagerness to come to the end of this journey had her sitting on the edge of her seat— every nerve and muscle vibrating with her concentrated energy. *Home! I want to get home!* She clutched at the door handle as the coach lurched through another pothole.

Clark turned from his conversation with the black-suited gentleman and gave her another understanding smile. "Won't be long now," he assured her, looking over her shoulder at the landscape. "Thet's Anderson's Corner just up ahead."

Marty knew he was right. Still, she told herself, it would seem forever before the stagecoach finally pulled to a dusty stop outside their local livery. She wondered if she would be able to keep herself in check for these last endless miles. In an effort to do so, she set her thoughts to imagining what lay ahead. Who would be there to meet them? Would firstborn Clare be the one driving the family team? Would he have his Kate with him? Or would it be Arnie who would be waiting for them? Would their youngest, Luke, be along?

Marty's thoughts switched to her home. Would it seem strange to her when she walked through the door? Would she feel she was entering the abode of someone else, or would she still have the delightful sense of fully belonging there? Would Ellie have supper waiting, impatient with the fact that the stagecoach was almost an hour overdue and things would be overcooked as the dishes waited on the back of the large, homey kitchen stove?

Marty thought of the farmyard, the garden, her chickens clucking about the pen, the spring, and the woods. She could hardly wait to see them all again. *Here I am, a grown woman, actin' like Lukey when he was a little shaver waitin' for an egg to hatch.* She smiled to herself.

She stretched her legs in an effort to relieve some of the stiffness from the long ride. Her glance fell on Clark's one booted foot placed firmly on the floor, and she knew his long leg must be even more cramped than her short ones. She did not look at the other side, the pinned-up leg of his trousers. *At least that one isn't complainin' about more room!* Clark had showed her how to treat his handicap lightly. *But it must ache, too, after this long period of forced inactivity,* she reasoned and wondered if Clark was suffering any pain with the shortened limb.

Clark must have seen her glance and read her question. He shifted his position and spoke to her. "Really takin' this jostlin' fairly well," he said, patting his thigh. "It will be as glad as the rest of me to be out of this rockin' stage, though. Seems we been shut in here 'most a lifetime."

Marty nodded and tried another smile in spite of the fact that she was hot and dusty and longed to be out in some clean, fresh air. Even the switch to the old farm wagon for those last few miles would be a welcome one.

Marty leaned for another look out the window and discovered they had covered some good distance since her last check. Right up ahead lay the last bend in the road before the small community they called *their town* would come into view. A quiver of excitement passed all through her—oh, to be home again! During the long trip home by train and stage, she realized just how much she had missed it—had missed all of them.

Her thoughts returned to Missie and Willie, Nathan and Josiah. How wonderful it had been to spend the time with them. She had learned to love and appreciate the West along with Willie's ranch and the men who lived and worked on it. She wondered how Cookie was doing. Was he progressing in his newly discovered faith? She remembered Wong and his last-minute gift of baking for their train trip home. And there was Scottie, the kind and patient man who needed to allow God to work in his life. She thought of the bitter Smith and hoped that it wasn't just wishful thinking on her part that the man's attitude was beginning to soften. Perhaps one day he would even venture to attend the Sunday services in the new church. Marty's thought of the new church brought all sorts of memories of the many people with whom they had worshiped and grown to love as neighbors and friends. How was Henry doing as he led the little flock in Bible study? Were the Crofts still coming faithfully, and had they found the peace that

Mrs. Croft especially had so longingly searched for? Did Juan and Maria. . . ? And then the stagecoach driver was yelling "whoa" to his horses, and the stage was sliding to a halt in a whirl of dust.

Marty's whole insides leaped with such eagerness she felt dizzy with the intensity. Clark's hand was supporting her as she struggled to her feet. *Which of the family will be here? How long will it be until we see the others? What if they didn't get the message of our coming and no one is here to meet the stage? How can I ever bear the extra hours until we can find some way home?* Her thoughts clamored for answers. Dared she look beyond the stagecoach door?

Momentarily she shut her eyes and steadied her jangled nerves with a little prayer. Clark's firm grip on her arm calmed her. She took a deep breath and sat back down to allow the other passengers to leave the coach ahead of her, then waited for Clark to step down so he might help her as she left the coach, now finally stationary. She felt as if she were still moving—swaying slightly with the roll of the stage. Marty steadied herself, reaching for Clark's outstretched hand, and stepped down as gracefully and calmly as she could. And then the air around her seemed to explode in cries and blurred movement as family members swept toward her. Marty was passed from one pair of arms to another, crying and laughing as she held each one close. They were all there. Clare and his Kate; Arnie, Ellie, and Luke; Josh and Nandry and the children. Only Joe and Clae were missing—missing because they were still in the East, with little Esther Sue, where Joe was finishing up his seminary training.

Marty finished the round of hugs and turned to hug them all again. Wiping away tears of joy, she stood back to marvel at how much the grandchildren had grown, how pretty and grown-up Ellie looked, how Luke didn't look like a boy anymore, and how tall and manly her two oldest sons appeared. They had changed, her family. In just one short—and long—year, they had changed so much. Josh was shaking Clark's hand now and telling him how much he had been missed. Marty saw anxious glances at Clark's pinned-up pants leg, and she knew that this was a difficult and emotional time for her family. Clark put them all at ease as he expertly maneuvered his crutch and picked up some of their belongings.

"'Member how we left this place? Stuff piled up high till I wondered iffen the poor horses would be able to pull the load. Well, we came back with far less than we left with." He grinned and slapped his short leg. "Even lightened *me* up a bit fer the return trip," he quipped.

The boys laughed some, and the tension eased. The menfolk started in on the luggage and soon had it moved to the waiting wagon.

Marty turned again to the girls. "Oh, it's so *good* to be home! It's such a long trip, an' I have so much to talk 'bout I'm fair burstin'." Then she spoke to Ellie. "Thought you'd be home stewin' 'bout the stagecoach bein' so slow an' ruinin' yer supper."

"We got together an' decided to just this once be real extravagant," said Ellie, her lovely face and smile warming Marty's heart once more. "We knew you'd be tired after yer long ride, and we thought ya might need a little break before climbin' in the wagon an' headin' on home. 'Sides, we're all anxious fer some talkin' time, so we decided to meet in town an' eat together at the hotel."

Marty was surprised but, after mulling it over quickly in her mind, agreed with their decision. It would be good to just stretch a little and then enjoy a meal with the family. She would simply put off the reunion with her home and its familiar surroundings.

Marty turned to talk with Nandry, but the young woman was standing as though transfixed, watching the men move off toward the waiting wagon. The grown boys appeared to jostle for position beside their father, all talking and laughing at once. It was obvious they shared the joy of having him back. Nandry's Josh, too, walked with them, carrying their youngest, Jane, along with them. Andrew bustled along with the men, hoisting high Marty's prized hatbox. But it was on Clark that Nandry's eyes were fastened, and

Marty saw deep pain in her face. Marty wanted to assure Nandry that it was all right, that the stump of leg no longer gave Clark dreadful discomfort, that he was still able to do all the things he used to do . . . well, almost all the things. He had made the adjustment well, and they had even been able to thank God for the life-changing event in their lives, since so many things had happened for God's glory from the results of the tragedy. But before Marty could even move toward her oldest daughter—this one whom she loved as truly as though hers by birth—Nandry had moved away, the pain in her eyes showing clearly on her troubled face.

It's a shock, thought Marty, *a terrible shock. She needs time to face it an' time to adjust. I didn't bear it very well at first, either.*

Ellie was speaking. "Mama, how is Pa? I know thet he seems . . . well, he seems his old self. Is he really? Does . . . does it bother 'im?"

"Yer pa is fine . . . just fine." Marty hoped her voice would carry to Nandry, who stood silently with her back to the group. "'Course it was hard on all of us. It's hard on you, too . . . I know thet. 'Specially at first. But ain't nothin' much yer pa puts his mind to thet he can't do. He's a big man, yer pa. A little thing like a missin' leg won't slow 'im down much. You'll—"

But Ellie was weeping. Quiet sobs shook her slight frame as large tears streamed unheeded down her cheeks.

Marty crossed quickly to her and held her close, patting her back and rocking her back and forth until Ellie had cried herself dry.

"It's okay," Marty whispered. "I had me a lot of cryin' time, too. It's all right."

Ellie dabbed at her eyes with her handkerchief. "Oh, Mama," she apologized, "I thought I was all through with such like. I promised myself . . . but when I saw 'im . . . when I realized it was really true, I . . ."

Marty held her close. "It's just fine," she assured her again.

"Why, I couldn't begin to tell ya the number of times Missie an' me cried together."

Ellie blew her nose and Kate did, as well. Marty hadn't realized Clare's young wife had also been weeping. She moved to Kate and held her new daughter-in-law for many minutes. Kate clung to her, no doubt sensing the love and strength that were being offered her by this newfound mother-in-law.

Marty turned next to Nandry. Taking the young woman in her arms, Marty could feel a stiffness in her body. No tears flowed. Nandry embraced her in return, but Marty could sense a with-holding there. *Go ahead. Weep,* Marty wished to say. *You'll feel better if you do, and we'll all understand.* But Nandry was drawing away, dry eyed and silent.

The men were returning. Ellie and Kate made another effort to dab at the tears and turned to face the family.

The walk to the hotel dining room was full of loving com-motion. Marty's mind went back to the morning so long ago when they had gathered together to say their good-byes. They had been noisy then, too. In fact, Clark had needed to silence his family in order to get the gathering under control. Just as these thoughts flew through Marty's mind, Clark turned to the chattering throng and held up his free hand. "Hold it," he spoke loudly. "How 'bout we git some order outta this chaos."

Tina, who appeared to have grown many inches, responded as she had a year before. "Oh, Grandpa—"

And Clark finished it for her. "I know . . . I know. How can you organize chatter?" He pulled her pigtail and they both laughed. Tina reached up for the hug she knew would be forth-coming.

Marty laughed, too, a tight little laugh that caught in her throat and brought her pain as well as gladness. *See,* she wanted to say to her gathered family, *nothing has changed—not really—at least nothing that really matters.* But perhaps they all got the message without her saying anything, for Marty noticed the changing expressions on the faces before her—the sorrow, then the acceptance, and finally the relief.

Pa was still Pa. This big man whom they knew and loved was still the same man. His accident had not altered his character. He was still in command. Oh, not of incidents, maybe, but he was in command of himself. He had not allowed something like a missing leg to shape who he was, the person he had become. He was, thankfully, still in control. No, that was not right. Clark had never claimed to be in control. That was the secret. The man who stood before them, the man whom they were blessed enough to call "Pa," the one whom they had loved and respected and learned early to obey, had always assured them that the real secret to life and its true meaning was not to try to take over the controls. The answer to a life of meaning and deep peace was to leave the controls in the hand of the almighty Father. And the fact that *He* was still totally and wisely in control was a fact not a one of them in the close little circle doubted.

Only Nandry, who stood slightly apart with eyes averted from the empty pants leg, seemed to have any doubts at all. Marty watched the expression on her face and knew Nandry was not allowing herself even to recognize any part of the situation. Marty prayed silently for this daughter who had always kept herself rather closed and alone. Nandry would need to deal with this new reality, but she probably couldn't manage it just now.

T W O

Catching Up

When the group reached the hotel dining room, Marty and Clark were pressed on every side by grandchildren who wished to sit as close to them as they could. Only Jane, who had been just a few months old when Clark and Marty left for the West, did not remember them, and she chose to cling to her father, her big blue eyes watching every move of the two strangers. Marty yearned to hold her but held herself in check, wanting to give the child enough time to get acquainted. There would be many days ahead to hold and cuddle her.

Tina, their oldest granddaughter, excitedly told them about her school and gave them a progress report on her schoolwork. Andrew boasted that he, too, was a schoolkid now and insisted on counting to ten to prove it. Mary moved closer against Marty and shyly whispered that she still had to stay home to help her mommy with Janey. Marty put an arm around her and hugged her tight.

"Well," broke in Arnie during a slight lull in the conversation, "let's hear all 'bout the West. Is it really what they claim it to be?"

Marty smiled, and Clark answered Arnie's question. "I have to admit to still preferrin' my spot right here, but the West draws one, fer sure. I can understand why Willie is so fired up 'bout his ranch. People out there are right neighborly, an' the land is wide an' open. Gives ya a feelin' of bein' free like."

"Still miles an' miles of country nobody has claimed?" asked Clare.

"Not much. Once the train tracks arrived, the available land was taken up real quick. Those ranches are so much bigger than the farms here thet one man needs far more land. There doesn't seem to be much acreage left to claim in Willie's area. 'Course, thet still don't mean a great abundance of neighbors, but they do have people all round them now. Ya just ride a ways to reach 'em, thet's all. The town has grown quickly, too. An' now they have their own little church, an' they are startin' school this fall—part-time, anyway, with Melinda teachin'—an', 'course, they have a doctor now, so things are lookin' really good."

Ellie shut her eyes. "Dr. de la Rosa," she said, trying out the unfamiliar-sounding name to herself. "Guess we owe him a lot, huh?"

Clark nodded solemnly. "Yeah," he said. "Guess we do. An' I'm countin' on 'im again, too. Countin' on 'im to safely bring into the world another of my grandchildren."

"Oh yes!" exclaimed Kate. "How is Missie?"

"She's fine. Just wished we could have been there to hold the wee one a bit 'fore headin' on home."

"Well," said Clare, reaching for his wife's hand, "maybe we can help out with thet . . . with a wee one, I mean. We thought maybe we'd just . . ."

"Ya mean. . . ?"

Kate blushed. "Oh, Clare, stop—"

But Clare, not to be deterred, went on. "Not yet," he said to the now-excited group. "We just think it sounds like a real good idea, thet's all. I can't wait to have a son of my own."

Marty sat back in her chair again, feeling a fleeting moment of disappointment. It would be so wonderful to have a grandchild right in her own yard. She wished Clare had actually meant . . .

She checked herself. There was no need to be in a hurry. She smiled at the still-blushing Kate. She was anxious to get to know her daughter-in-law better. "Never mind his teasin' none," Marty assured her. "Clare always has been an awful tease. We know him well enough to pay 'im no mind."

She could see Kate relax, and Marty decided to turn the attention of the group elsewhere.

"An' what of you, Arnie?" she asked, smiling knowingly at her son who sat across from her, acting as if he had no interest in the previous conversation.

"What of me?" Arnie repeated, as though not understanding Marty's question. But Marty could see the slight color creep into Arnie's face, and she knew he understood her well enough.

Ellie giggled. "Go ahead, Arnie. Tell 'em," she encouraged.

Arnie pretended to ignore the whole group and intently studied the pattern of the tablecloth.

In Arnie's defense, Luke spoke up slowly. "She's nice," he stated. "I don't blame Arnie none at all."

"Nor do I," Ellie added, giggling again.

Marty watched her son squirm and decided now was not the time to discuss the issue at hand.

"I will want to hear all 'bout her," she said, "just as soon as we have us a chance to talk. Right now I guess we should be decidin' what we want fer supper."

With the attention taken from Arnie, Marty turned instead to Luke. "I'm anxious to hear what plans you have, son, an' how things have been goin' with Dr. Watkins."

"Great!" was all Luke said, but he put a lot of meaning in the word. Marty assumed that Luke's plans for doctoring had not changed.

Clark turned to Nandry. "When did you last hear from Clae?" he asked.

Nandry busied herself with brushing Mary's already clean front. "About a week ago," she said without returning Clark's gaze.

"Everythin' fine?"

"Seems to be. Joe's almost finished now."

"The last we heard was 'bout a week before we left Missie's," Marty commented. "I was so glad to hear they have the boy they've been wantin'. Nice thet he arrived 'fore they have to make their move, too. Clae wrote about Joe takin' a church in the East, though. I hate the thought. Wish they were comin' back here, but I understand how Joe feels 'bout it. It would be a good experience for 'im, and he could git those extra classes at the same time, iffen it all works out fer 'im," she concluded.

Nandry only nodded.

The white-aproned waitress came for their orders then, and by the time the family group had sorted out what they wanted and the poor, confused-looking girl had left their table, the discussion had turned to other things.

Marty glanced out the window and noticed the sun no longer shone down heartily on the world. It had moved far to the west and before too long would be sinking into bed for the night. She longed to be home before dark so she might see their beloved farm, but she realized now they would not make it in time. Part of the last leg of the trip would be made by moonlight, and the men would do the remaining chores by lantern light. The boys no doubt had done all they could before leaving for town. Marty hoped silently that the meal would not take too long. She forcibly turned her attention back to the conversation, listening to the men talk of the crops, the needed rain, and the outlook for the next harvest. Marty pulled Mary up close against her and smiled across at Tina and Andrew, who sat quietly, one on each side of their grandpa. She let her eyes linger over the faces of all the family who shared the large table and inwardly thanked the Lord for bringing them home safely and for keeping the family in their absence.

Looking at Clark sitting across from her with one hand resting on Andrew's shoulder, she saw the same man with whom she had left the long year before. Marty saw the same strength, the same leadership, the same twinkle of humor, the same depth of character, and the same love for his family. These were the things that really mattered, not the stub of a missing leg beneath the table.

Marty hoped these were the qualities her family saw in the man, too.

————

Just as Marty had suspected, daylight had been long gone by the time they arrived home. She quietly mourned the fact that she could not look around her beloved farm immediately. Though the night was moonlit and cloudless and the stars twinkled brightly overhead, she knew that to stumble around in the semidarkness would be ridiculous. So from her perch in the farm wagon, she contented herself with simply peering through the gathered night at the shapes of the buildings in the yard. She picked out the barn, the henhouse, the first little log home she and Clark and their growing family had shared, now the home of Clare and Kate. With a sigh, she allowed Clark to help her down and followed him to the house, straining as she looked out toward the garden. She wondered just what Ellie and Kate had planted and in what quantity, but the darkness of the night kept its secrets.

Ellie had already lit a bright lamp, and she watched carefully as her mother looked around at her familiar kitchen. There was Marty's beloved stove, her neatly organized cupboards, the large family table that had graced their home for years. The curtains and the pictures on the walls were just as she remembered them. Even the towel bar with its assortment of dishtowels looked the same, and familiar potholders hung from the pegs near the stove. Only the lone calendar on the wall had been changed, it now being a year later than when Marty had left her home. She sighed and turned to smile her pleasure at Ellie.

There was great relief to find everything just as she had left it. Contentment settled over her like a warm comforter. She put down the things she had been carrying and began her home-coming tour, hurrying from room to room. Yes, Ellie had kept it just as it had been. It looked like home—it felt like home. As Marty's eyes flitted over the furnishings, her mind was noting things that needed to be done in the near future. The living room could do with some new wallpaper, and the kitchen woodwork should have some fresh paint. Marty sighed contentedly again; her home still needed her. She must get busy right away and care for it—but not tonight. Suddenly she ached for her own bed. How tired she was! Because of the excitement of getting home, she had not realized her extreme weariness. Well, she knew it now. She secretly wondered if she would find the strength to climb the stairs to her own room.

Clark noticed. His eyes sought hers with an unasked question.

"I'm fine," assured Marty quietly. "Just didn't realize till right this minute how tired I am, I guess. Think I'll just go off to bed and leave the rest of the visitin' fer the morra. Plenty of time to catch up then."

Clark nodded, tucked her cases under one arm, and, with his crutch under the other, expertly maneuvered the stairway.

Marty slowly climbed after him, all her excited energy depleted. She stood at the door of her own bedroom—hers and Clark's. It had been so long since they had slept here. Her eyes lovingly caressed every inch of it. The delicate pattern of the rose wallpaper, the deep, rich look of the polished wood floor, with its thick handmade rugs, the full whiteness of the curtains at the windows, the inviting bed with its quilted coverlet. She loved this room. She wouldn't trade it for any amount of money, even for the rich hotel room where they had stayed on their trip west.

She remembered now that she had forgotten to tell the girls about the hotel room. She hadn't yet told them about her thinking Clark's watch was lost to thieves, or about the night spent with the bedbugs, or the sight of the real western Indians with their furs for sale. There was still so much to talk about, but talk would just have to wait.

Clark had placed her cases in the corner and returned to the family below.

Marty turned at a movement behind her and saw Luke

approaching with the portable bathtub.

"Thought ya might be wantin' to wash off some trail dust before retirin'," he said simply and placed the tub on one of the large rugs in the middle of the floor. "I'll be right back with a couple of pails of warm water."

Marty gazed at their youngest son with deep love. It was just like Luke to realize she would want to soak in the tub before retiring.

True to his word, he was soon back, and Marty thanked him as he emptied the buckets of water into the tub.

"When yer done just leave it sit," Luke said, "an' I'll take care of it in the mornin'."

Marty nodded and Luke started to go. At the door he stopped and turned to her. "Good to have ya home, Ma," he said softly. "Been awfully lonely around here without ya. I missed ya."

"An' I missed *you*," Marty said with emphasis. "I was so afraid you'd be off fer yer trainin' an' me not here to send ya. I was so thankful when ya decided to wait fer a year. I do hope it ain't caused problems fer ya."

Luke smiled. "Did me lots of good, I'm thinkin'. Doc has been a great teacher. Can't believe what he's taught me over the last year. It did somethin' else fer me, too, Ma. There's not a doubt in my mind but thet I want to be a doctor. Some fellas have a hard time at first knowin' fer sure, Doc said, an' then it's a lot of time an' money wasted."

"An' you have no doubt?"

"Nope, none whatever."

"Then yer Pa and me will give ya our blessin'—even though I hate to think of ya goin' so far away."

Luke smiled. "Thanks, Ma," he said. "I'm ready to go now. I wouldn'ta been last year."

He was gone then, and Marty turned to her bath.

Oh, how good it feels! she thought as she climbed in and sank into its warmth. She let it wash away all of the travel grime and the extreme weariness from her aching muscles. A clean, warm night-gown, a few brushstrokes of her hair, and she was ready for her bed.

She had no more crawled in than there was a light tap on her door. After Marty's "Come in," Ellie entered.

"Just had to say good night an' welcome home," she whispered and leaned over to kiss Marty on the cheek. "It's so good to have ya home, Ma. I missed ya."

"An' I missed you. Ellie, I'm proud of the job ya did when I was gone. Everythin' looks so good, so well cared for. Makes me very proud . . . an' a little scared, too."

"Scared?"

"Yeah, scared. I have to admit, an' I hate to, thet yer truly able to make some lucky man a good wife. I don't even want to think of thet, Ellie. I hate to lose ya."

Ellie laughed softly.

"Ma, the worrier," she said as she stroked back a lock of stray hair from Marty's forehead. "Don't ya go frettin' none 'bout thet. I'm in no hurry at all to set up housekeepin' on my own."

"Yer not interested in a home of yer own an'—?"

"Now, I didn't say thet. Sure, I want a home of my own . . . an' a family of my own. I just haven't found the one I wish to share it with yet, thet's all." Then she leaned and kissed Marty's forehead. "Now, you go to sleep an' sleep as long as ya want in the mornin'. I'll care fer the family's breakfast."

Marty was just closing her eyes when again her bedroom door squeaked and Arnie tiptoed over to her bed. Marty forced her eyes to open.

"'Fraid ya might already be sleepin'," Arnie said softly. "Didn't want to waken ya iffen ya were. Clare an' Kate said to tell ya good night for them. They came over to say it in person an' found thet you'd already come up to bed."

"I shoulda thought to wait—"

But Arnie interrupted, "You've had a long, tiring day. Pa says thet yer 'bout beat. He'd chase me outta here right now iffen he knew I was botherin' ya."

Marty smiled.

"I better git," Arnie continued and bent to kiss Marty on the top of her hair. Then he whispered softly, "She's really special, Ma. Yer gonna love her. I'll tell ya all 'bout her tomorra." And Arnie, too, was gone, stepping from her room as quietly as he had come in.

Marty's weary eyes would no longer stay open. Her last thought was of Clark. Where was he? He should be in bed, too. He was just as tired as she was. And then her mind would no longer function, and Marty slipped into a deep and peaceful sleep.

THREE

Taking Stock

Clark's side of the bed was empty but still warm when Marty's eyes first opened next morning. She had not slept late. After the rest received in her own bed, she was ready to get reacquainted with her farm home. As soon as she had enjoyed Ellie's breakfast and helped with the dishes, she went out to the garden. Ellie and Kate had indeed planted it well, with more than they would be able to use. Marty smiled as she looked at the quantity and variety of growing things. She had no argument with the types of vegetables the girls had planted, and there no doubt would be neighbors who would be happy to use some of the extras. The garden was already flourishing and productive looking. Though it was still early in the season, Marty could see the potential for a good yield. Here and there she poked a plant upright or patted some extra earth around it or complimented one on its exceptional size for the time of year.

She turned from the vegetable garden to the flowers. The early blooms were already nodding in the morning breeze, dew-sparkled in the sunlight. Marty breathed deeply of their sweet scent as she moved from plant to plant. Honeybees buzzed about the flowers, sipping sweetness from the open petals.

Marty then went out toward the fruit trees. It had been a good spring for the blossoming, and Marty saw that the trees promised a wonderful harvest if the needed rains arrived in time. She prayed they would as she moved on toward the spring.

The woods were cool and green, and Marty's heart quickened with joy as she inhaled the fresh scent of the trees and the wild flowers beneath them. She hadn't known how deeply she had missed the coolness and the scent of her woods. In Missie's West they had not seen a truly wooded area. Marty stopped and watched a robin as it flew to a nearby limb with a worm in its beak. Soon tiny heads and open beaks appeared and began to chirp in unison to be fed. Marty smiled, but she sympathized with the busy mother.

Down the path she walked until she could hear the soft gurgle of the spring. The stream was down some because of the lack of rain, but the water still ran clear and sparkling. Marty bent to touch its shimmering coolness as it whispered its way across the smooth stones that formed the bottom. How inviting it looked!

Marty reached the spring, lowered herself to the ground, and reached out to trail a hand in the water. It was cold to her touch— so cool, in fact, that it made her fingers cramp. Marty wondered as before at this small miracle. How could waters gurgling forth from this tiny hillside in the woods be so cold? Where did the water come from, and how was it kept so cool in its underground travels? In her mind she could taste the sweetness of the cream and butter as they were lifted from the icy waters, even in midsummer.

She cradled her hand in her apron to restore its warmth and sat still, watching the swiftly flowing water. A woodpecker drilled on a nearby tree. There was a scampering in the grass as a wood mouse scurried past. Marty watched a dragonfly dip and swirl over the creek waters. The woods were teeming with life, much of it out of sight and sound, she knew. She continued her silent vigil, listening and watching for any movement that took place about her.

Marty loved the woods. It was such a refreshing place. Marty needed refreshing. Physically she was still bone weary from the long trip home. Emotionally she was drained from all the excitement of rejoining her family and exploring her beloved home and farm. She'd had many adjustments to make over the last year. She knew that life was full of adjustments; to live meant to change. But Marty, from the depths of her heart, thanked the Lord for the things that stayed constant in a changing world—even things as simple as a quiet stream and a gurgling spring.

And Clark. She smiled and waved as his familiar figure appeared over the hill. She could tell he was concerned about her as he drew near and searched her face for the signs of extreme fatigue that had been there last night.

"Mornin'," he greeted her as he lowered himself to a spot at her side, using his crutch for support. "Ya didn't sleep very long. How ya feelin' today?"

"I'm feelin' some rested an' *so* glad to be home, Clark!" Marty slipped her arm through his. "I'll be good as new in just a few days, 'specially iffen I can sit here by the spring a spell."

"So yer aimin' fer a life a' leisure," he teased, his loving squeeze on her hand belying his words. "Ya just go on sittin' here long as ya like," he assured her. "Ellie's got everythin' well in hand, an' she likes bein' busy."

"Thanks, Clark," Marty said and kissed him good-bye as he rose.

"I'll be gittin' back to the barn," he said, brushing her cheek with his hand. "Ya can sit here till dinnertime iffen ya want."

Yes, Clark is an unchanging part of my life, Marty thought as she watched his tall figure disappear from sight. "Thank ya, Lord," she whispered.

Eventually Marty lifted herself from the grassy bank and headed back toward the bright sunlight and the house. She looked about her as she walked, understanding better the comments she had been hearing from one person or another ever since they had arrived home. The land needed rain. The fields needed rain. The streams needed rain. Marty's eyes looked out across the neighboring pasture. The grass was short and beginning to turn brown. After coming from the arid West, even these parched meadows looked green. But Marty's memory served to remind her that things should be much greener than this in the middle of June. She looked up, but the sun shone with a dazzling light out of a cloudless sky. Then Marty looked toward the horizon. No clouds appeared anywhere over the distant hills. There was no sign of rain in the immediate future.

Marty crossed to the barn and reached a hand over the corral fence to stroke the neck of the big bay. Its teammate sauntered over for her share of the attention, and Marty patted her on the neck, too. She snorted at Marty's outstretched hand, annoyed that it held no piece of apple or lump of sugar, and walked off—heading for the shade to escape the fierceness of the sun.

Marty, too, walked on, past the chicken coop. The hens squawked and squabbled and fought over the watering trough. A big rooster strutted across the enclosure and crowed his challenge to the smaller male members of the flock. Marty noticed a number of hens with good-sized chicks scurrying about them. Ellie had cared well for the flock. There would be a fine supply of chicken for the fall and winter.

Marty slowed as she came to the little log house she had called home for so many years. She still felt nostalgic as she looked at the fluffy curtains blowing in the open kitchen window. Kate was out back hanging some wash on the line. Marty called a good morning, and Kate waved in return.

"I'm almost done. Can ya stop fer coffee?" her daughter-in-law invited.

Marty could and did. She was anxious to see the home that Kate and Clare had made for themselves in the little log house. She followed Kate through the entry and into the tidy kitchen. There had been some changes at Kate's hand—changes for the better, Marty reflected—but much of the cozy room was just as Marty remembered it.

Kate poured the water into the kettle for coffee and measured the grounds. "I was hopin' you'd have time to drop by today. I was achin' to show ya our home. Isn't it just perfect?"

Marty agreed with a smile. That's how she had always felt about this little home.

After Kate had placed the water on to boil, she offered Marty a tour, and Marty was quick to accept. They entered the family living area, and Marty looked from the fireplace to the bookshelf—familiar things—to the couch and two armchairs, the small table and the grandfather clock—all unfamiliar things. The rugs on the floor and the curtains at the window were new, as well.

They moved through the door to the room that had been Marty's bedroom, the one she had first shared with the young Missie and later with baby Clare and then with her husband Clark. Marty stopped for a moment to remember that first year with Clark and his wonderful patience with her, his gentle caring, which had broken through the walls she had built around her broken heart.

Marty looked about her at Kate's bed covered in a deep, down-filled quilt. The chest against the wall held more drawers than the chest Marty had used. There was a comfortable chair beneath the window, with a cozy cushion embroidered in butterflies. A cedar-lined chest stood in the corner. Marty openly admired the room and Kate looked pleased.

They moved on then to a simply furnished spare bedroom. It contained only a bed, a chair, and a small table with a lamp on it. It was clean and airy, and Marty was sure a guest could feel quite comfortable and at home there.

With a bit of a flush to her cheeks, Kate led her to the next room. A small workbench and a few tools lay scattered about, and Marty looked at several pieces of turned wood stacked neatly in a corner.

"Clare makin' somethin'?" she asked, and Kate flushed a bit deeper.

"A crib," she said. "We still aren't quite sure yet if we'll be needin' it, but we're hopin'. I scolded Clare last night fer speakin' up when we aren't really sure yet ourselves, but he's just so excited, an' iffen it's true an' we really are, then—well, we want our two mas to be the first to know. Clare promised I could drive on over to see my ma this afternoon."

Marty put her arms around Kate and gave her a quick hug. "I'm so happy fer ya—fer ya both. I hope with all my heart thet yer right."

"Me too," sighed Kate. "Clare would be so happy. He's been waitin' an' waitin'."

"But ya haven't even been married a year yet," Marty reminded her.

"A year is a long time when yer waitin' fer somethin' ya want so badly," Kate said in frustration and then laughed at herself.

Marty laughed with her.

"Well, I guess it really hasn't been so long," Kate went on, "but it has sure seemed long to Clare an' me."

They returned to the kitchen to enjoy their coffee, and Marty listened as Kate talked about their plans for the coming baby—if one was really on the way. As Marty left Kate's kitchen to return to her own, she prayed that Kate was right and that their dream would soon be fulfilled.

Ellie looked up from kneading some bread dough as Marty entered. Marty felt a bit chagrined when she realized what her daughter was doing.

"Oh, Ellie," she said, "I should be doin' thet instead of wanderin' about like a thoughtless schoolgirl."

"Look, Ma, I've been doin' this fer a long time now."

"I know—an' it's time ya had a break. Here I am back again, an' ya still have to do all the work."

Ellie smiled. "The work's not hurtin' me none. Do ya feel a little better now thet you've seen everythin' is as it should be?"

"Guess I do. Not thet I doubted it would be. . . . It's just thet I wanted to see iffen my memory served me accurately or if I'd built it all up to some fairy-tale dream."

"An'?"

"It's just as I remembered it. My memory played no tricks on me."

"Good," said Ellie as she continued to knead the bread dough.

"Had coffee with Kate," Marty went on.

"I saw ya go in."

"She has made Clare a nice little home. They do seem happy."

"She's been a perfect wife for Clare. Iffen she isn't in agreement with everythin' he does, I never hear about it. Kate's a dear."

Marty smiled. "It means everythin' to a mother to hear thet her children are happily married to mates who love 'em just the way they are."

Ellie nodded and kept up her rhythm with the bread. "You'll like Arnie's girl, too," she said. "Arnie's a lucky guy."

"Arnie came in to see me last night and said he'd tell me all 'bout her as soon as we find some talkin' time."

"Then I won't spill any of his secrets," assured Ellie as she efficiently placed the kneaded dough in the greased pan together with the rest of the batch. She covered it all with a white cloth and set it near the stove on a tall table built for the purpose.

"I think I'll go on up and unpack an' care fer the things from the trip," Marty said. "I was just too tired to do anythin' with 'em last night."

"Ya still look a mite tired," observed Ellie. "I think this has all been a heap harder on ya than ya will ever admit."

"I'm fine," argued Marty. "In a day or two, after I catch up on a bit of sleep, I'll be right as rain."

Ellie looked out at the brightness of the day. "Speakin' of rain," she said, frowning, "we sure are in need of some. I've already been totin' water fer the garden, an' it needs it again. We planted far too big a garden to be waterin' it by the pailful."

"It sure is lookin' fine right now," Marty encouraged. "But yer right, it does need rain."

Ellie must have read Marty's mind as she glanced at the clock.

"Ya go on with yer unpackin'," she urged. "I'll look after gittin' dinner on."

Marty thanked her and went on up to her room. As she climbed the stairs, she had to admit to herself that she *was* tired. Why, after dinner she might do an unheard of thing and lie down for a little nap. She wondered at Clark's vigor. *He must be just as tired as I am, but he seems to keep goin' with no problem,* she chided herself lightly. Marty then excused herself with the promise that after a day or two of adjusting, she would be her old self again.

FOUR

Happenings

Marty and Arnie eventually found their talking time. Since Marty still had not felt too perky the next day, Ellie convinced her to sit on the porch with some hand sewing while Ellie herself continued with the duties of the kitchen. Arnie found his mother busy with some mending and sat down to talk to her about his Anne.

Anne came from a family of four and was the daughter of Pastor Norville, who was in charge of the small church congregation in the nearby town. Anne had lost her mother when she was only eleven years old, and, being the only girl in the family, much of the running of the household had fallen upon her at that very young age. Arnie spoke of her with love in his voice, and Marty was more anxious than ever to meet the girl.

"Do ya s'pose ya could bring her to dinner on Sunday?" Marty asked.

"Sure thing. I'll be seein' her tomorra night. I'll ask her then."

"Has she met most of the family?"

"All but you an' Pa."

There was a brief pause.

"Do ya have any plans?" asked Marty quietly.

Arnie colored slightly. "Sure, I got plans—but I haven't spoken of 'em yet. I wanted you an' Pa to meet her first."

"I see," smiled Marty. "Sunday, then."

Arnie, whistling, left for the barn, and Marty watched him go with both pride and a little sorrow. Soon they would all be married, her children. How would she ever endure an empty and quiet house?

———————

Zeke LaHaye stopped by that evening. He wanted to hear all about his son Willie, about Missie and his two grandsons, and about the West they loved so much. Marty and Clark welcomed Zeke warmly, and as Marty put on the coffeepot, Zeke and Clark pulled chairs up to the kitchen table and settled in for a long visit.

Clark's enthusiasm was clear in his voice as he spoke of Willie's ranch and described the spread in detail. He told about the herd, the buildings, the cowboys, the neighbors, the small but growing town, and the prosperity that Willie had worked so hard to achieve. When Marty joined them at the table, the talk turned to the family members. They laughed as they told Zeke about the antics of their shared grandchildren. Zeke joined in the laughter, but as he listened, the hungry look in his eyes deepened.

"I think I'm just gonna take me a little trip out there," he announced at length.

"Thet's a mighty fine idea," encouraged Clark. "They'd like nothin' better. One of the last things Willie said was fer us to send ya on out."

Zeke swallowed with difficulty. "Think I'll head on into town tomorrow an' book me a ticket," he said, his head nodding slowly. "I've waited too long already."

———————

It was hard for Marty to wait for Sunday. First of all, it would mean seeing all her friends in the Sunday morning worship service. Marty thought of Ma and Ben, and Wanda and Cameron. Though Ellie had filled her in on news of the community, it wasn't like seeing her neighbors in person.

After the service, the family would be together for Sunday dinner. They had not seen Nandry and Josh and their family since the night they had arrived home, and Marty was most anxious for another visit and a chance to get reacquainted with her grandchildren.

She was eager to meet Arnie's Anne, as well. What would she really be like? Marty trusted Arnie's judgment, but was he seeing the girl through star-filled eyes? Ellie and Luke, too, had spoken well of Anne. Marty dared to hope that Anne was all her family had claimed her to be and that God, in His love and goodness, had brought them together. Marty could hardly wait to give her blessing to the two of them.

Sunday was another bright, warm day. Ellie had worked long and hard to prepare the family dinner. Marty tried to help, but she found she still tired far too easily. Surely she wasn't *that* tired from her trip from the West! Maybe it was just that she needed to adjust to the climate again, though the weather hadn't seemed to affect Clark one little bit. He was busy every day and managed, with no apparent difficulty even with a crutch, to keep up with his energetic sons.

Marty often felt Clark's eyes upon her, but he seldom made comment except to encourage her now and then to sit for a spell or even to take an occasional nap. Marty fussed inwardly, though she dared not protest too vigorously. In fact, she forced herself to admit that she really had no energy even for argument. She was anxious to be back caring for her family again. But now it was Ellie who had to bear most of the load, though she never mentioned the fact and often asked Marty, "Now, what shall we have?" or "What shall we do?" or even "What would ya like?" so Marty might feel she was in charge.

And now, because of Ellie's capable hands in the kitchen, they were ready for Sunday and the family dinner that would follow the service. Marty wondered, a little guiltily, if she was more excited about being back in her own church and seeing her friends again than about the worship service itself. She decided that the Lord understood her feelings and didn't mind that today most of her attention was on her friends. As Marty and Clark entered the churchyard, their friends welcomed them back to the little congregation with happy smiles and warm embraces.

Wanda ran to meet Marty and clung to her; tears dampened the eyes of both women.

"Oh, I've missed you so much . . . so much," she whispered to Marty over and over. "Can you come for a nice, long visit soon, so's you can tell me all about Missie and her family?"

Marty promised she would.

Ma Graham, too, held Marty for a long time. A sob caught in her throat as she spoke of their deep sorrow when they had learned of Clark's accident. She told how, on three occasions during the ordeal, the church members had met for special prayer on his behalf. Marty thanked her sincerely and assured her that God truly had honored their prayers. Ma looked at Clark, busily shaking hands with the neighborhood men, and nodded her head slowly. "Yeah," she affirmed, "I can see thet He did. I don't see one ounce a' bitterness in the face of thet man."

The church bell called them to worship, and Marty and Clark took their familiar places with their family. It was strange not to see Pastor Joe leading the service, but the new young man whom the church had appointed did a fine job. Marty looked across at Josh and his family and realized that Nandry was not with them. She felt a moment of concern. Perhaps Nandry was busy elsewhere, she told herself, but after the service when she inquired, Josh informed her that Nandry just wasn't feeling herself and had decided to stay home. Marty felt a bit anxious, but Josh assured her that Nandry was all right, just not feeling her best. Marty promised herself that she would check on Nandry in a couple of days just to be sure. In the meantime, the family would miss them at the dinner table. Marty had counted so on all of her nearby family being there.

Anne was all that Arnie had described and more. Marty and Clark both loved her immediately. She was a rather quiet and serious girl, but her spirit was kind and gentle, and when she smiled, her whole face lit up and one could not help but smile in return. She loved Arnie—Marty could see it in her eyes and hear it in her voice. Just before Arnie left to take Anne back to town, Marty answered the unasked question in Arnie's eyes with a quick smile and an almost undetectable nod of her head. Arnie caught it and grinned. Marty had a feeling that when Arnie returned, he would have some news for the family. As a matter of fact, he did. He shared it with great gusto, and there was lots of back slapping and congratulatory hugs. He couldn't announce a wedding date yet, but he grinned and said it would be soon.

Marty did call on Wanda. They had a long visit and caught up on all of the happenings since they had last been together. Marty could see no change in her son, Rett. Though he lived in the body of a man, he had not really advanced beyond the small-boy stage. He still evidenced his uncanny ability with animals, and his menagerie had grown steadily over the years. Marty wondered how Wanda, who still clung to some of her eastern city-girl ways, managed to put up with the strange assortment of creatures with which she was asked to share her home. *Only a mother's love,* she decided with a smile as she watched the two of them.

Ma Graham came to call. She came alone now. All her children were married and had homes of their own, though Lou and his wife did live in a small house in the Graham yard and shared the farming duties with Ben. Marty caught up on all of the news of the family members and shared with Ma the latest happenings concerning Missie and her household.

Marty began rather slowly, but eventually she told in detail about the trying days following Clark's accident. Ma was the only person to whom Marty felt she could really bare her soul. As they talked and the shared tears fell, Marty felt that maybe Ellie was right. Maybe the whole ordeal had been harder on her than she had dared to admit. Maybe now that she had voiced it all, she would get back some of her old energy.

———————

July came. Still no rain—except for a few scattered showers that didn't really count for much on the thirsty land. Daily, as a family, they prayed that the rain might come. Ellie kept busy with her watering pail trying to keep the plants from wilting. Even her brothers were not above carrying water for the very dry garden. The fields, as well, began to show the effects of the long dry spell. There was no way to bring water to the fields without the help of the Master of wind and rain.

———————

A telegram from Missie set the whole household buzzing. It stated: *PA LAHAYE ARRIVED—STOP—SO DID MELISSA JOY, 7 POUNDS 10 OUNCES—STOP—THANK GOD FOR BOTH—STOP—ALL FINE—STOP*

The whole family rejoiced at the news, but Clare's eyes shone the brightest of all.

"Have ya told 'em?" he asked, giving Kate a nudge and a squeeze.

She answered with a shake of her head and a cheery, though embarrassed, smile. "Dr. Watkins said yesterday thet we're gonna be parents, all right."

And so there was more reason for rejoicing. Everyone in the family heartily congratulated Clare, who grinned at each comment, and hugged Kate as she flushed prettily. Marty looked at the girl's shining violet eyes and thought she had never looked prettier.

FIVE

Confessions

The storm moved in from the west with low-hanging clouds and a strong wind. Marty worried that the wind might drive the clouds right on by before the land had a chance to rejuvenate with the much-needed water. Her fears lessened as she stood at the window and watched the wind abate and the clouds hang low and heavy over the countryside. And then for three days, a continual steady rain emptied itself on the thirsty soil. When the sun returned, the growing things lifted high their drooping heads, all strength renewed. Marty felt like shouting praises. In fact, the whole family gathered together for a special thanksgiving prayer.

———————

Kate was experiencing morning sickness. Marty felt sorry for her, but the girl only smiled. "It won't be for long," she insisted, "an' it will be worth it." Clare fussed over her and insisted that she take it easy and care for his "boy."

Already the two of them were busy with preparations for the coming baby—even though that "comin'" was more than seven months into the future. Marty, sharing their joy and enthusiasm, would welcome the wee baby, too. She suggested several home remedies to Kate that might help her over those often difficult early months of a pregnancy.

———————

Marty continued to feel dragged out—not herself at all. She tried not to let it show, but the harder she tried to keep up with Ellie, the more it was obvious she couldn't. Clark suggested a trip in to see Dr. Watkins, but Marty shook her head. She had a suspicion that her age was showing and it bothered her some. She was an awfully young woman to be going through *that,* she kept telling herself. She did not express her concerns, but she felt her family's eyes upon her, watching with loving care.

"I'll be fine—just fine," she kept assuring them all, and she tried to be—tried with all her might to walk a little brisker, lift her feet a little higher, hold her head a little straighter. But most of the time it just didn't work. She felt tired before the day had hardly begun.

One morning she felt sick to her stomach. She passed it off as a touch of the flu. Then after an hour or two, she felt fine. But the next morning it recurred. She shrugged it off that time, too, but when it happened again on the third morning, even she was a bit worried, though she would not admit it.

"I'm as bad as Kate," she remarked to Ellie with an attempt at a light laugh.

"Well, I don't like it," Ellie said seriously. "Kate has a very good reason."

A wild thought suddenly went racing through Marty's mind, though she did not voice it to Ellie. *Ya don't s'pose. . . ? No, thet's impossible. Thet's unthinkable.* But it nagged away at her all day.

Each time it unwillingly returned, Marty tried to drive it away. *I'm past my forty-third birthday,* she kept telling herself. But inwardly she knew that really did not preclude this extraordinary possibility.

It's so silly . . . so foolish, she reminded herself. *Here I am—a grandmother many times over. I would be so embarrassed. . . .* And Marty's cheeks burned at the very thought of what might be.

The feeling of sickness continued to occur. Marty tried to hide the fact from her family. She made even more of an effort to look perky and carry her end of the household tasks. But even as she fought against it, she knew she was really being foolish.

It must be so, she finally admitted to herself and went to her room to have a rest and a good cry.

Whatever will Clark think? Here I am, a woman my age . . . and this!

Her thoughts moved on to the rest of her family. *What will Ellie think? And Missie? And Kate? Here Kate is expecting a baby of her own, and her mother-in-law, who should be long past such things, is joining her—stealing her thunder!*

And Arnie? Here he is planning his wedding, and his own mother will show up at it quite obviously with child. It'll embarrass him nigh to death!

Marty refused to share her worries with any of her family. It was the first time in her years of marriage to Clark that she kept something from him. *Maybe I'm mistaken,* she kept saying to herself. *Maybe I'm all wrong. Or, if I'm right, maybe I'll lose it. Women my age often do.*

But deep within, Marty knew she was probably correct and that the day would soon come when she would have to tell Clark. She dreaded it. Dreaded his reaction. Would he laugh? Or would he actually pity her? Marty could not stand that thought. *If he should look at me with eyes that say, "You poor thing," I'll be so mad. . . . But he just might,* Marty decided. *He just might. Especially the way I've been feeling.*

Marty decided she couldn't tell Clark—not yet. She'd wait awhile until she was absolutely sure.

———

Kate was now feeling a little better daily. Every time Marty saw Kate or Clare, it seemed they were talking about the coming baby. Never had Marty seen a couple anticipate a new arrival with such longing and joy. She envied them in a way. *It must be nice to be looking forward so—*

But Marty stopped herself. Hadn't she also looked forward to the arrival of each of her babies? *Each of them, but . . .* She didn't allow herself to finish it. She felt guilty about the way she was feeling toward this child. After all, this baby had not asked to be brought into the world.

She wondered what Kate and Clare would think if she suddenly were to announce, *Isn't it wonderful? I'm expecting a baby, too, and I think both babies will likely arrive about the same time.*

My, would eyes ever pop then!

But there was no way Marty would announce it like that.

———————

Josh and Nandry were joining the family for Sunday dinners again. Marty was so glad to have them back, but she was concerned about Nandry. Something was troubling her. Quiet and withdrawn, she never looked directly at Clark unless he was seated at the table, and then her eyes seemed to slide over him. Was Nandry feeling all right? Was Marty imagining things? Was Clark's new appearance really troubling her in some way? Marty tried not to borrow trouble. At least Nandry and the family were with them, and for that she was thankful! Perhaps with a little time things would be as before.

———————

"I've made an appointment with Dr. Watkins."

Clark made the statement matter-of-factly one night as he and Marty prepared for bed. Marty's head whipped around, concern filling her mind.

"Have ya been feelin' okay? Is yer leg—?"

But Clark interrupted. "Ain't fer me. It's fer you."

"Fer me?" asked Marty. "Whatever fer?"

"I've been worryin' 'bout ya, thet's what fer. Thought it might just take a while fer ya to get back on yer feet like, but ya haven't, Marty. Ya still have to push yerself an'—"

Anger colored her voice and face as she cut in. "Wish ya wouldn't have done thet. Nothin' wrong with me, an' there's no use troublin' Doc over somethin' thet—I'm fine, an' ya really had no call makin' an appointment without even talkin'—"

Clark reached for her and pulled her to him. Marty seldom responded in such an angry way, and when she did now, she knew he felt even more convinced that something was wrong.

He tried to hold her close, but she stubbornly stiffened her body. He did not speak, only stroked her hair.

She could not resist him for long. She began to relax against him. He went on holding her, gently kissing the top of her head. Suddenly, to his surprise, she crumpled up against him and began to cry.

Clark's grip on her tightened, and Marty knew he now was genuinely worried that something was seriously wrong.

"Please, God, please," she heard him whisper.

Marty did not weep for long. As soon as she had quieted, Clark spoke softly into her hair. "Somethin' is wrong, isn't it?"

Marty nodded her head against him, indicating that, yes, she thought there was.

"Have ya already been to the doc?"

Marty shook her head no.

"Then yer guessin'."

"I . . . I . . . don't think so," she sniffed.

There were a few minutes of silence.

"An' what are ya expectin'. . . ?" Clark didn't finish.

Marty waited for only a moment before she spoke through renewed sobs. "A . . . a . . . baby."

Clark pushed her back to arm's length, perplexity showing in his face. "A what?"

"A baby," she cried, her face crumpled with weeping.

"A *baby*?"

She nodded, wishing she could bury her head against his shoulder again so she wouldn't need to look into his eyes.

"A baby?" Clark repeated with only a shade less shock in his voice.

Marty just let the tears run down her cheeks. She closed her eyes. She wished to see neither reproach nor pity in his eyes. She stood silent and mute.

"Oh, Marty," Clark said, giving her a little shake.

Marty opened her eyes and looked directly and deeply into the eyes of her husband. There was no worry there. There was no pity. But there was love. Lots of love. Marty answered his look, and then she flung her arms tightly about his neck and wept again, tears of relief.

Clark held her for a long time, then pushed her gently from him. There was the trace of a smile on his lips.

"Thet's a bit of a wonder, ain't it?"

"A wonder?" repeated Marty, puzzled.

"Yeah, a wonder. Here I was a worryin'. Arnie's gittin' married soon an' movin'. Luke is goin' off to become a doctor, an' we both know there's no way we can hang on to Ellie fer long. An' here now, as I was hatin' to lose the last one, God is sendin' us another!"

Marty hadn't been giving God much credit for the whole event. She wasn't sure she liked the idea, even yet. She was a little old to be a mother again, and what in the world would her family and all of the neighbors think?

"I'd still like ya to keep the appointment," Clark was saying. "We wanta be sure thet everythin' is all right."

"Iffen ya want me to," Marty agreed, but she dreaded to face even the kindly doctor. She wished there was some way to keep her news to herself indefinitely.

"All of the family will be relieved," Clark went on. "We've all been worried thet somethin' might be wrong. It'll be a real relief—"

"A real embarrassment, ya mean," Marty interjected.

"What d'ya mean—an embarrassment? Yer simply bein' a

woman the way the good Lord made ya. Nothin' wrong or embarrassin' 'bout thet."

Marty argued no further. She knew it would do no good. She also knew she was extremely tired. It was not difficult for her to agree to go to bed at Clark's gentle prompting.

SIX

Announcement

Clark pulled the team up before the house and helped Marty into the wagon. He drove to town more slowly than usual. Marty knew it was out of concern for her—and their unborn baby. She could feel her cheeks warm slightly as she wondered what Clark would think if he knew of the many times she had secretly hoped she would lose the child. Clark certainly wouldn't be having any such thoughts, she was sure.

It was a beautiful summer day. A rain shower had freshened their whole world just before dawn, and everything smelled green and growing. Marty pushed back her bonnet so she might get a better look at the familiar countryside. It had been a while since she had made this trip to town.

They passed the Grahams', and Marty waved to Ma, who was out in the garden, hoe in hand. Marty thought again of how very little of the hoeing in this year's garden she had done. Poor Ellie! She certainly had been carrying the load.

When they arrived at the doctor's, Clark helped Marty down over the wheel and gently steadied her on her feet. "I'll be in as soon as I tie the team," he promised.

Marty nodded and moved on to enter the small office. Three others were waiting, and Marty was glad to postpone her visit with the doctor for even a little while.

Clark soon joined her. The time went by too quickly, and before she was emotionally ready, it was her turn to step into the inner office. The doc began with a few preliminary questions. Marty prepared herself for the shocked look on his face when she told him what she had concluded, but it did not come. He seemed to feel it was quite the most ordinary thing in the world for a woman of forty-three, with a number of grandchildren, to be sitting in his office chair quietly informing him that she believed another child was on the way.

After the examination, Doc calmly assured Marty that she was right and that everything seemed fine. He made a few suggestions about what she might do to assure proper progress for the baby and renewed energy for herself. Marty solemnly promised to eat right and get plenty of rest.

Doc Watkins then called Clark into the room and offered his congratulations to the father-to-be. Both of the men seemed rather pleased with the fact of the coming baby, and for a moment Marty felt a trace of exasperation with them. She pushed it aside. They were right and she was wrong. There should be joy over the coming of a new life into the world. She must get her thinking into proper perspective.

When the Davises left the office, they did their needed shopping—not really all that much. In fact, it was Ellie who had prepared the list for Clark.

As they left the general store, Clark wouldn't allow Marty to carry even a small bundle. Instead, he insisted on making two trips himself, his crutch beating a rhythm on the wooden sidewalk. Marty waited rather impatiently in the shade until the groceries were carefully stored away.

"Why don't we git ya some tea?" Clark offered, and Marty agreed that it would pick her up a bit.

They headed slowly for the hotel dining room.

"Been wonderin'," Clark said as they walked, "iffen you'd like to git some things fer the new young'un while we're here. Seems to me there couldn't be much left from our previous babies."

Marty looked up at him in shock. She hadn't even thought

about starting all over with the sewing of baby clothes and the making of diapers! Here Kate was as busy as could be, and their babies were due about the same time—and Marty didn't have one thing. But she took a breath and put a check on her thoughts. She just wasn't ready for that yet.

"There'll be plenty of time" was all she said.

Clark nodded and held the door for her.

———

All the way home, Marty's head spun. Her family knew she had been to the doctor today and were worried there might be something seriously wrong. They would need to know. She couldn't possibly continue to let them worry when nothing at all was "wrong" with her. It just wouldn't be fair. They would need to know the truth. Marty thought of asking to go to her room to lie down and letting Clark share the preposterous news. That really wasn't fair, she knew, and was the cowardly way out. Oh, how she dreaded it! How did one say it? What did you tell fully grown children? It used to be so easy. One gathered the little ones around and informed them joyfully, "We're gonna git ya a new baby. Only God knows whether it will be a new brother or a sister." And there was great rejoicing, and they would take sides as to who wanted it to be what. It was sort of like casting votes. On the day of the actual arrival, there were always winners and losers—but that was soon forgotten in the excitement of the new baby. After the initial announcement and a viewing of the new little one, everyone realized God had sent just what each one had really wanted.

Only this time, thought Marty, *we don't all want this baby. Maybe nobody really does. Oh, I know Clark will accept the new arrival all right, but is this what he really wants? Will the family really want a new baby? I know I don't. Not really.*

Marty was ashamed at the direction of her thoughts. But it was true. She hadn't planned on this baby. As much as she had enjoyed raising their family, she didn't want to start all over again with night feedings and diapers and round-the-clock care of a little one. It would not be happening had the choice been hers.

She pushed those thoughts aside and concentrated on the lazily drifting clouds overhead. It looked as though they might get a bit more rain. Well, she supposed they could use it. It seemed they never really got too much.

They passed the Grahams' again, and Marty was glad Ma was no longer in her yard. Somehow she felt that even in driving by and waving, her secret would be revealed. *Oh, what will Ma think?* And then Marty remembered that Ma had been her age when her last child was born.

But that was different, she argued with herself. *There wasn't a big gap between children, and she didn't have a whole passel of grandchildren by then, either.*

Marty's inner self quickly countered, *No, and you don't have a grandchild yet from any of the family you have actually given birth to. Nandry and Clae are both Tina's girls, and Missie is Ellen's girl. True enough now, though, you seem to be running a race with your firstborn son.*

In spite of herself, Marty smiled at the humor of it. It *was* rather funny. Why, she and Clare's Kate could well be confined at the same time. Imagine a child sharing a birthday with an aunt or uncle! She was sure there would be plenty of teasing ahead for both the little ones.

All too soon Clark was pulling the team up before the house and hopping down to help Marty. She dreaded it. Would they all storm her with questions the minute she entered the kitchen? She turned to go up the walk alone, but Clark was at her side.

Ellie met them at the door. Her eyes held her questions. She looked right past Marty and sought the eyes of her father.

Clark responded. "Ma's fine," he said with satisfaction, and the look of fear left Ellie's face, though Marty could sense that questions still remained.

Marty was surprised that Clark let it go at that, and she went on up to her room and changed into her housedress. Supper was almost ready.

It wasn't until the next morning at family worship that Clark brought up the subject. He had read a portion on the rich promises of God and the thankful response that His children should feel toward His loving-kindness. Each member of the family was invited to share something for which they were especially thankful. Clark stated that he was thankful for each family member that God, in His wisdom and love, had sent into the home, and then he led the family in prayer. After the prayer, he motioned for the little group to remain seated.

"When ya were all little an' we had a special announcement to make, we used to gather ya round us like this and share it together. Now, Luke here has never gotten in on any of those special announcements. Well, we are 'bout to correct thet. Lukey," he said, using the pet name of years gone by, "yer ma an' me got somethin' to tell ya. All of ya." Clark stopped to look around the circle. "We're missin' some of the family to be sure, but fer those of us here together, we want ya to know thet yer ma an' me are gonna git ya a new baby. Boy or girl, we not be knowin', but . . ."

Three pairs of eyes turned in unison to look questioningly at Marty. She felt herself squirm under the intensity of it. Arnie was the first to catch his breath. He gave a whoop and leaped from his chair. Luke was next. "Finally!" was what he shouted. "Finally I git my turn."

Marty couldn't believe her ears. She turned from her grown sons to Ellie, but she was crying. Oh no, did it really bother Ellie that much?

Marty moved toward her in concern, but Ellie met her halfway. "Oh, Mama," she wept, "I was so scared. So scared." And then she began to laugh through her sobs. "An' it's just a *baby*! 'Magine thet. A baby." Then she turned to her brothers. "I hope it's a girl," she stated emphatically.

"A boy!" they shouted in unison.

"A girl," insisted Ellie. "We already got more boys than girls."

"Thet don't matter," said Luke. "I still don't have a baby brother."

Clark held up his hand as a signal for silence. "Hold it," he said into the commotion. "Hold it. What it will be is already determined, an' no 'mount of yellin' on yer part is gonna change it none. I suggest we just wait an' see."

Marty looked around at her incredible family. They didn't seem to mind. They didn't seem to mind one bit. Of course, Arnie had always loved babies, and Ellie had always shown a tendency toward mothering. Luke maintained that he didn't get the fair end of things in not being a big brother to *someone*.

Marty shook her head. She might as well have purchased the materials for the making of the little garments. With a family like she had, there would be no peace until everything was prepared for the little one who was to bless their home.

SEVEN

Planning

Marty and Ellie had been invited over to Kate's for morning coffee. Marty was glad Kate was now feeling well enough to again think of serving them at a midmorning break. As yet, Marty still had no desire to eat until later in the day. She didn't say that to Kate, though. But when Kate began pouring the coffee and cutting the coffee cake, Marty asked for only a part of a cup and then generously poured cream in the cup to soften the bitter taste. Even then she was only able to sip at it. She passed up the dessert, as well. She was glad the girls did not press her.

Kate enthused about her coming baby. She seemed to expect Marty to be every bit as excited about her pregnancy as she was herself. Marty tried to show some enthusiasm. She hoped it came through as sincere. She was able to share in the joy that Kate's face held as she showed them garment after garment she had stitched.

"Clare insists it will be a boy," she laughed. "But I told him it could just as well be a girl."

"Men!" said Ellie. "They scare ya half to death with their knowledge of things to come! I'm glad when it finally does arrive, they are just as pleased with one as the other."

Marty wondered momentarily where Ellie got all her understanding of the subject. Well, she certainly had lived in a community—and a family—where there were lots of babies.

Kate showed them the nursery room, wallpapered in light green. The fluffy curtains at the windows were white, as was the painted trim. The yet-unfinished crib was quickly taking shape at the hands of Clare, who spent every available minute working on it. Kate herself was now sewing a crib quilt. To match the wallpaper, it was in a pale green calico print.

"Clare tried to talk me into blue," she laughed, "but I said I was gonna play it safe."

A small chest stood against the wall. As Kate opened the drawers, Marty saw many more already-completed baby items.

My, thought Marty, *it is still many months away. Whatever is she gonna do with all the extra time?*

Kate seemed to read her thoughts.

"I know we're gittin' ready awfully early, but iffen I get the necessary things outta the way, I can spend the rest of the waitin' time sewin' some 'specially fancy things. I wanna knit up some sweaters, too, an' I'm awfully slow at thet."

"Mama," said Ellie as they walked the short distance back to the big house, "are ya feelin' up to a trip to town?"

"I guess so. Why?"

"I'm a thinkin' it's 'bout time we got busy on this baby of ours. We don't want her comin' 'fore we're all ready."

"Baby of *ours*?" Marty repeated the words under her breath. Yes, she supposed that was the way Ellie thought of it. It would belong to all of the family.

"There's still plenty of time—" began Marty, but Ellie cut her short.

"Sure, there's lots of time, but we want lots of things fer her. I want her to be the best-dressed baby thet ever—"

"Now, hold on," laughed Marty. "She'll be properly cared fer, fer sure, but we ain't gonna go overboard. 'Sides, how any baby could ever have more'n thet little one of Kate an' Clare's is beyond my knowin'."

"Aren't they excited? Never seen a couple so eager fer a baby!

Kate was an only child, ya know. She wanted a baby of her own from her weddin' day on. She'll make a good mother, too—I know she will."

Marty agreed. Kate seemed to be cut out for motherhood. She rejoiced with everyone who had the joy of a baby. Even the announcement of Marty's coming child had made her almost silly with happiness. Marty was glad. She didn't want the fact that she was also expecting a baby to rob Kate of any of her own anticipation. It hadn't. Kate seemed to bloom enough for them both.

"Well," insisted Ellie, "can we go shoppin'?"

Marty still hedged. She hated going into town and looking for material for baby things. Everyone would know and whisper and . . . No, she just didn't want to do that until there was simply no way of hiding it anymore.

"I'll buy it iffen ya want me to," Ellie offered.

"You?" Marty said, shocked. "Now why would I be wantin' folks to think thet *you* had need of such things?"

"Pshaw," responded Ellie. "It might be fer Kate, fer all they need to know. Or we might be sewin' fer Missie or Clae—they've each had a baby recently. An' anyway, Nandry might even—"

"Ya know somethin' 'bout Nandry thet I don't know?" asked Marty, half hoping she did. She wished with all of her heart that Nandry's somber withdrawal could be traced to something as simple as a baby on the way—although having a baby had never seemed to bother Nandry any before.

"Nope," said Ellie, "but somethin's strange, don't ya think?"

"Yeah," replied Marty with a deep sigh. "I've noticed it, too. I was hopin', though, thet I was imaginin' it."

"Yer not imaginin' it," Ellie responded. "It's there, all right. I haven't yet been able to figure out why, though. Iffen it were a baby . . ." Ellie let her thoughts hang in the air between them.

They reached the house, and Ellie continued around to the backyard to see if the wash on the line was dry. Marty went into the kitchen for a dry bread crust, in the hope that it might settle her queasy stomach. It didn't seem to help, so she went on up to her room to lie down for a spell. She would be so thankful when this dreadful morning sickness had run its course. Why was she having problems with this child, when none of her others had ever bothered her in this way? Well, Kate seemed to be fine now. If she could just hang on, perhaps the day would come when she, too, would feel well again.

––––––––––

Fall had brought with it both blessings and sorrows. Marty did finally feel better. It was so good to actually be hungry again. With the satisfied hunger came added strength. Marty could help more around the house without feeling completely exhausted. It was Ellie now insisting along with Clark that she slow down and not try to tackle everything in a day.

Fall was also the time for Luke to leave. Marty dreaded it. She tried to push the thought of the approaching day to the back of her mind, but it persisted to nag at her.

Again and again she reminded herself that Luke was no longer her baby. He was a young man and well able to care for himself. She had a hard time convincing herself, and as she sewed new shirts or knit new socks for him to take with him, tears often fell upon her work.

Luke was excited about his coming adventure, and it seemed to Marty that he spent far more time with Doc Watkins poring over medical books than he spent at home with his family. The doc was quite convinced that Luke would be the star pupil among the doctors in training and made no bones about telling his eastern colleagues so. Luke was to get special attention as the older doctor's protégé. Marty was glad there would be those who would be watching out for him, but it was still difficult to let him go.

She reminded herself often that Luke would be home with them again at Christmastime. Not only would it be Christmas and the family would be together, but it had been chosen as the time for Arnie's wedding, as well, so Luke could be the best man. Clark had agreed to pay for his train ticket home. Marty was glad. She would be able to judge for herself if Luke was standing the pressure of the medical training, and if he wasn't, then there surely would be some way to keep him at home.

She comforted herself with these thoughts as she worked the heel of the newly forming sock. She also faced again that it was only a matter of days until Luke and his belongings would board the stage to go meet the eastbound train.

One consolation for Marty was the fact that at the other end of the train trip, Joe and Clae and their family would be waiting. Although there was not room for Luke to be able to board with his eastern family, at least he would be able to visit them from time to time should he get lonely, Marty comforted herself. Luke had no such fears, and if Clark had, he did not voice them. He seemed to understand Marty's feelings, though, and he was gentle and re-assuring as he spoke often of the short time until Christmas would be upon them.

All of Arnie's thoughts seemed to be taken with his Anne and the farm to which they would be moving following their wedding. The house that was located on the property needed repairing, and Arnie spent many hours with hammer in hand getting it ready. When other duties freed him, Clark, too, helped his son. On occasion, even Clare had some extra time that he used to help his brother with the task. The house soon began to shape up, and with it, Arnie's impatience seemed to increase.

The hammers and saws had to be laid aside for the harvest. There was a good crop to be taken in, and Luke would be around for very little of the time. Clark did a fair share. He had rigged enough contraptions together to be able to operate almost any of the farm equipment with just his one leg. The boys marveled as they watched him. He could keep up with almost anyone they knew.

All too soon the day of Luke's departure arrived. The whole

family drove him into town to meet the stagecoach. Doc and his wife were there, too. Luke, near bursting with excitement, endured all kinds of good-natured teasing from his older brothers. The kind doctor had lots of last-minute advice. Marty wondered briefly if she even would get a turn at telling her son good-bye. Just before he was due to leave, he stepped over to her and hugged her close. Marty had to look up now, for her youngest was taller than she by a considerable amount.

"Ya take care, now," Luke whispered for just the two of them. "I don't want anythin' to happen to thet baby brother."

A sob caught in Marty's throat. *I'd gladly give up this baby if I could just keep you,* she wanted to say. But she didn't. Luke wouldn't want to hear that kind of talk.

Instead she held him close and said motherly things about caring for his health and getting lots of rest. She also assured him that she would be counting the days until Christmas, and he promised in return that he would be doing the same. His luggage was tossed up onto the waiting stagecoach as the restless horses stamped and pulled on the bits. The driver called, and Marty knew she must let him go. She stepped back and attempted a smile, a rather lopsided one. Luke's was broad in return. He let his hand touch her cheek, and then he wheeled and swung himself into the waiting stage. With a shout from the driver and a scattering of dust from the wheels, the coach jerked away. The horses were in a gallop before the driver had firmly settled himself. The lump stayed in Marty's throat, but she refused to allow herself to cry. There would be plenty of time for that later.

Why was life so full of good-byes? She looked over at Arnie. He would be the next one. And he was even more excited about the prospect than Luke had been. Why were they always in such a hurry to leave home?

Before Marty's thoughts could continue in this direction, Ellie was taking her arm and moving her down the street.

"Now you an' me are gonna do some shoppin'," she was

saying, "an' I'm not gonna be put off any longer."

Marty nodded numbly. It was time. With Luke gone, she would need some kind of sewing to keep her hands busy. Besides, she was beginning to show—just a bit. She supposed that if people were going to talk, they would already be at it. She might as well settle their minds once and for all.

She allowed Ellie to lead her into the general store and over to the yard goods.

Little one, she apologized to the child she carried, *if you're really there—and I still have a hard time accepting the fact—you'll have to forgive me some. I just can't get excited about you—I didn't plan for you, and—* But Marty got no further, for a strange thing happened. With a suddenness that startled even her, the baby within answered with a fluttery movement. It was unmistakable, and with the movement came the clear knowledge that Marty did indeed carry within her another life. At that same instant, a love for the unborn child filled her being. Whoever this baby turned out to be, he or she was special, individual, and hers—hers and Clark's. And even though she hadn't planned it, the fact that this baby was growing, warm and safe, inside her body and would one day snuggle in her arms, impressed itself upon her.

"I hope thet yer a girl," she whispered under her breath as a tear slowly formed in her eyes.

"What'd ya say?" asked Ellie, busy laying out soft flannels and cottons for selection.

"Oh, nothin'," answered Marty, quickly disposing of the telltale tears. "Nothin' much. I'm just on yer side, thet's all. I hope it's a girl, too."

EIGHT

A Visit With Ma

Marty decided she would make a call on Ma Graham. Before word started to circulate throughout the community that the Davises were to be parents again, Marty wanted to tell Ma herself. She asked Clark for the team and bundled up snugly against the brisk fall breeze.

Even before she had the team tied at the Grahams' hitching rail, Ma was on her way across the yard, arms outstretched in welcome.

"How did ya know I've been achin' fer a good visit?" Ma called. "We haven't had us one since just after ya got home."

"I know," responded Marty. "I couldn't wait any longer."

"How ya been?" Ma asked, arm around Marty's waist on the way to the house.

"Fine—just fine."

Ma apparently let the answer go and ushered Marty into her kitchen, hanging up her coat on a peg by the door.

"Sit ya down," she said, "an' I'll put on the pot. Ya carin' fer coffee or tea?"

"Tea, I'm thinkin'."

Ma put another stick of wood in the firebox of the big kitchen stove and shoved forward the kettle. Then she joined Marty at the table.

"Yer lookin' better. Ya had me worried there fer a while. Every time I saw ya at church, I'd say to Ben, 'Somethin' ain't quite right 'bout Marty.'"

"Ya said thet?"

Ma nodded.

"My," said Marty. "I didn't have me any idea how many folks I had a worryin'. My family was frettin', too."

"But yer lookin' better."

"Feelin' much better, too." Marty smiled.

"Seen the doc?"

"I did, as a matter of fact."

"He able to tell ya what was wrong?"

Marty nodded in agreement.

"An' he was able to give ya somethin' to get ya over—?"

"Not exactly," Marty put in.

Ma's face again showed concern. "But ya said yer feelin' better."

"Oh, I am," Marty quickly affirmed.

Ma looked puzzled.

"Ya see," said Marty, "all thet is . . . I mean, the only reason I wasn't feelin' my best is thet . . . I'm . . . I'm in the family way."

Ma's eyes grew large and then her face grew into a broad smile. "Well, I'll be" was what she said. "Now, why in the world didn't I guess thet?" She chuckled and reached across the table for Marty's hand.

"Guess, like me, ya wasn't really expectin' it. I couldn't even believe it myself fer a long time."

"Well, I never," said Ma again, shaking her head with another chuckle.

"I'm showin'," said Marty and stood to her feet so that Ma could see for herself.

"Well, I declare," said Ma. "Ya are, yes, ya are."

Now Marty began to laugh and Ma joined her.

"Isn't thet somethin'?" asked Marty. "A woman of my age— an' a grandma?"

"Ya ain't so old. I had me another young'un after I was older'n you."

Marty quickly nodded.

The teakettle began to steam and Ma pulled herself up to go and prepare the tea.

"An' what does yer family think 'bout it?" she asked over her shoulder as she cut some gingerbread.

Marty shook her head. "Would ya believe thet every one of 'em thinks it's just fine?"

"Clark?" Ma asked as she rejoined her guest at the table.

"I'm afraid he has a hard time keepin' himself from bein' downright proud. He only holds hisself in check fer my sake."

Ma smiled, poured the tea, and passed Marty her cup.

"Well, thet sure beats fussin' 'bout it."

Marty knew that Ma was right.

"An' you?" asked Ma, passing Marty the gingerbread.

Marty was slow to answer. "Well, me," she said, "thet's a different story. I wasn't all thet happy 'bout the idea."

"Embarrassed?"

"Embarrassed! Scared! Worried!"

"Bein' sick like had ya scared?"

"Not really. I hadn't even figured out what was wrong with me fer a long time. When I did reckon it might be this, I was scared and worried 'bout what folks would think, not 'bout iffen I could make it okay."

"I know the feelin'," said Ma. "I felt thet way with my last one. Then I just got busy an' told myself thet it weren't nobody else's business anyway."

Marty laughed. "People make it their business," she said. But, to her amazement, she found she really didn't care anymore.

"Ya feelin' better 'bout it now?"

Marty looked into the teacup before her and watched the wispy steam rise upward. "Yeah," she said at length, raising her eyes to Ma's. "I feel better 'bout it now. After Luke left, there was a big emptiness, and then . . . well, Ellie insisted on shoppin' in town since we was already there. She's been pesterin' me 'bout gittin' some garments ready fer this here new one—an' a strange thing happened. It was the first time I felt movement. An' suddenly . . . well, I just felt a real love, all through me, fer this little stranger. I wanted the baby, Ma. I can't really explain it—I just knew I loved an' wanted this baby."

Ma nodded her understanding. "I know what yer meanin'," she said. "It's powerful hard to keep fightin' it once ya feel 'im really there."

The two women sat silently for a few moments, each deep in her own thoughts.

Finally Ma broke the silence. "Must have been awfully hard to let Luke go."

"It was. It really was. An' he was so excited 'bout it thet he could hardly contain hisself. . . . Might have been easier iffen he'd clung to me just a bit," Marty finished, her voice low.

Ma smiled. "Might have made ya feel better fer a minute, but it woulda made ya feel worse in the long run."

"I s'pose. I mighta cried all night iffen I'd felt he was hurtin', too."

"Seems they grow up too fast. Ya just git yer heart set on 'em, an' they're gone."

"It's Ellie thet frightens me."

"Meanin'?"

"Just don't know how I'm gonna stand it when it's Ellie's turn to go. She has been so good, Ma. Takin' over the runnin' of the house an' coaxin' me on. I just don't know how I'll ever manage without her."

"Ellie got a beau?"

"Not yet—but it'll come."

"I know what yer meanin'. Girl like Ellie can't hold off the young fellers fer long."

"She's never really paid thet much attention to the young men who've hung around, but one of these days . . ."

"I must confess," said Ma, "I been lookin' round me at church tryin' to sort out just which of the neighborhood fellers is good enough fer Ellie."

Marty nodded and admitted that she had been doing the same thing.

Then she prompted Ma, "An'. . . ?"

"Ain't spotted 'im yet," answered Ma frankly. "Somehow it seems Ellie should have someone special like."

"Guess she'll think he's special when the time comes."

Ma reached for Marty's cup to refill it. "I know I fought it some when my young'uns were gittin' theirselves all matched up with their mates. Kinda glad it's all over now an' settled. They all chose ones I can be proud of, too. Kinda a good feelin' to know it's cared fer. They did a good job of it, too. I can sorta just sit back an' relax—an' enjoy the grandchildren."

"But yer grandkids are all nearby. Me, I've already got 'em scattered from the East to the West. I just don't think I could bear it iffen any more of 'em move so far away from home."

"Must be hard. I'd sure miss mine if they weren't here."

"Nathan an' Josiah are such sweethearts. An' there's the new little Melissa now. Who knows when I'll see her? An' Clae with her two little ones—we haven't seen her baby yet, either. Oh, I wish she could come home—even fer a short visit. It's hard, Ma. Hard to have them scatter. I miss them all so much."

Ma looked searchingly into Marty's face, then brightly and promptly changed the subject.

"An' how are Arnie's weddin' plans comin' along?"

The remainder of the time together was spent in discussing the family members who were close at hand, and Marty's spirits rose as she thought of the coming events and the happiness that was in store for each of them. And for her and Clark.

Winter settled in, and Marty was glad she had no good reason to be out as she watched the swirling snow and biting wind. Ellie was daily encouraging her on the sewing for the new baby, and it wasn't long until Marty's enthusiasm matched Ellie's.

Kate dropped in often. She obviously found great pleasure in the planning and preparations for the two babies. Clare shared Kate's eagerness, and he, too, was involved on the long winter evenings finishing the bed for the new little one who would make them truly a family.

Clark was finding it difficult to be as active as he had been in the summer and fall. The icy patches were often causing his crutch to slip, and after one or two near falls, he was content to let his grown sons handle most of the chores. He had always been easy to have around, and Marty enjoyed being with him more often.

Daily, Marty's love for her unborn child grew. She wondered how she could have ever *not* wanted it. The whole family was waiting for this baby with far more interest than they had shown for any of the others.

Most of Arnie's time and attention were given to his upcoming wedding. His little farmhouse was ready now. Anne had even hung the curtains in the windows and scattered a few rugs on the floor. Because Anne had no mother to help her with her preparations, Marty had been pleased to piece quilts and hem dishtowels and assist in any way she could. Already she felt very close to her new daughter-in-law-to-be. She was sure that Arnie and Anne would be very happy.

And so the wintry days and evenings passed, one by one. The house was brightened by friendly chatter, much coming and going, and busy activity shared by the family. Marty felt it was one of the most pleasant times she could remember, in spite of those members who were not with them.

A welcome letter arrived from Luke, and Marty opened it eagerly and read it aloud. He assured them he was fine and enjoying his studies. He stated that Doc Watkins had certainly given him an advantage over his other classmates; he understood so much that they had never been exposed to. He was boarding with a kindly old couple who fussed over him and pampered him. They had never had children of their own, and the woman was trying to catch up on all the years of missed mothering in just a few short months, Luke wrote.

He missed the family, he said, though he really had very little time even to think about it. He was going to a nearby church and had never seen so many young people gathered together before. Most of them were very kind and friendly. He hadn't seen Clae and her family very often. There just wasn't time for much visiting, but he was to join them for Thanksgiving, Clae insisted. They were all fine. The new baby was really sweet, and "Esther Sue had grown like you wouldn't believe." She had been shy with Luke at first, but she had gotten over that quickly. Joe was enjoying his seminary classes. He wondered how the little church back home had ever put up with his lack of knowledge. He couldn't believe how much there was to learn.

Luke ended his letter with a message for each of them. Marty was admonished to take care of herself and that coming baby. He would be home soon for Arnie's wedding and Christmas, and he wanted everything to be just as he remembered it.

There was a postscript on the bottom addressed to Ma. "I really won't mind if it's a girl," the sentence read, and Marty brushed at unbidden tears as she folded the letter and replaced it in its envelope.

Dear, dear Luke, she thought. *Alone and so busy—and lovin' every minute of it.*

But Luke was right. Before they knew it, Christmas would be upon them.

NINE

Ben

Marty felt like she had just snuggled down and closed her eyes when there was a pounding on the front door. Clark bounded from the bed and was pulling on his clothes while Marty struggled to a sitting position.

"What is it?" she wondered.

"Don't know—but someone seems to want us powerful bad."

Clark left the room, his crutch beating a fast rhythm as he hurried toward the stairs.

"Light the lamp," Marty called after him. "You'll be fallin' in the dark." But Clark was already on his way, no doubt feeling his way through the hallway and down the steps.

Marty left her bed and reached for her wrap. She could see Arnie beyond her door, and he had taken the time to light a lamp.

Ellie called to him from her room. "What is it?" Marty heard her ask.

"Not knowin' yet," answered Arnie. "Pa has gone to see."

He moved on down the stairway, and Marty slipped into her house socks and quickly followed after him.

Arnie turned when he heard her coming. "Ma, ya shoulda stayed in bed," he said.

"I'm all right," she insisted.

"Watch yer step," said Arnie, reaching out a hand to assist her.

Lou Graham was in the kitchen talking with Clark when the two entered. Clark looked up, and when he saw them he moved to Marty and put an arm around her shoulders. "It's Ben," he said softly.

Marty had many questions, but she could not find voice to ask any of them. Her heart was pounding as she looked from one face to the other. Surely it was serious to bring Lou out in the middle of the night. Ellie joined them, a puzzled frown on her face.

Clark moved a chair toward Marty, and she sat down.

"What happened?" It was Arnie who finally was able to speak.

"His heart," answered Clark.

A moment's silence, and then, softly, "How is he?"

"He's . . . he's gone."

"Gone?" It was Marty now. *There must be some mistake!* Her thoughts whirled. Why, she had seen Ben herself just a short time ago, and he looked perfectly well. He had taken care of the team when she was over to visit Ma and had even given out some good-natured teasing. There must be some mistake. It couldn't be Ben. Not Ben Graham.

Clark was speaking. "It happened just as he was gittin' ready fer bed. I'm goin' over, Marty."

Marty's stunned mind and emotions were scrambling to sort out what was being said—what was going on. *Ben was gone—Ben Graham—their good neighbor of so many years. Ma was a widow again. Clark was going to her.*

Marty shook her head and tried to stand. "I'm goin', too," she said quietly yet with insistence. "I'm goin', too."

She could feel their eyes upon her. Each one in the circle seemed to be saying no, even though no one had actually said it. Marty wrapped her robe more closely about her and took a deep breath. She squared her shoulders and looked at them.

"I'm goin', too," she said evenly. "Ma needs me—an' I'll be just fine."

Still no one voiced an argument, and Marty went back to her room to get dressed. Ellie followed her.

"Mama," she said, "be sure ya dress warm. It's cold out there."

Marty nodded and mechanically went on laying out her clothes.

When she went downstairs again, Clark was waiting. Lou had already gone on to take the sad news to others in the family. Arnie was heating a brick in the fireplace, and Marty knew that it was to keep her feet warm as they traveled. The team was ready, and they stomped and blew impatiently. They did not cotton to the idea of leaving their warm stall on such a night.

Without comment Clark helped Marty in, and Arnie placed the wrapped brick at her feet and tucked a heavy robe securely about her. His feelings showed without words in his extra care for her comfort and safety. Clark picked up the reins, clucked to the team, and they were off.

Marty had never experienced such a silent trip to the Grahams'. All the way there, she attempted to accept the truth that Ben Graham was dead—but it did not seem real. She wondered if Clark was wrestling with it, as well, but she did not ask.

A pale moon was shining, reflecting off the whiteness of the snow-covered fields. A million stars seemed to be blinking off and on overhead. Vaguely she wondered if anyone knew for sure just how many were up there—no, she supposed not. There were too many. Only God himself knew the actual count.

And God himself knows about each one of His children. Marty closed her eyes. He knew what had happened this night. He knew of Ben. Why, He had already welcomed Ben into the courts of heaven. Was He glad . . . pleased to have one more child at home? Marty would be. If one of her far-off children were suddenly to walk through her door, she would be celebrating. Maybe God was celebrating—celebrating because Ben was home.

But what about Ma? her thoughts went on. She was alone again now. Did God know that, too? Did He know how empty and lonely Ma would be feeling? What was it that Ma had said to her long ago about losing her first husband, Thornton? Ma had said she had wanted to die, too, that a part of her seemed to be missing or numb or something. Well, Ma would be feeling that way again. She had loved Ben so much, had shared with him for so long. Ma would be empty and hurting, and there wouldn't be any way that anyone—anyone in the world, no matter how much they loved her—would be able to help that hurt.

Suddenly Marty was crying—tearing sobs from deep inside. *Oh, Ma. Oh, Ma! How ya ever gonna bear it?* she mourned inwardly. It was true. It really was true. Ben was gone.

Clark let her cry, though he placed an arm around her and drew her closer to him. He didn't try to hush her. He knew as well as she did that she needed the release of the tears.

By the time they reached the Graham farmyard, Marty had herself under control. Lights shone from each window. Teams and saddle horses milled and stomped in the yard, doors opening and closing quietly as family arrived.

Clark helped Marty down and then moved the team on farther into the yard to tie them at a corral post. Marty waited for him, dreading that first meeting with poor Ma. She didn't want to go in by herself.

When Clark returned to take her arm and lead her to the house, they spoke for the first time.

"Looks like the whole family's here," said Marty softly.

"Yeah, Lou said he was lettin' 'em know."

"Good thet they're all close by."

"Lem was away—don't know iffen they got in touch with 'im yet."

They reached the house, and without knocking, Clark ushered them in. The big farm kitchen was full of people. Coffee cups sat on the table, but no one seemed to be drinking from them. Tear-stained faces were turned toward Ma, who sat before an open Bible and, with a quavering yet confident voice, was reading to her family.

"'. . . for his name's sake. Yea, though I walk through the valley of the shadow of death, I will fear no evil: for thou art with me;

thy rod and thy staff they comfort me. Thou preparest a table before me in the presence of mine enemies: thou anointest my head with oil; my cup runneth over. Surely . . .'" Ma's voice broke. She waited a moment and then went on, her voice ringing out stronger than before: "'Surely goodness and mercy shall follow me all the days of my life: and I will dwell in the house of the Lord for ever.'"

She placed both hands on the Book and closed her eyes, and everyone in the room knew she was believing its promises and silently making them her own in prayer.

When she opened her eyes again, she saw that Clark and Marty were there. Without a word she held her hands out to them as a fresh collection of tears spilled down her worn cheeks. Marty moved quickly to her and took her in her arms. They clung and cried together. Marty was vaguely aware of voices and movement about her. She knew that Clark was offering his sympathy to other family members. She must speak to them, too, but Ma came first.

After the initial expressions of sorrow, they sat around the kitchen sharing memories of Ben and discussing plans for his funeral service. There wasn't a great deal of preparation to do. The new undertaker in town would prepare the coffin. The young minister had not been called in the dead of the night—Ma insisted that he be allowed to sleep. She had her family and her neighbors, and there was plenty of time to make the arrangements. Besides, she declared, the poor young man had already lost three nights' sleep sitting up with ailing Maude Watley. Her condition seemed to have improved somewhat, and the minister finally had been able to get a night's rest.

The neighborhood men would dig another grave in the little yard beside the church. Clark offered to make sure that was done. Tom thanked him for his kindness. "But," he said, "the boys an' me been talkin', an' we'd kinda like to do it ourselves."

Clark's understanding of their desire was clear as he nodded his agreement.

Sally Anne was weeping the hardest. Marty found her in Ma's bedroom, Ben's old farm work hat crumpled up against her, the sobs shaking her entire body.

Marty tried to comfort her, but Sally Anne just cried all the harder.

"I'll be all right," she finally gasped out between sobs. "Just please leave me be." So Marty left. Sally Anne was going to need time to sort out her grief.

The day of the burial was cold. But the wind had gone down, for which all were thankful. Still, the sky was gray and the air frigid. Marty clasped her coat about her and prayed for the group of family members who were clinging tightly to one another. It would be a hard day for each of them. And when they scattered again to their various homes, what would become of Ma then?

Marty was glad that Lou and his wife and two children lived near her. At least Ma would have someone close. Still, it would be hard for her—hard to face an empty house, hard to lie alone in a bed that had been shared for so many years, hard to sit at a table where no one used the adjoining chair. Yes, she had many difficult days ahead of her. Marty was glad Ma had a deep faith in God that would help her through the days of intense sorrow. She must remember to pray for her daily. And visit her as she could. Maybe Ma would like to be included in some upcoming family dinners.

But Marty also knew that Ma wasn't likely to sit around and feel sorry for herself. What an example of faith in trying times she was to the whole community.

TEN

Good News

Life required that everybody carry on, so even though their hearts were heavy, family and friends of Ben put their minds on living and the everyday tasks that called for their attention.

It was only a few weeks now until Christmas and Arnie's wedding. Marty tried her hardest to keep an atmosphere of anticipation for the sake of her family, even though she could not get out from under the heaviness she felt for Ma and her family. Ma was often in her thoughts and prayers.

Clark returned home from town one day and hurried into the kitchen, his expression telling Marty he had news.

"Yer not gonna believe this. Guess what I just heard."

Marty looked up from the small baby gown in which she was making dainty tucks. "Couldn't guess," she said. "What's goin' on now?"

"Willie's pa has been so impressed with the West thet he's talked the whole family into goin' out fer a look."

"Yer joshin' me," said Marty, laying down her handwork in disbelief.

"Not joshin'."

"Ya mean they're *all* movin' out?"

"Not movin'. Not yet anyway. They're just goin' on out fer a look-see."

"Callie an' the kids, too?"

"Yep."

"Who's to care fer the farm?"

"Now this yer *really* not gonna believe."

Marty felt her eyes widen, wondering what in the world could be more difficult to believe than what she had already heard.

"Lane," said Clark.

"Lane?"

"Lane."

"Our Lane? I mean Willie's Lane?" Marty was stunned.

Clark laughed. "Told ya you'd never believe it."

"I can't imagine—Lane comin' back here! Are ya sure?"

"I'm sure. Zeke LaHaye showed me the letter hisself. Fact is, Lane's s'posed to arrive tomorra so's he can learn all he needs to know 'fore the LaHayes leave next Tuesday."

"Yer right—I can't believe it!" exclaimed Marty, excitement taking hold of her. "Lane comin' here. Isn't thet somethin'?"

"Ellie," she said, hurrying to the kitchen, "Ellie, Lane's comin'."

Ellie lifted her head from the potatoes she was peeling.

"Who's Lane?" she asked.

"Lane. Willie's Lane. We told ya 'bout 'im."

"Lane," repeated Ellie and frowned as she tried to remember. Clark joined them in the kitchen.

"Want some coffee, Pa?" Ellie asked, and Marty was just a trifle irritated that Ellie hadn't responded more enthusiastically to the wonderful news of their friend's arrival.

Without waiting for her father's answer, Ellie moved to reach for two coffee cups, which she placed on the table and filled.

Clark thanked her and sat down, pulling one cup toward him, and Marty took the chair opposite him and accepted the other cup. Ellie had already gone back to peeling potatoes.

"I just can't believe it," Marty said again, not willing to let the matter drop. "Lane comin'."

"How so?" asked Ellie.

"The LaHayes are goin' out to see Willie an' Missie. Gonna be there in time fer Christmas and then stay on a spell," Clark explained again.

Finally Ellie's hands stopped their busy paring, and her head bobbed up. "Really? Missie will be so excited she'll near go crazy. 'Magine thet. Havin' all thet family fer Christmas!"

Marty smiled as she pictured Missie's excitement and busy preparations. "And we can send some Christmas presents with them—"

Clark's laugh interrupted her. "Yeah, well, ya better go easy on how much you send—the LaHayes are gonna have enough luggage of their own."

"Who's gonna look after their place?" asked Ellie, and Marty noted silently that the girl hadn't been listening.

"Lane," she answered patiently.

"Oh, *thet's* why Willie's sendin'—what's his name?"

"Lane."

"Lane who?"

Clark began to laugh. "His name's Lane Howard. He's one of Willie's hands. Guess he must know somethin' 'bout farmin', or Willie wouldn't be sendin' 'im."

"I see," said Ellie, and her hands began to work on the potatoes again.

"He's such a fine boy," Marty said. "He's the young cowboy who was the first one to come to Willie's services, an' he was the first one to believe."

Ellie nodded her interest in that piece of news.

"He's a mighty fine young man," Clark agreed. He looked off into space as though seeing some events in his memory.

"It was Lane who knelt down beside Jedd Larson and joined me in prayer when Jedd was in such a bad way."

"It was Lane who rode through the cold night to get Doc de la Rosa fer Jedd, too," added Marty.

"Yeah, an' Lane hitched the team and drove back through the night to take Jedd over to Doc's house," Clark continued.

"He rode with ya, too, when ya went on over on Christmas Day," Marty reminded Clark.

"Yeah, he did, didn't he?" Clark smiled. "I can still see him climbin' down off his horse an', without sayin' a word, takin' his blanket to cover up my stub of a leg. Boy, was it cold! I think thet I'd a froze it fer sure iffen Lane hadn't done thet. An' me—I was too dumb to even think 'bout it needin' coverin'.'"

Ellie looked back and forth between her parents as they remembered their experiences with Lane out west.

Marty said, her voice low and husky, "Don't know iffen ya even knowed it, but Lane was the one who helped the doc when he took off yer leg. Willie wanted to, but he was afraid he couldn't stand it, so he went fer help—an' it was Lane who volunteered."

"Didn't know thet." Clark shook his head, looking thoughtful. Then he sighed. "Shoulda known it, though, thet Lane would be the one—"

"It'll be so good to see 'im again. When did ya say he's comin'?" Marty asked.

"S'posed to be tomorra."

"We'll have 'im over right away!"

"Now, hold it," laughed Clark. "Willie is sendin' 'im out here to look to his family's farm, not to spend his time—"

"I know thet," retorted Marty, "but surely we can have 'im visit now an' then without any harm bein' done. He has to eat, now, don't he?"

Clark stood up and ruffled her hair.

"Reckon we can," he said. "I was thinkin' myself thet it'd be awful nice to give 'im an invite fer Christmas."

"I hope we don't need to wait thet long to see him. I'd nigh bust by then."

Clark laughed again. "Got me a feelin'," he said confidently, "thet he'll be lookin' us up."

Marty hoped Clark was right. Lane was almost like family, like he'd be bringing a little piece of their beloved Missie's family with him.

————

"Look at thet sunshine," Ellie commented to Marty. "Think I'm gonna go out an' git me a little of it."

Marty followed the girl's eyes to the window. It was a truly glorious winter day.

"I was just thinkin' the same," she said. "Think I just might go on over an' have me a cup a' tea with Kate."

"Good idea. I might even join ya iffen I git my chores done in time, but don't wait on me. I might git to enjoyin' the sun so much I'll decide not to come in."

Marty smiled. Ellie had always loved the out-of-doors.

"Go ahead," she said. "It'll do ya good."

"Ya git ready," said Ellie, "an' I'll walk ya on over to Kate's so ya won't slip on the ice."

"Ya fret too much," Marty countered. "Just like yer pa. I've been walkin' on ice fer a good number of years now, an' I don't recall takin' a tumble yet."

Ellie shook her head without saying anything further, put on a light coat, and stood waiting, so Marty pulled a warm shawl about her and they started off together. The sun reflected brightly off the snow and made them squint against the glare. It felt warm on their heads in spite of the cool air.

"Hard to believe we're 'bout due fer Christmas. Feels more like spring," observed Marty.

"Doesn't it, though?" answered Ellie. "But I'm so glad it's nice. Makes it better fer Lady and her puppies."

"How are they doin'?"

"Oh, Mama, they're so cute now. 'Specially thet little black-an'-white one. He has the biggest eyes an' the floppiest ears. I hope Pa will let me keep 'im."

"We hardly need another dog around here, I'm thinkin'."

"But he's so cute."

"Puppies are all cute," reminded Marty. "When they grow up they're just another dog."

"Now, ya can't be tellin' me thet ya aren't partial to dogs," Ellie remonstrated, and Marty laughed, knowing Ellie was right. She had always loved dogs, and each time there had been a new batch, she was the one who suffered the most as she watched the puppies going off to new homes.

They reached Kate's house, and Marty was warmly welcomed in, while Ellie went on to care for her chickens.

———

The young man swung off his horse, tied it to the rail fence, and walked up to the door. Several knocks received no response, so he turned toward the barn, where he saw the door standing open.

After Ellie had finished feeding the chickens, she had gone on to the barn to see the puppies. The day had become so delightfully warm she hadn't gone far before removing her coat.

She had thrown the barn door wide open and let the sun stream into the building. Lady ran to meet her, four pudgy puppies tumbling and stumbling along behind her. Ellie tossed aside her coat and fell down on her knees in the warm, sweet-scented straw.

"Oh," she crooned, picking up her favorite and pressing it against her cheek. "Yer just the sweetest thing."

A small tongue licked haphazardly at her nose, and Ellie kissed the soft fuzzy head and reached for another puppy. A third one began to tug at her skirt, growling and pulling as though tackling something unknown and dangerous. Ellie laughed and playfully pushed at the puppy with her foot. The puppy swung around and attacked her shoe instead. She pulled him into her lap and reached for the last one, a shy little female, the smallest of the litter. "Come here, you," Ellie said, coaxing the little one closer. She settled herself into a sitting position and cuddled the puppies in her lap. Lady pressed herself close, taking a lick at Ellie's face, her arm, her hand—wherever she could get one in. Ellie lifted her feisty little favorite again and pressed him close against her cheek. "I must ask Pa iffen I can keep ya," she told him.

Ellie was so busy with the puppies she hadn't seen the shadow that crossed the door; nor did she notice the figure who stood there, looking at the shining golden head bowed over the squirming puppy. He watched silently. She lifted her face to the sun, and it fell across her cheeks, highlighting their glow and the deep blue of her eyes. Still she had not seen him, so enraptured was she with her little friends. She stroked the curly fur gently with slender fingers and caressed the fluffy, drooping ear.

"Yer just the sweetest thing," she went on, lifting him so she could look the puppy in the face. "How could anyone give ya up?"

Lane had not moved. He knew he shouldn't be standing there watching her with her unaware that he was present, but he couldn't bring himself to break the spell of the scene before him. Who was she, this delightful young woman? She was as pretty and wholesome as . . . as . . . Lane had nothing to compare her to. He had never seen someone like her.

It was the dog who gave away his presence. Lady turned toward him and whined, her tail beginning to wave ever so slightly. Ellie lifted her eyes from the puppy to the door. At the sight of the young stranger, she gave a little gasp and hastened to her feet, scattering the three puppies playing on her skirt into the soft straw.

Lane quickly found his tongue.

"I'm sorry, miss—to startle ya like thet. I wasn't meanin' to. I'm . . . I'm lookin' fer the Davises."

"In a barn?" she asked, but her tone held more banter than blame.

"I knocked at the house an' didn't get an answer."

When she didn't say anything, he explained, "I . . . I saw the barn door open an' I thought someone might . . ." He trailed off. "I'm sorry if I've imposed, miss."

"No harm done," she said finally and put the puppy back down with its mother.

"Am I at the right farm or——?"

"We're the Davises," said the young woman before him, reaching down to brush straw from her skirt. "Who was it ya wished to see?"

"Missie's folks," he responded. "Clark an' Marty."

Ellie felt her eyes grow wide with shock and some embarrassment, and she took a good look at the young man who stood before her, hat in hand. *This must be the Lane Ma and Pa were talking about,* she thought as she looked him over.

He was tall and rather thin, though his shoulders were broad. He had a clean-shaven face and deep brown eyes. His jaw was firm set, as though once he had made up his mind it might be hard to change it. He wasn't what Ellie would call handsome—his somewhat crooked nose prevented him from being that—but he had a certain bearing that made you wonder if he wouldn't be a nice person to get to know.

Ellie let her gaze drop, further embarrassed by her bold scrutiny of the stranger.

"Mama is at Kate's right now, an' Pa is about the farm somewhere," she explained quickly.

She moved to lead the way to Kate's house, and he fell into step beside her.

They walked to Kate's without speaking further, and Ellie rapped lightly on the door but didn't wait for Kate's answer before she entered.

"Mama," she said, "there's someone here to see ya," and she stepped aside to let the young man enter.

Marty gave a little cry and sprang up from the table.

"Lane!" she said as she greeted the young man with a motherly embrace.

Marty turned from hugging the young man to Kate.

"An' this is Kate, Clare's wife," she introduced him warmly. "An' ya already met our Ellie."

Ellie stood rooted to the spot, feeling rather self-conscious and silly under Lane's gaze. He stepped forward.

"Not really," he said. "I sorta found her—but we weren't introduced proper like."

"Ellie," said Marty, "this is Lane, the one we've told ya so much 'bout."

Lane moved closer to acknowledge the introduction.

Ellie held out her hand. "I'm pleased to meet ya," she said softly. "I'm sorry I didn't realize who ya were."

Lane took the hand and looked into Ellie's blue eyes. Neither of them spoke. Ellie was rather surprised and not a little dismayed by her tumbling thoughts. She'd had no shortage of young men who would have stood in line to come calling if she'd given the slightest hint of interest, but none of them had made her feel like this. *You only just now met this Lane,* she told herself sternly. *Now get yourself back in hand,* she finished her silent lecture.

Marty insisted that Lane stay for supper. It hadn't been too difficult to persuade him. He said he was anxious for a good, long visit with Clark and Marty. He had news concerning Willie and Missie and their family. He had up-to-date reports on the new little church and its growth since they had left. There were messages from the ranch hands. And then, he said, there was his number-one reason for being in their home that evening—the package from Missie that he was to hand deliver. He reached into his shirt pocket. "Missie sent this, an' she told me not to dare fergit."

Lane withdrew a piece of carefully folded paper.

"Missie sent ya a lock of Baby Melissa's hair." He handed the small packet to Marty. Marty unwrapped it carefully, and a tiny scrap of soft, fluffy baby hair lay snuggled against the paper.

Ellie watched her mother struggle to hold back the tears.

"Far away in the West I've got a little granddaughter," Marty whispered as she held up the tiny baby curl. She lifted it up and it wrapped around her finger. There was just a tint of red to the golden lock. Marty held it to her lips and the tears began to fall.

Marty wiped her eyes as she turned to Lane. "Thank ya," she murmured. "She must be beautiful."

"We think so," Lane said. "We all think so."

"What a place fer a little girl to grow up," Clark spoke up. "There on a ranch with a dozen men to spoil her!"

They all laughed.

ELEVEN

Ma Graham

Marty wanted to see Ma one more time before Christmas, so she asked Clark to hitch up the team for her while there was still a pleasant break in the winter weather. He reluctantly agreed because he knew how important it was to her, but his eyes showed his concern.

"Sure yer not wantin' me to drive ya on over?"

"I'll be fine," Marty assured him. "Really, Clark, I'm feelin' just fine now. Best I been feelin' fer months."

Clark eyed her rounded body. "Well, be extra careful," he cautioned.

But Marty stopped him with a playful toss of her wet dishrag. "I won't be doin' any racin'," she promised with a smile.

Though the wintry sun was shining, the air still held a sharp chill. Marty had not gone far when she was glad for the extra blanket tucked about her at the insistence of her family.

She wondered who might be meeting her in the Graham yard to take the team now that Ben was gone. He had always been so quick to greet her and hurry her off to see Ma while he tended the horses. The thought of Ben not being there made Marty's heart ache once more for the empty place left in their lives.

She thought of Ma and wondered just how she was handling the long days and nights alone. It must be awfully hard on her and even more so with Christmas approaching. Christmas was a beautiful time of year but also a very lonely time if a person had recently lost a special loved one.

When Marty turned the team into the Graham yard and alighted from the sleigh, she was soon greeted by Lou, who came from the barn. He welcomed her warmly and sent her on in to see Ma, just as his father had done on so many previous occasions.

Marty did not have time to knock, for Ma had seen her through the window and came to meet her.

"Been so hopin' ya would come!" Ma said. "Been needin' ya somethin' awful."

Marty removed her heavy coat, hugged Ma, and crossed to warm her hands at the kitchen stove.

"I was thinkin' ya might," she said, her own tears close to spilling. "My thoughts are of ya so much, an' I'm prayin' so often . . . but thet . . . even thet doesn't help much, I'm afraid."

"Oh, it helps. To be sure, it helps," Ma assured her. "I've just been feelin' the prayers of those who are upholdin' me. I have no idea how I'd ever make it without 'em."

They both were silent for a moment.

"It sure does git lonely, though," Ma went on as she motioned Marty toward a chair at the table. "Even with my family nearby— an' they've been so good, always invitin' me fer supper or coffee or just to talk. But I've got to make the adjustment on my own, Marty. At first I was over there 'most every day. Thet was fine fer a while, but I can't keep on like thet. I've just gotta make the adjustment to livin' alone."

Marty sat down, and Ma pulled out a chair across from her.

"Ya know, in some ways," Ma went on, "this time is harder than when I lost Thornton."

Marty was surprised.

"What I'm meanin' is this: when I lost Thornton, even though it was terrible hard—'cause I loved him so much an' he was so young, and I was so unprepared—still I had my young'uns, an' I knew thet I couldn't give up—not fer a minute. They sorta kept me goin', if ya know what I mean. I scarce had time to think of my own sorrow. Well, this time I'm here all alone. My young'uns are grown now. It seems there just isn't a good reason to keep on a goin' a'tall."

"Oh, but there is," Marty quickly put in.

"I know. I know. I preach myself all those sermons many times a day, but I have a hard time believin' 'em."

"Ya said thet it takes time," Marty reminded Ma. "Remember? Ya haven't had much time yet, Ma." Marty reached across to grasp the work-worn hands folded one on top of the other.

Ma sat with head bowed, and Marty feared Ma would suddenly begin sobbing. Instead she squared her shoulders and looked up with a shaky yet brave smile. "Time?" she said. "It do take time, all right. Time an' God."

Marty toyed with an edge of the table, running a finger back and forth on the wood grain. "Wouldn't hurt none, either, iffen ya tried to look ahead," she said. "Christmas is comin'. Ya got a whole passel of grandchildren. Got their gifts all ready?"

Ma shook her head.

"Best ya git out yer knittin' needles and yer crochet hook, then, 'cause they're all gonna be expectin' Grandma to come up with the usual passel of scarves an' mittens."

"Oh, Marty, I just have no heart fer Christmas!" Ma mourned.

Marty rose and moved around the table to lay her hand on the shoulder of the older woman. "The hardest Christmas I ever faced was the one just after I lost Clem," she stated. "But ya know what? In lookin' back now, I see it as my most meanin'ful Christmas. Never have I felt the true meanin' of Christmas more'n I did thet year.

"I've often wondered why," she went on, sinking into the chair next to Ma, "but I think maybe it was because thet year I decided to use Christmas as a growin' time. I didn't even understand what it was all 'bout at the time, but I knew God had a far deeper meanin' fer Christmas than we usually give it. I wanted it. I wanted to find an' understand thet meanin'. At the time, all I knew was thet I wanted to give Missie a special Christmas. She had already lost so much, an' I wanted to help heal some of those painful memories. In givin' to Missie, I got far more myself. I kinda think thet's the true meanin' of Christmas. . . ." Marty paused and looked into Ma's face.

"Now, ya got a family," she continued after a moment. "A family thet ya love very much." Marty's voice was low but clear. "They are all hurtin' in their own way, but mostly they are feelin' deep sorrow fer you. Christmas isn't gonna mean much to any of 'em— unless *you* can give it meanin'. They need ya, Ma. They need ya ever' bit as much as they did when they lost their other pa."

Ma was crying softly as Marty spoke. When Marty finished, the older woman blew her nose and wiped her eyes.

"Yer right," she said. "In my sorrow I just haven't seen it. They do need me. All of 'em."

She left the table and went for the boiling coffee.

"My lands!" she exclaimed as she poured two cups and lowered herself wearily back into her chair. "I'm way behind. By this time most years I already had four or five pairs of mittens finished. I'm really gonna have to hustle, ain't I, Marty?"

TWELVE

Lane Helps Out

The LaHaye family got away on their visit west as planned, and Lane settled in to oversee their farm. There really wasn't all that much to do over the winter months. The stock needed tending, and there were two cows to milk night and morning, but he still wondered if he'd have empty hours hanging over him.

Glad that he had an excuse, he went to see the Davises and explained his predicament to Clare and Arnie. He began with, "What ya usually doin' with the long days of winter when there be no field work?"

"Well, we more'n have our days full with cuttin' the year's wood supply," answered Clare.

"The LaHayes got wood stacked a mile high," Lane informed them. "Told me not to be botherin' 'bout gittin' out any more. They gotta use thet up before it goes rotten."

"Then we've got all of the stock to care fer."

"They don't keep much stock. One sow, a few chickens, some milk cows, and a few beef cattle. They don't even have 'em a dog."

Arnie laughed. "Hope ya like readin'," he joked.

"Don't mind readin'," answered Lane, "but I sure don't wanna be doin' it all the time. Mind iffen I give ya a hand with yer cuttin'?"

"Yeah, we're gonna be gittin' out a little extra wood this year. Gonna have three fires of our own to keep burnin', what with the folks', mine, an' Arnie's here," said Clare. "'Sides, we kinda thought we'd like to add a bit to Ma Graham's woodpile, as well. Sure could use some extry help. Wanta swing an axe fer a few days?"

It was more than Lane had dared to hope for. His days would easily be filled with activity, and, in working with the Davis boys, he might even catch a glimpse of Ellie now and then. He promised Clare and Arnie he would be over the next morning as soon as he had finished the farm chores.

The chores took Lane a little longer than he had hoped, and he was concerned about the time as he hurried to the Davis farm, not even stopping for breakfast. He wondered if Clare and Arnie would be waiting or had already left for the woods without him.

He need not have worried, for the hour was still early and the Davis men were busy with the livestock when he arrived.

"Go on in an' say mornin' to Ma," Arnie called to him. "I'll be in shortly fer another cup of coffee an' my lunch. Ya might even be able ta talk the womenfolk into a cup for yerself."

Lunch, thought Lane, disgusted with himself. *I never even thought 'bout fixin' myself some lunch.*

Ellie opened the door to his knock. Trim and attractive in a dress of blue gingham with white cuffs and collar, a stiffly starched apron tied around her, Ellie smiled when she saw him, and Lane could feel his heart thumping.

"Won't ya come in?" she welcomed him. "The boys said thet ya had kindly offered to help git out the wood."

Lane entered and flipped his hat onto a peg near the door.

"Ma'll be right down," said Ellie. "She just went up to git her knittin'. Care fer some coffee?"

"Thet'd be powerful nice, ma'am," answered Lane, suddenly realizing just how hungry he was.

Ellie wrinkled a pert nose at him. "An' don't call me *ma'am*," she teased. "Ya make me feel like an old-maid schoolmarm."

Lane grinned. "Well, ya sure don't look like one," he dared to say and quickly added "miss."

"Ya needn't say *miss,* either," retorted Ellie.

At Lane's raised eyebrows, Ellie said, "Just 'Ellie' will do."

Lane nodded and Ellie indicated a chair at the table. Lane sat down and wondered what on earth to do with his hands. They seemed too big for his lap and too awkward for anything else. Ellie was no doubt too busy pouring a cup of coffee and selecting some morning muffins to notice.

"Those sure do look good, miss . . . Ellie," he said as she set the fresh-baked pastries before him.

"Bet ya didn't even stop fer a decent breakfast," she chided. "I know how my brothers batch. They'd starve to death iffen someone didn't look out fer 'em." And so saying, Ellie went for her frying pan and some eggs and bacon.

Lane was hungry, but he sure didn't want her to go to all the trouble. Still, he wasn't quite sure how to stop her, so he just sat and watched her as she fixed the plate of food.

"There, now," she said as she placed the plate before him. "Iffen yer kind enough to work for the Davises, the least thet we can do is to feed ya." She reached for his cup to refill it but discovered he had not yet touched it.

"Ya don't care fer coffee?" she asked him.

"Oh no. I do. I love coffee. Don't know how I'd ever git by without it. Why, on the ranch—" Lane stumbled to a stop. "I was just too busy to start drinkin'," he finished lamely.

"Busy?"

"Watchin' ya," he said softly. He could feel his face turn red at the boldness of it.

Ellie flushed, too, and turned back to the cupboards. "Best ya eat 'fore it gits cold," she said, sounding a little flustered. "I've got some lunches to make."

Lane busied himself with his plate and soon had cleaned up the bacon and eggs and finished the muffins. He crossed to the stove to refill his own cup. Ellie raised her eyes from her sandwiches. Lane took a sip and then lifted his cup to her.

"Thet's good coffee," he stated.

"Coffee's always better when it's *hot*," she countered, and Lane knew she was teasing him.

Arnie came in then. He tossed his mittens in a corner and moved to the cupboard for a cup.

"Boy, but she's cold out today! Gonna hafta really work to keep the blood circulatin'."

Clare was just behind him. "Thought ya had yer love to keep ya warm," he kidded.

Arnie colored.

"Ellie, got an extra cup of coffee there?" asked Clare.

"Help yerself," Ellie responded. "Ya know where the cups are."

He reached out and messed her hair. "Boy," he said, "yer as sassy as ever. Got no one to keep ya in line since I moved outta the house. What ya need is a good boss—"

But Ellie did not let him finish.

"There," she said, putting the last bundle into a small box. "There's yer lunch. I put in enough fer the three of ya."

Clare hurriedly downed a few swallows of coffee and then set aside the cup.

"I'm gonna run over and say good-bye to Kate. Meet ya at the barn," he said to the men and was gone.

Marty entered the kitchen, her knitting basket on her arm.

"Oh, mornin', Lane," she said. "I didn't know ya had arrived. Heard about yer kind offer to help the boys cut wood. Made Clark feel better. We need a lot of wood this year, and swingin' an axe with just one good leg is a mighty hard job. 'Specially when things are all wet and slippery underfoot. With you helpin' I'm hopin' to be able to keep him at home." She hesitated for a moment. "Did Ellie invite ya to stay fer supper?"

Lane flushed again.

" 'Fraid I didn't," said Ellie. "I wasn't thinkin' thet far ahead."

"Thank ya, ma'am," Lane said to Marty. "But I don't—"

"No problem," Marty assured him. "Iffen yer gonna be helpin' us out, the least we can do is to see thet yer proper fed."

Lane reddened even more. "Miss Ellie already fixed me my breakfast," he confessed, "an' sent along lunch fer my noon meal. I think thet'd be quite enough."

Marty laughed good-naturedly. "I'm glad she took care of ya. Now, ya just pop on in here an' have ya some supper 'fore ya be headin' fer home. We'll have it ready when ya get in from the hills."

Lane thought he should argue further, but he looked over at Ellie. It would be nice to see her just a bit more.

"Much obliged," he said to Marty and moved to follow Arnie out the door.

———

Ellie had a bad day. Something about Lane upset her. She had never met a young man who affected her that way before. Every time she thought about the way he looked at her, her cheeks felt aglow. He seemed as though he was trying to read her very thoughts—to send her strange messages with no words. It troubled Ellie and excited her, too. Why did he have to come from so far away and upset her neat and orderly world? In a few months' time, he would be heading back to the West, and what then? Would things fall back into the snug and familiar routine as though he had never been? Ellie was afraid not.

"He's nice, isn't he, dear?" Marty interrupted her swirling thoughts, and Ellie jumped.

"What?"

"Lane's a nice boy. Willie is so lucky to have him. He's been such a help on the ranch and in the church, too.

"An' then he comes on out here an' offers to go help cut wood—one of the hardest jobs there is. Sure takes a load off a' me where yer father's concerned."

Ellie agreed with her mother without committing herself in any way.

"Wonder how long he'll stay," Marty mused. "S'pose he's anxious to git on back, but they did say thet the LaHayes are gonna stay beyond Christmas, didn't they?"

"Guess so," murmured Ellie.

"Well, we should be real nice to him while he's here. Don't think he has a family of his own."

Marty went on with her knitting, and Ellie continued her kitchen tasks.

"Would be nice iffen he could go to the social at church next week," Marty speculated out loud. "Nice iffen he could meet some of our young people. Don't s'pose he's been in with fellas his own age fer ever so long. Some of those western cowboys can be a little rough. Would be nice fer him. Why don't ya ask him, Ellie?"

"Me?" Ellie's voice squeaked in astonishment at the very idea.

Marty's head came up, surprise on her face.

"Oh, now look, Ma," said Ellie defensively, "I don't go round askin' fellas to take me—"

"Oh," said Marty thoughtfully. "I wasn't thinkin' of it thet way. No, I guess ya don't. Would sorta sound thet way, I s'pose. I was just thinkin' of Lane as a friend of the family, thet's all. I'll have Arnie—"

"Arnie will be goin' with Anne."

"'Course."

"Well," said Marty, obviously not willing to give up on her idea, "I'll think of somethin'. Wish Luke was gonna be home in time. He could take 'im."

Marty busied herself counting stitches, and Ellie slipped a cake into the oven.

"Who ya goin' with?" Marty asked suddenly, and Ellie shook her head, wondering why her mother hadn't dropped the subject.

"Wasn't sure thet I would be goin'," answered Ellie honestly, thinking of the two boys who had asked her and not really wishing to go with either of them. She shrugged. "Not sure thet I want to," she continued.

"But ya should," encouraged Marty. "Ya need to git out more."
Ellie was highly relieved when her mother let it go at that.

Supper was ready when the men came in from the woods. Lane knew he really should go directly home and care for the LaHaye chores before it got too dark, but he couldn't resist spending a little more time in the same kitchen as Ellie. All day long he had thought of her. Her efficiency in the kitchen, her thoughtfulness in fixing his breakfast and sending along his lunch, her sparkling eyes and teasing smile. He couldn't get her off his mind, and he wasn't sure he really wanted to.

She served the meal, and once, when she had to replenish the plate of biscuits, she had bent near him to reach the empty dish. Lane thought surely everyone at the table must have seen how it affected him. He looked around quickly, but in truth, no one seemed to have noticed. No one but Ellie perhaps, and she was not letting on.

Lane left long after he should have and much before he wished to. It was dark riding home and a cold night for being out. He still had chores to do and cows to milk. He hoped that nothing on the LaHaye farm had suffered because of his tardiness. He wouldn't do it again, he told himself. He'd tell the Davises that he must go straight home from the wood cutting.

The next morning he was up even earlier than usual. He did the chores thoroughly and promised the milk cows that he would not keep them waiting that night.

He pushed the horse a little faster than normal on the way to the Davis', though still careful not to ask too much of it. If anyone knew how to care for his horse, it was Lane.

Again Ellie met him at the door, and Lane was surprised when he entered the kitchen to see that there was a place set at the table. Ellie pointed to it and asked him to be seated. She then busied herself at the already hot grill on the big kitchen stove, frying up a plate of pancakes. The very fragrance of them made Lane's mouth water.

She didn't pour his coffee until she had placed the stack of pancakes before him.

"Ya weren't gonna chance it gittin' cold, huh?" Lane asked softly, teasing in his voice.

If his words surprised Ellie, she chose not to show it. "Eat yer breakfast," she said in mock firmness, her words carrying with them an acknowledgment that she was aware of the strange under-current that existed between them.

Ellie went to make the lunches, and Marty soon joined them in the kitchen. They talked of the weather and the soon-approaching Christmas, and Marty extended an invitation to Lane to join them for Christmas Day, which he gratefully accepted.

Clark came in from the barn carrying a pail of fresh milk.

"How ya enjoyin' bein' a farmhand?" he joked with Lane. "Is it kinda nice to milk 'em rather'n brand 'em?"

Lane grinned. "Guess I'm 'bout the only cowboy who would ever admit he don't mind milkin' a cow."

Clark laughed. "Well, I don't mind admittin' it none. I kinda enjoy it myself. Had me an idea, too," Clark went on. "Since yer out there doin' my work, how 'bout I do a little of yers?"

Lane looked puzzled.

"Well, iffen ya wouldn't have to hurry on home fer the chores, you fellas could chop a few more trees. I thought I'd just ride on over and do up yer evenin' work so's you could stay on to supper here an' not be worryin' none 'bout the time thet ya git home."

"Oh, I couldn't—I was gonna tell ya thet I wouldn't be stayin' on fer supper. I'll just go on home after we finish in the woods. It won't be too late iffen I—"

"Nonsense," said Clark. "Me, I've got all day here with very little to do. I can do up the chores here and still have plenty of time to do yers, too, 'fore it gets dark."

"Oh, but I hate—"

"Won't have it any other way. Not gonna let ya work in the woods all day an' then go home to git yer own supper and do chores in the dark."

Lane could tell there was no use in arguing. He wondered if Ellie was listening to the conversation and if she was, what she thought about it.

" 'Preciate it," Lane said and determined that he'd work doubly hard felling trees.

THIRTEEN

Marty Makes a Date

Supper that night was chicken and dumplings, and Lane thought he'd never tasted anything better. Ellie wore her hair pinned up, but tendrils floated loose about her face, and her cheeks were flushed from working over the stove. Arnie was anxious to eat and be off to see his Anne, and Clare had gone directly home to Kate.

After the meal, Ellie tried to shoo everyone into the family sitting room before the big fireplace. Clark and Marty were quick to respond. Lane went, too—rather reluctantly. He chatted with Clark for a few moments, more aware of the activity in the kitchen where Ellie was clearing away the table than in the responses he was attempting to make in the conversation.

When Marty started a new subject with Clark, Lane saw it as his opportunity and slipped back to the kitchen.

"Mind iffen I dry?" he asked quietly, and Ellie looked up in surprise.

"I'd think yer muscles would be tired enough after yer long day," she stated.

"I'm thinkin' thet it might take a different set of muscles to dry a few dishes."

"Then I accept the offer," Ellie said and smiled. Lane's heart did a flip.

She handed him a towel and showed him where he could stack

the dried dishes. She led in the conversation, keeping it light and sticking to general subjects.

They were finished all too soon. Lane hung up the towel.

"An' how's yer young pup?" he asked.

Ellie looked surprised and then must have remembered the first time Lane had visited the farm.

"He's growin' like a weed," she said. "Pa has already given away two of the others."

"But not yer favorite?"

"Not yet. But he will. We already have enough dogs. I know thet. Pa's right. We can't keep 'em all. We'd soon be overrun."

She moved to stack dishes in the cupboard.

"It bother ya?" asked Lane.

"Guess it does." Ellie's smile looked a little forced. "But I'll git used to it."

"Anybody asked fer 'im yet?"

"I hide 'im," Ellie admitted sheepishly. "Every time someone comes to look at 'em, I hide 'im."

It was like the game of a little girl.

"An' don't ya tell," she quickly admonished, and then they were laughing together.

"How long d'ya think ya can keep doin' thet?" Lane asked when they were serious again.

"Till he's the last one," she said soberly. "Soon as the next one goes, I'm a goner."

"They don't have a dog at the LaHayes'," Lane said quietly.

"So ya said. I can't 'magine livin' on a farm without a dog."

"I've never had a dog of my own."

"Never?" Ellie's tone said she could scarcely believe that one could live without a dog.

"Never!"

"Don't ya like dogs?"

"Love 'em." Lane handed Ellie another stack of dishes, and she placed them in the proper spot in the cupboard.

" 'Specially took to thet little one of yourn out there. I been thinkin', iffen ya have to give it up anyway, would ya mind if I took it?"

Ellie's eyes widened. "Not . . . not iffen you'd like 'im."

"I'd love 'im—I really would."

"He's an awfully good dog," Ellie enthused. "He's gonna be real smart—you can tell by the brightness of his eyes. An' he's from real good stock an—"

"Hey," cut in Lane, "you don't have to sell me on the pup. I'm already askin' fer 'im."

Ellie smiled. "When d'ya want 'im?" she asked.

"Well, I was wonderin'. With me gone all day, would it be too much to ask ya to keep 'im fer a while? I mean—till I'm done cuttin' logs so's I'll be home with 'im. Seems a shame to take 'im from his ma an' then not have any company fer 'im."

Ellie's grin widened. "I'll tell Pa," she said.

Lane turned to go back into the living room because all the dishes were done and there really didn't seem like any good reason for him to stay around longer. Ellie stopped him midstride by calling his name. "Lane."

He turned quickly, and she spoke softly. "Thank you," she said.

Lane wondered just how late he dared stay without being an unwanted guest. Clark challenged him to a game of checkers, and Lane was surprised that he was able to play as well as he did with Ellie sitting across the room from him, hand stitching a baby blanket. Marty was working on a tiny sweater, but Lane was scarcely aware she was there until she suddenly spoke.

"The young people of the area are havin' a little gatherin' in the church next week," she said. "Would ya be interested in goin' an' gettin' acquainted, seein' yer goin' to be in our area fer a time?"

"It'd be nice," Lane answered absently and moved a checker out of range of Clark's.

"Arnie an' Anne will be there," went on Marty, "but I don't s'pose you'll be knowin' many of the others."

"Don't s'pose," said Lane.

"Thought maybe ya wouldn't mind takin' Ellie on over. She could show ya the way an' introduce ya to the rest of the young people."

Lane moved a king directly into the path of one of Clark's men and said calmly, "Be obliged."

The game went on. Lane lost soundly. From that move on, his mind was not on the game. He didn't dare look at Ellie. He had heard a little gasp and her shocked whisper, "Mama." He was surprised she hadn't outright refused her mother's suggestion. Would she back out gracefully later? Did she already have a date for the night? Lane feared it might be so. Clark moved to put away the checkerboard, and Marty kept her knitting needles *click-clicking* in a steady rhythm. Lane rose to excuse himself, and after a mild protest on Marty's part, which Lane countered with thanks for the evening but he had to go, Marty suggested that Ellie show him to the door.

Ellie rose obediently and laid her sewing aside.

They walked silently through the room and into the kitchen, and Lane took his heavy jacket from the hook and slipped his arms into it. He pulled his mitts out of his pocket and reached for his hat. Still Ellie had not spoken.

"That wasn't yer idea, was it?" Lane asked softly.

"No," answered Ellie, not meeting his eyes.

"Iffen it's a problem, I understand."

Ellie looked at him then. "Is it a problem fer you?" she asked sincerely.

Lane looked at her steadily. "It's an honor fer me," he stated.

"Then it's no problem fer me," said Ellie simply. Lane left with his hat in his hand and his heart singing.

On the night of the social, Lane was in early from the woods, for Arnie, too, wished to be home in plenty of time to properly get ready before going to pick up Anne. Clare gave them both some good-natured teasing, but Arnie quickly reminded Clare of how he had acted when he was courting Kate.

Lane did not stop for supper, having already informed Marty not to expect him. He hurried on home, thinking of a warm bath and a quick shave. He wasn't too sure that what he had to wear was appropriate, but he would do the best he could with what he had. He couldn't believe his good fortune—that he would actually be escorting Ellie! He still wasn't sure just how it had all come about or why Ellie hadn't turned him down.

———

Ellie rushed through the supper dishes and hastened to her room.

Marty went up to see what was taking her so long and returned to Clark, shaking her head. "Never seen Ellie fuss so," she said. "She's had herself a bath, and she's put on and taken off more'n one gown."

"Every girl fusses when she's goin' out with a young man," Clark responded.

"Lane?" Marty's head swung around to stare at Clark. "Why, he's just like one of the family."

"And so he is," agreed Clark.

———

Lane was plenty early, and when he looked at the radiant Ellie, his pulse beat more rapidly. She wasn't just pretty—she was lovely.

They walked out to the sleigh, and he helped her to be seated and tucked her in carefully against the cold of the winter night.

They talked of this and that on the way to the church. When they passed a neighbor's farm, Ellie would tell Lane something of the family who lived there.

When they arrived at their destination, Lane helped Ellie down and went to tie his horses among the milling, stomping teams of the neighborhood youth. He spotted the team of bays that Arnie drove and gave one a pat on his broad rump as he walked by.

Ellie was standing just inside the door when he entered the church. She showed him where to put his hat and coat and then began the introductions.

The young people were friendly and the games lively. The evening went quickly, and Lane, who was not used to such gatherings, was surprised at the fun they had. After a snack served by the girls, it was time to go home.

Lane felt several pairs of eyes on him as he helped Ellie into her coat. He knew there were a number of neighborhood boys who greatly envied him. He could feel it in their looks and their curt manners. It made him even more conscious of the fact that he was escorting the prettiest girl in the room.

Lane did not push the horses on the way home. If Ellie realized it, she did not say so. Instead, she talked about the party, the people he had met, and his thoughts concerning the evening. He reached to tuck the blanket securely around her, wishing with all his heart that he could leave his arm around her, too. Reluctantly, he withdrew it.

"What do ya think of our country?" asked Ellie, making a real turn in the conversation.

"It's different," he answered her, "but I like it fine."

"Ya miss the West?"

"Not as much as I thought I would," he said honestly.

"But you'll be glad to git back?"

Lane thought of the wide-open spaces, the mountains in the distance, the night-crying of the coyotes, and the wind in his face and answered her, "Reckon I will."

"Guess Missie has learned to love it, too," Ellie said, gazing up at the wide, star-studded sky as she spoke.

"I think thet she does," answered Lane.

"Seems so long since I've seen Missie."

"She speaks of ya often," Lane said and went on to think about the young sister Missie had referred to and wondered what Missie would think if she could see Ellie now.

"I still miss her. She was a wonderful big sister."

"Why don't ya come on out an' see her?" *With me,* he wanted to add but thought better of it.

Ellie laughed softly. "Sometimes I get the feelin' Mama isn't too anxious fer me to go visitin' out west. I think she's afraid I might not come back."

"Do you think ya could like the West?"

Ellie sighed. "I think I could like anywhere iffen . . ." But she did not finish.

"Iffen—?" Lane prompted.

"Well," she said matter-of-factly, "no use thinkin' on it now anyway. Mama needs me at home with the new baby comin' an' all. Maybe Missie will be able to come on home fer a visit 'fore too long. I'd love to see her—an' her babies."

Lane's heart sank a little. Was there a hidden message here? Was she warning him that he had no part in her future? Mama needed her. Lane loved her for her consideration, and she was right. Marty did need her now, but surely she wasn't planning to spend the rest of her life caring for her mama's kitchen and never giving consideration to having one of her own. He wanted to ask her—to tell her—but she pointed out a falling star and began to talk of other things. He clucked to the team. The night suddenly seemed much colder.

FOURTEEN

Christmas

Marty, filled with excitement about the nearness of the Christmas season, was also anticipating Arnie's upcoming wedding. But she was absolutely overjoyed by the fact that Luke would soon be home.

Oh, how she had missed him! His letters, which seemed all too infrequent, reminded her of how lonesome she was for their youngest son.

She baked his favorite cakes, fussed over cleaning his room, insisted that his favorite foods be on hand. And even when all this had been accomplished, she still bustled about trying to think of something more to do to make sure of his welcome.

"Why don't ya just sit ya down and relax?" Clark asked her. "Yer gonna be wearin' yerself out. It's *you* the boy is comin' to see, not the house or the pantry."

Marty knew Clark was right, and she tried to hold herself in check. But it was awfully hard.

On the day of Luke's arrival, Marty suffered a disappointment. She had planned all along to travel into town to meet his stage, but the day was bitterly cold with a strong wind blowing. And Clark firmly announced she would best stay home by the fire and let them bring her son to her.

She knew there was no use arguing, but how she chafed and stewed! She finally consented, insisting that Clark and Arnie—the two making the trip to town—promise to hurry home just as fast as the team would bring them. Clark agreed and left in time to do any shopping beforehand so they could leave for home as soon as they could load Luke and his luggage.

The day went awfully slowly for Marty. Ellie shook her head at her mother's pacing back and forth to the window. "Yer gonna wear out the floor," she teased, but her tone said she understood.

At last the team was welcomed by the dogs, and Marty ran to open the door for Luke.

At first appearance, Marty felt Luke had not changed much in the few months he had been away. He had really not grown taller, and he was about the same weight. His grin was as broad and his hug still as hearty. It wasn't until they had been together for some time that Marty began to recognize little changes. Luke was no longer her "little boy." He was well on his way to being a responsible man. The knowledge both saddened her and made her proud. She felt that he was seeing her in a different way, too. Luke had always been her compassionate and caring son. Now he looked at her, as well, with the concern and practiced eye of a doctor. Oh, true, Luke had a long way to go before he would be qualified, but he was already seeing the world through a physician's eyes.

The trips to the woods were put off during the busy time of Christmas celebration and Arnie's wedding. Lane hated to think of not having an excuse to visit the Davises for a whole week, but Marty seemed to feel he was a part of the family and always found some reason for him to come over.

Lane helped Ellie set up and decorate the tree in the big family living room. The boys were busy with other things, Marty said, and it was a big job for the girl to do all alone. Lane was happy to assist and enjoyed the evening immensely. Ellie was in a carefree mood, and her light chatter and silvery laugh rather went to Lane's head. *What would it be like to share this task with this girl for the many years ahead?* he asked himself and readily admitted that he liked the idea.

Christmas Day found the house crowded with family. Children

ran in and out, laughing and shrieking and exclaiming over Christmas surprises. The menfolk gathered in front of the open fire and roasted fall nuts and told jokes on one another, with much hearty laughing and good-natured backslapping. Women bustled about the kitchen, stirring and tasting and seasoning the huge pots that spilled savory odors throughout the whole house. Lane, who could not remember ever having been a part of such a Christmas before, joyfully absorbed every minute of it. Gifts from the tree were lovingly distributed, and Lane had been thoughtfully included. Marty's warm knit stocking cap would keep his head protected on cold winter days in the woods.

Eventually they were all gathered around the extended table. Chattering children were silenced for a season, joking men became serious, and the busy women laid aside their aprons and sat with hands folded reverently in their laps. Clark lifted down the family Bible and read aloud the Christmas story, as he had done on each of the preceding family Christmases, and then led his household in prayer. He remembered each of the absent ones by name—Willie and Missie and their children, and Clae and Joe and their little ones. He thanked the Lord for bringing Luke back to them for a visit. He prayed for the new family members who were yet unknown and asked that God would bless the mothers who carried them and make the new babies a blessing to many in the years to come. He asked God's blessing on Arnie and Anne as they shared the family table and would soon be establishing a home of their own. He prayed for Josh and Nandry and each one of their children. He thanked the Lord for Lane and his presence in their home and his friendship that meant so much to the family. He remembered the Graham family and this first difficult Christmas without the husband and father of the home. Last, he remembered Marty, his helpmate over the years. He thanked the Lord for her return to good health and asked God to give them both wisdom and direction as they guided the new little life with which He had seen fit to bless them.

It was a lengthy prayer, spoken sincerely. Even the children sat quietly, for Grandpa was talking to God.

In direct contrast, the meal itself was a noisy affair. Over the steady hum of chatter and loud laughter, one could scarcely hear oneself think. Lane stole a glance at Ellie. Cheeks flushed, golden hair wisping around her face, eyes sparkling with happiness, she answered some teasing coming from Clare. Lane was unable to hear her words, but from the look on Clare's face, he could guess Ellie was able to give as good as she received. After Clare's initial look of surprise at her quick response, he began to laugh and exclaimed loudly, "Well, ya got me there, little sister."

The children were excused to go back to their toys, and the adults settled down with another cup of coffee. The talk was not as boisterous now.

Clark leaned back and looked at his youngest son. "Yer lookin' good, boy. They must be takin' good care of ya."

"The Whistlers? They do all right, that's for sure. Aunt Mindy fusses even more than Ma." Luke looked at his mother with a grin.

"An' yer likin' the studies?" Clark went on.

"I love it. Learning something new every day."

"Like?"

"Ya wouldn't believe what they are able to do now—in surgery, for treatment. I'm just getting a glimpse into it, but it's a whole new world out there. In a few years' time, with what they are learning, they'll almost be able to make a man over again if something goes wrong with him."

"Guess I was born a few years too soon," Clark moaned in mock despair and brought laughter around the table.

"No fooling, Pa," said Luke. "You ought to see the artificial limbs they've got on the drawing boards now."

"Ain't no help on a drawin' board," replied Clark, and his sons laughed again.

But it looked like the doctor in Luke was not to be put off with joking. He began to explain the advancements in artificial limb design. Before he was finished, he was kneeling before Clark with the pinned-up pant leg containing its stub of a leg unself-consciously held in his hand. He explained to the gathered family what could soon be done. "You'll forget you even have a leg miss-ing!" he exclaimed. "I told Dr. Bush you were a natural to be one of the first to try it out. I want you to have one, Pa."

———

Nandry left the table. Marty thought she was going to check on the children. But when the meal was finished and the dishes were being cleared away, Nandry still had not returned.

The afternoon was spent in playing games, toasting nuts, and visiting.

"Remember the Christmas at Missie's when we all joined together in carol singing?" Marty asked Lane.

He nodded his head, remembering it well.

"Henry played his guitar," Marty went on and then interrupted herself. "Ya played your guitar, too."

"You play the guitar?" asked Arnie, immediately interested.

"Some," answered Lane.

"I always wanted to play a guitar," continued Arnie.

"Henry taught me. 'Fraid I wasn't too great a pupil, but I learned enough to sorta git a kick outta it."

"Do you have yer guitar with ya?" asked Ellie rather shyly.

"At the LaHayes'," he answered.

"I'd like to hear ya play sometime."

Only Lane and Ellie seemed to be conscious of the undercur-rent flowing between them. None of the other members of the family seemed to notice that Lane's eyes followed her about the room or that her cheeks flushed when she found him looking at her. Her simple words now were more to him than a statement. They came as a request, and without a spoken word his eyes made a promise.

Nandry returned—from where, Marty did not know. Perhaps she was not feeling well. Marty hoped she wasn't coming down with something that would keep her from Arnie's wedding. Nandry stayed on the fringe of things, keeping a close eye on the children and even bustling about in the kitchen some.

The day itself was clear and bright, though the air was cold. The children begged to go out to play, but Nandry stated it was far colder than they thought it to be and the outside could just wait.

Lane, too, longed to get out. He ached for an opportunity to be alone with Ellie. He had done some shopping in the nearby town and had purchased a locket, which he had withheld from the Christmas gift exchange. He wanted to give it to her privately. But where and when would he ever find privacy on a day when the family had gathered together? He wished he were daring enough to ask Ellie to go for a walk, but he couldn't gather the courage. The day was swiftly passing, and still he had found no opportunity to speak with her. Ellie herself, perhaps unknowingly, gave him the opportunity he had been longing for.

"I'm gonna take a few goodies to the barn fer Lady and yer pup," she said. "Ya wanna see 'im?"

Lane bounded to his feet. The whole group must have thought he was uncommonly fond of his young dog.

"Better wear yer coat. It's cold out there," Ellie cautioned at the door, for Lane would have left the house in his shirt sleeves, so unthinking was he at the time.

He flushed slightly and pulled on his coat. Ellie was already bundled and ready to go.

"Yer gonna be surprised at how he's grown," Ellie told him as they walked to the barn.

Ellie threw wide the door, and the two little pups pounced upon her, licking and yapping excitedly. Ellie giggled as she tried to get them under control. Lady watched from the sidelines with a mother's pride.

"My, ya do fuss over a body!" she exclaimed and worked to settle them down so she could give them the pan of turkey meat, gravy, and dressing scraps.

"They love it," she said, watching them wolf it down. "Pa says I spoil 'em."

The pup really had grown. He was still curly haired, and he still had his long, droopy ears, and he still looked awfully good to Lane. In his mind was the picture of a beautiful girl cuddling a small puppy. He reached down and picked it up, holding the wriggling body to his chest as he stroked the soft fur. Ellie stepped closer and touched the puppy, too.

"He doesn't have a name yet," she told him. "Thought of one?"

"How 'bout iffen you name 'im?" asked Lane.

"Me? He's yer dog."

"I'd still like yer name fer 'im," Lane said, looking steadily at her. Ellie stopped stroking the puppy and stepped back.

"I dunno," she said. "I haven't really been thinkin' on it."

"What would you have called 'im iffen ya coulda kept 'im? I bet ya had a name all picked out."

Ellie's smile admitted that she had.

"C'mon," said Lane. "Out with it."

"Don't s'pose you'd want my silly name none. It's not a very sensible name fer a man's dog."

"Why? What's a sensible name fer a man's dog?"

"Oh, Butch. Or Pooch. Or Ol' Bob. We used to name our dogs Ol' Bob. We had one Ol' Bob, and when we got a new puppy, Arnie named it Ol' Bob, too. Mama told me 'bout it."

"Don't think I care fer Ol' Bob," said Lane. "Or Butch or Pooch, either. This here's a special dog. He should have a special name."

He looked at her, coaxing her to share the name that she had picked for his dog. She still hesitated.

"C'mon," he said again.

"You'd laugh."

"Never!"

Ellie began to laugh softly. "Well, ya might not laugh, ya bein' so polite, but ya sure would *want* to."

"A good laugh is good fer a body," replied Lane, and Ellie's laughter sounded like she agreed.

"Okay," she said. "An' have a laugh iffen ya want to. I woulda called 'im Romeo."

"Romeo?" and Lane did laugh.

Ellie joined in. When they had finished chuckling over the name, Ellie said more seriously, "Why don't we just call 'im Rex?"

"Rex. I kinda like thet. Though it sure be a comedown from Romeo."

They laughed again.

"Promise ya won't tease?" asked Ellie.

"Tease?"

" 'Bout Romeo."

"Promise," said Lane. "I might even call 'im thet myself—once or twice—in private." And he put the puppy back down beside his mother.

Ellie picked up the pan and turned to go, but Lane stopped her.

In response to the question in her eyes, he reached into his pocket and pulled out a small package.

"I wondered when I would git to give ya this," he said softly. "I didn't want to put it under the tree with the others. It's my Christmas gift to you."

Still Ellie said nothing. He passed it to her and she took it, looking down at it with confusion in her face.

"Open it," prompted Lane, and Ellie's trembling fingers began to do his bidding.

As she lifted up the delicate locket, her eyes filled with tears.

"Oh, Lane, it's beautiful," she whispered, and then the tears did spill. "But I can't take it."

It was Lane's turn to be bewildered. "Ya mean . . . what I was hopin' . . . was dreamin' . . . I didn't see a'tall?"

Ellie just stood mute, the tears continuing to fall and the fingers gently caressing the locket.

"Ya don't care fer me?" asked Lane.

"I never said . . ." sobbed Ellie.

"Then there's someone else."

"No," said Ellie emphatically.

"Then I don't understand—"

"It's Mama. She needs me."

"I know," said Lane gently, reaching out to take her hands. "I'll wait. I'm not meanin' to take ya away *now*. It won't be long—"

"But ya don't understand!" cried Ellie. "It would near kill Mama. She misses Clae and Missie so. It would break her heart iffen another of her girls were to move so far away. Can't ya see. . . ?"

"But surely—"

"No," said Ellie, shaking her head again. "I just couldn't do it to Mama. I wouldn't." And she pushed the locket back into Lane's hand and ran from the barn, leaving her pan behind her.

Lane felt a sickness sweep all through him. He loved her. Until that moment of losing her, he had not realized how deeply. He looked at the locket lying in his open hand and longed for the comfort of tears. He did not allow them. Instead he sank down upon the straw and reached for the small dog. He pressed his face against the soft fur and remembered how Ellie had looked with her face against the puppy.

"Oh, Romeo," he groaned. "I just don't know how I'll live without her. Yer a mighty poor substitute, I'm a thinkin'."

It was a long time before Lane felt composed enough to return to the house.

———

Arnie's wedding day turned out not to be a fair day weather-wise. The wind was blowing and light snow was swirling as Clark tucked the blanket securely around Marty in the sleigh and headed for the church. All of the others had gone on before, and Marty fretted over last-minute concerns.

"Ellie has everythin' under control," Clark reminded her. "Ya needn't worry yerself none. The weddin' dinner will happen all proper like."

Marty knew that was true. She had worked on the dinner preparations in the kitchen with Ellie as much as her family would allow her, and then her physician-to-be son had gently but firmly shooed her to bed.

"You've been on your feet long enough," Luke insisted. "I'll help Ellie with whatever she needs."

And now the rest of the family were all at the church making the final wedding arrangements and waiting for the preacher to give the signal that the long-awaited hour had come.

Clark let the horses pick their own pace. Because they hated the cold and were in a hurry to get the journey over, they trotted briskly, Marty noted with some relief as she held the blanket up to her cheeks to prevent frostbite.

Other teams belonging to family and friends stood waiting in the churchyard when Clark swung his team in close to the steps and helped Marty alight. Luke was there to assist her in and hang up her coat. She was then seated in a spot reserved for the mother of the groom and had only moments to wait until Clark joined her.

The wedding party began to take their places in the front. Marty had never seen Arnie looking happier nor Anne more radi-ant. Ellie seemed a bit pale and strained, and Marty chided herself. The girl had been working much too hard. She must see that Ellie got a good rest when all of this excitement was over.

It was a beautiful ceremony. The young pastor was able to give it the proper dignity and warmth of feeling that a wedding service should have. Before a caring congregation, the young couple exchanged their vows, looking at each other with expressions that said they meant deeply everything they promised.

Marty swallowed hard and blinked back her tears. Another of their children was establishing a home of his own. Soon there would be none of them left to share the big house that Clark had built for his family. And then a little jab under her ribs reminded Marty that it would be a while yet before the house would be empty, and she smiled through her tears and reached down a hand to touch the spot where her unborn child was making its presence known.

FIFTEEN

Back to Routine

Luke now had to board the stage once again and return to school. Marty sighed deeply at the thought of seeing him go, but somehow it seemed easier this time than before.

The household settled back into its routine. Arnie and his new bride took up residence in the little home that he had been so industriously preparing for them. The day Arnie had walked out the door carrying the last of his belongings from his lifelong home stead was very hard for Marty, but the broad smile on his face made her realize the truth: that all was as it should be when Arnie was looking forward to starting out on a life of his own. The thought gave her a measure of peace.

How glad she was to have Ellie as she watched Luke and Arnie leave the home. What a comfort to have at least one of her children still with her. Then Marty looked carefully at Ellie, and her eyes told her that something was not quite right. Ellie still looked pale and overtired. She had been working far too hard, with all the family at home for Christmas and then the added burden of preparing for Arnie's wedding, as well. Marty decided that what Ellie needed was to get away from the kitchen for a while. She had heard some of the neighborhood young people talking about a skating party on Miller's pond. That was what Ellie needed. A chance to be out having fun with young people of her own age.

Marty tucked the information away in her mind, with the intention of doing something about it at her first opportunity.

Marty was not concerned about who would take Ellie to the skating party. True, the girl no longer had big brothers in the house to escort her to such activities, but that would be no problem. Lane would be happy to take over that role. He was such a nice young man, and he and Ellie seemed to get along just fine. Though she would miss her brothers, Lane would be good company and sort of an "adopted" big brother.

Marty smiled as she concluded these thoughts. She tucked the small sweater that was taking form under her quick needles back into her knitting basket and went to the kitchen. She had heard the dog bark, and that must mean the men were back from the woods. This was their first day back on the job since Arnie's wedding. She hoped Arnie would stop for a brief chat before he went to his new home and waiting bride.

Ellie was busy at the big stove, stirring a pot of wonderfully fragrant stew. Fresh biscuits sat in a pan at the back of the stove, smelling as good as they looked. Marty noticed the table. It was set for four. For a moment, Marty thought Ellie had forgotten that Arnie would no longer be eating with them, and then she remembered Lane. Of course—Lane always ate with them after he spent a day in the woods. It had been a while since the men had all gone out together, and she had forgotten. She smiled again, thinking this would be a good chance for her to tell Lane about the skating party.

Marty was disappointed when Clark came in saying Arnie had been in such a hurry to get home to his Anne that he had sent his mother greetings and excused himself from coming in. He'd see her sometime soon, he promised, and told Clark to give her his love.

Lane did come in, but he seemed edgy somehow. This was the first they had seen him since Arnie's wedding, and Marty had been all prepared for a good chat. Lane, though he politely answered all the questions that were put to him, just didn't seem much in the mood for chatting. Ellie didn't seem to be too talkative, either.

Perhaps they were both weary after the rush and busyness of Christmas, Marty concluded. Well, things should slow down now.

———

Lane had been nervous about appearing as usual at the Davis table. He had not really seen Ellie since Christmas Day, except for a few brief glimpses of her on the day of Arnie's wedding. She had been so busy then that there was no opportunity at all for him to speak with her. Lane felt it was important for them to get a chance to have a real talk. He couldn't leave things as they were when he had presented his Christmas gift to her.

Some way he had to make her understand he would never take her from her mother while Marty needed her but would wait as long as was necessary if Ellie would just give the word. But what had Ellie said in her rush of tears? *It would kill Mama iffen another of her family was to move so far away.* Did Ellie really mean that? Would it really be that hard on Marty? Lane had to know. He needed a chance to talk things out. That is, if Ellie cared—if she cared at all about him. Could he have been so wrong? Maybe Ellie didn't even—

Lane's thoughts were interrupted by Marty's words. She was asking how the logging was going. Lane answered her. He hoped that what he said in response sounded sensible. He stole a glance at Ellie. She seemed perfectly unaware that he sat across the table from her. She was completely absorbed in cutting a piece of meat into a smaller portion before serving herself.

"Ellie tells me you've laid claim on thet last pup," Clark stated.

Lane looked back to Clark and fumbled some with his fork. "Right," he finally was able to answer. "I always wanted a dog of my own an' never had me a chance."

"Think ya picked a good one," Clark continued. "Those be awful good stock dogs, an' I think thet pup be the pick of the litter. A little trainin' an' he should be 'bout able to read yer mind where stock are concerned."

Lane could feel his face get warm. What was a cowman to do with a trained stock dog? Sure wouldn't use one to be rounding up the herd. No one seemed to notice, and Lane shuffled his feet some and cleared his throat.

"Yes, sir," he said. "He does look smart, all right."

It was time for Ellie to serve the apple pie. Though Lane's favorite dessert, somehow he had no appetite for it tonight. He did manage to swallow it, washing it down with his second cup of coffee. He stole another glance at Ellie. She still looked cool and aloof.

Clark was pushing back his chair.

"Care fer a game of checkers?"

Lane gathered his scattered wits. "No . . . no . . . I think not. Not tonight. I need to git me on home—"

"The chores are all done," Clark reminded him. "I been over and took care of everythin'. No need fer ya to—"

But Lane was standing to his feet and excusing himself. "Thanks," he said, "but I think I'd better git on home just the same. Christmas has a way of wearin' one out, an' it's a little hard to git back to work again afterward. Think I'll just go on home an' catch up a bit."

Lane was glad Clark did not argue further as he thanked them all again for the supper and the evening and turned toward his coat hanging on the peg.

"Speakin' of Christmas wearin' one out," Marty said, moving closer to address herself to Lane as he shrugged into his coat, "I been noticin' thet Ellie needs a bit of a change from all her hard work, too, an' I overheard some of the young folks talkin', an' they said this Saturday they're gonna have 'em a skatin' party on Miller's pond. Ellie knows where thet be, iffen you'd be so kind as to drive her on over."

Ellie was pouring hot water into the sink, her back to them.

"I'd be most happy to," Lane answered evenly.

Marty began to smile.

"No," Ellie said sharply without turning. "No."

Marty swung around toward her, a look of concern replacing the smile.

"No," said Ellie again. "I'm not goin'."

"What d'ya mean?" asked Marty, confusion in her tone. "Ya need to git out with the young people more. Why, ya hardly had a chance—"

But Ellie cut in with, "Mama, do you know just how *young* those young people are? Why, I wouldn't even fit in! All the young girls my age are married an' busy keepin' house. Those young people . . . they . . . they're just *kids*. I don't belong with 'em now, an' besides . . . I don't want to go . . . really I . . ." Ellie turned away. "Let's just ferget it, can we?"

Marty looked dumbfounded. She turned back to Lane with a helpless look and a shrug of her shoulders.

"Guess it won't be necessary," she said in a low voice, putting her hand on Lane's arm. "Thanks anyway, though."

Marty turned to the cupboard. "Here," she said. "Take ya home one of these fresh loaves of Ellie's bread." She hastened to wrap a loaf and hand it to Lane.

Lane took one last lingering look at Ellie. Her head was bent over the dishpan. He couldn't tell for sure, but he wondered if it was a tear that lay upon her cheek. He muttered a good-night to all of them and went out the door.

———

Clark followed Lane to the barn to get his horse. The young man had declared it unnecessary, but Clark insisted. He wanted to check the barn doors anyway, he declared.

As Lane went to mount his horse, he turned to Clark. "Been thinkin'," he said. "S'pose it's time fer me to do my own chorin'. Willie sent me on out here to be takin' care of things, an' I feel a bit guilty not doin' it myself. Tell the boys I'll just meet 'em in the mornin'. A bit closer fer me iffen I go straight on over from the LaHaye farm. And then iffen I go right on home at night, I'll have plenty of time to do my own chores."

Clark knew this time that Lane had made up his mind to care for the LaHaye chores himself. He didn't know what it was that had made the younger man decide as he had, but Clark put it aside as none of his business. He was sure Lane had a good reason, whatever it was. No mention was made of the meal that was always waiting at the Davis household.

"Sure," Clark said, "iffen thet's what ya want. Come anytime ya can. We're always most happy to have ya."

Lane said his good-night and urged his horse forward.

Clark returned to the warmth of the kitchen. Ellie was busy scrubbing at an awkward pan, and Marty was placing dried, clean dishes on the cupboard shelf.

Clark leaned his crutch against the wall and steadied himself on his one foot while he pulled out of his heavy coat.

"Lane won't be here fer breakfast tomorra," he said to the two women.

Two heads came up and two pairs of eyes held his. Only Marty voiced a question.

"Why?" she said simply. "What might keep Lane from breakfasting with us?"

"He thinks he should care fer the LaHaye chores hisself."

"Maybe," said Marty in a puzzled tone, "though I really don't think it matters much to Willie as long as they're taken care of." Marty paused long enough to place some cups on hangers. "Maybe he's not feelin' well," she wondered. "I noticed he didn't eat well tonight. Perhaps a few days off from cuttin' will do 'im good."

"Oh, he's still cuttin'," Clark explained. "He's just goin' straight from the LaHaye farm, thet's all."

Marty looked at him, her eyes holding more questions. Then she turned back to the cupboard. "Well, we'll see 'im tomorrow night. Maybe he'll—"

"'Fraid not," Clark said. "He told me he would be goin' straight home from the cuttin' from now on, so he won't be takin' supper with us anymore."

Marty put down the plates she was holding and placed her hand on her hip, her frown deepening. "I wonder—" she began, but Clark stopped her.

"He was sent to care fer the LaHaye farm, not to cut the Davis' logs. Guess he feels a bit bad 'bout how things been goin', thet's all. I like a fella who looks after his own responsibility."

Marty still frowned but turned back to the plates. "I'm not arguin' thet," she said. Then she continued, "But it was so nice havin' 'im round, 'specially with Arnie an' Luke both leavin'. It was like havin' another son—an' it was gonna be 'specially nice fer Ellie to still have a big brother."

Ellie swung around, her eyes large and tear filled. "Mama, please," she begged, and then she was crying in earnest.

"What—?" began Marty, her utter bewilderment evident in tone and expression as she started toward her daughter.

"I'm . . . I'm sorry," stammered Ellie, backing away. "I didn't mean . . . I never meant . . ." She brushed roughly at her tears with a corner of her apron. "I don't need . . . I don't need another big brother." And saying the words, Ellie almost ran from the kitchen.

Marty's eyes were filled with concern. "I'm worried 'bout her, Clark," she said, slowly lowering her round body to a kitchen chair. "I've never seen Ellie with all the sparkle gone from her so. I just never dreamed it would be so hard fer her to say good-bye to both Arnie and Luke."

Clark had no explanation.

SIXTEEN

Secrets

In the days that followed, Marty kept a close eye on Ellie. She still looked pale and seemed listless, but she attacked each of her many household duties with the same determination and energy she'd had before. There just didn't seem to be the joy that had previously marked her character. Marty was hoping it would return when Ellie got accustomed to being the only child left at home.

Ellie seemed to yearn to be outside. It appeared to Marty that she used every excuse possible to leave the confines of the kitchen. She was always taking food and water to the chickens. She even insisted on hauling water from the outside well—a chore Clark had never expected of his womenfolk. Mostly, though, she spent time with the young pup. The dog was of training age now, and Ellie seemed to get what little pleasure was left to her in teaching him the basics in obedience.

Whenever Marty inquired about how things were going with the dog training, Ellie's answers contained a measure of enthusiasm. Marty felt these were the only times that the heaviness lifted for Ellie—her times with that small dog. Maybe even an animal could make one forget just how much one missed an individual, Marty concluded. *It must be Arnie thet Ellie misses so much,* she continued, *because I didn't notice this 'bout her 'fore Christmas, and Luke was gone then, too.* Marty hoped for a chance to talk to Arnie. Perhaps he could just pop in a bit oftener and say a few words to his sister. That might help her in her adjustment period.

They saw very little of Lane. He seemed to make out fine as a bachelor. Marty heard via the country grapevine that many of the neighbors—especially those with marriageable daughters—were inviting him in for meals. The only time the Davises saw Lane was at the Sunday services, and then it seemed he always had somewhere else to go. Marty did notice, though, that he was looking a bit thinner than when he had first come to their area.

"I wonder iffen Lane is missin' his West?" she said to Clark one night as they sat before the fire, Clark with a book and Marty with some sewing.

Clark lifted his head.

"Why do ya think thet?" he asked.

"Well, he don't seem as jolly—an' he looks to be losin' some weight. An' . . . an' we never see him anymore," she finished lamely.

"The fact thet we don't see 'im anymore could prove he feels more at home here—not less," Clark responded. "From what I'm hearin', he's gittin' round real good."

"Well, he still don't look happy to me," insisted Marty.

"I would love to argue with ya," said Clark slowly, "but I been thinkin' the same thoughts. Iffen it's just thet he's anxious to git on home, thet will soon care fer itself. I hear the LaHayes will be back in a couple weeks or so. Thet won't be long fer 'im to wait."

There was a soft stirring as Ellie quietly left the room. Marty could hear her in the kitchen. By the sounds that came to her, Marty knew Ellie was lighting a lantern and putting on outside wraps.

"Where ya goin', dear?" Marty called. "It's cold out tonight."

"Just gonna go check on Lady an' Ro—Rex."

"I made sure they was all shut up warm an' dry in the barn," Clark called to Ellie. "Even gave 'em some extra milk tonight."

If they expected Ellie to sigh with relief and return her coat to its peg, they were disappointed. "Still gonna go out an' see 'em," she answered, and the door opened and closed.

"She sure is powerful concerned 'bout those dogs of hers," Marty said to Clark. " 'Magine goin' out this time of night just to check on 'em."

Clark picked up the book he had laid in his lap, but his eyes didn't return immediately to the open page. Instead, he sat thinking, the frown lightly creasing his forehead. Something was amiss here, but as yet Clark wasn't sure just what it was.

Ellie walked quickly to the barn, her swinging lantern making streaks of light and shadows on the snow-covered farmyard. Her heart was heavy, and she felt the tears stinging her eyelids. The truth was, she had learned to love Lane. Maybe it had been unwise, but it had been impossible for her to stop herself. She was sure he had cared for her, too. She could feel it in the way he looked at her, the unspoken and the spoken messages he had passed to her. And the locket? A man like Lane would mean a gift like that as a promise of his love—and Lane would not hold love lightly. They could have been so happy together—if only . . .

But what was the use of *if onlys*? Her mother needed her. Not just for now before the baby came but in the future, too. Marty had suffered as each of her children moved away from the family home. First, it had been Missie, and she had gone so very far away. When she had left, Marty had not even been sure she would ever see her again, would ever hold the children that would bless her home, or sit in her kitchen sharing thoughts and feelings along with cups of tea. Then Clae had gone and taken with her one grandchild and a well-loved son-in-law. Now Clae had another baby, one Marty had yet to see. Ellie knew Marty ached to see Clae and Joe and the little ones. Then Clare had married and moved out on his own. True, he was close by, and Marty could share in his life in lots of ways. Why, Marty was as anxious for that new baby of Clare and Kate's as they were themselves. Ellie checked her thoughts. *Well, not quite,* she corrected herself and even managed a wobbly smile. Nobody could be quite as excited at the prospect of a new baby as Clare and Kate were.

Ellie's thoughts continued with her brother Luke's leaving. Her mama's baby. At least for so many, many years, Luke was the baby, though his time with that position was quickly coming to an end. Ellie had seen just how hard it was for Marty to let Luke go. And close behind Luke's leaving was the marriage of Arnie. And Arnie was always so anxious to get home to his Anne that he scarcely had time for even a hello anymore. Ellie loved Arnie and was touched by his love for his Anne. When—or if—Ellie ever had the joy of being someone's wife, she hoped someone would feel the same way about her.

Again Ellie's thoughts turned to Lane, and the tears continued to stream down her cheeks. She loved him. Oh, how she loved him! How proud she would be to be the wife of such a man. But she couldn't; she just couldn't. It would be more than she could ever bring upon her mother. To ask her to lose another daughter to the West would be too much. Ellie would never do such a thing.

She fumbled with the latch to the barn door and heard excited yelps. Already the dogs were ready to greet her. She let herself in and carefully hung the lantern on the hook by the door before allowing herself to respond to their wild greeting.

"Oh, Rex," she sobbed, taking the nearly grown Rex into her arms and pulling him close. The dog seemed to sense that something was troubling her, and instead of his usual frenzied play, he crowded up against her, softly licking her tear-wet cheek. A low whine escaped him.

"Oh, Rex," she said again, the tears running more freely. "He's soon goin' back. He's goin' back west, an' I may never see 'im again. Never." Ellie buried her head against the fur of the only friend with whom she felt she could share her burden and cried out all her sorrow.

———

Lane, too, was in a state of torment. He had reached home from the wood cutting, done the chores, and spent a miserable evening pacing the floor. Finally he went to bed, but his troubled mind would not let him sleep. Quickly the days were passing by. It would not be long until it was time for him to return to Willie's ranch. Once back west, he would be many miles and many days away from Ellie. How could he stand never to see her again? Oh, if only he had never met her, then he would be unaware of how much he had missed—how much he loved her. She was the kind of woman he had always dreamed of sharing his life with. Her gentle spirit, the sparkle in her eye, her understanding . . .

He had felt that they were so right for each other, and he had been foolish enough to hope and dream that she felt that way, too. *She does, I'm sure she does,* Lane argued with himself. *I'm sure she could love me if only* . . . There it was again. The situation did not change in spite of Lane's yearning. It would be unfair to even ask Ellie to go west, knowing that she felt it would bring such pain to Marty. No, it would be wrong. For Ellie, being as sensitive as she was, could not know true happiness herself if she knew her mother was suffering. It was unthinkable. Even Lane, with his aching heart, knew that.

But wait, Lane checked himself. *Who says I have to go back west?* He could stay right where he was. He could farm or get a job in town. Ellie would not need to leave her mother. That was it! They would stay, and he would be free to express to Ellie his great love and his desire to share the rest of his life with her.

For a moment Lane felt wild with excitement. He could hardly wait to talk with Ellie. If it hadn't been so late at night, he would have gone to her immediately. What would the Davises think if he came riding madly into the farmyard at midnight, crying out that he had solved the problem? No, he must wait. But could he wait? Yes—wait, he must. He would go see Ellie at the first opportunity. Saturday night. In fact, he would beg off log cutting early so he could hurry through the chores. A feeling of deep relief passed through him, so thankful was he to have found a way through the muddle. "Thank ya, God," he whispered. "Thank ya fer makin' a way." And Lane turned over and slept well for the first time since Christmas.

SEVENTEEN

Letters

The long days of a snowbound January dragged slowly by. Marty had finished her preparations for the baby and now was impatient for it to arrive. On January the twelfth, she stood and stared at the calendar on the wall. *Surely the month must be further along than this,* she told herself. But no. It was right there in black and white. It was truly just January the twelfth. Marty moved about restlessly, wondering what to do with herself. She knew there were little jobs about the house she could busy herself doing, but nothing caught her interest or seemed to be worth the effort. She paced back to the window and stood looking out at the softly falling snow. Would it never quit snowing? It seemed to Marty that she had been looking at mounds of snow for months and months. She turned from the window with a sigh and stared at the calendar again. How many more weeks must they—?

Ellie must have been watching Marty's restlessness for a while. She said, "Why don't ya go an' have coffee with Kate? She's prob'ly as restless as you are."

Marty turned to Ellie in surprise. "I'm sorry," she apologized. "I'm a case, ain't I? I never remember bein' so impatient with any of the rest of ya."

"Ya were too busy lookin' after the others an' the house an' all the laundry an' the feedin' of—"

Marty's cheery laugh broke into Ellie's comments, and Marty thought Ellie looked up at her with relief.

"It's good to hear you laugh, Mama," she said. "We haven't had enough of it round here lately."

"Yer right," Marty said. "I was too busy. Havin' you here has made a lazy complainer outta me."

Ellie protested, but Marty went on. "Boy, ya must find me hard to live with. Feelin' sorry fer myself, when I've got so much to be thankful fer. But yer right. I will go see Kate. Maybe she is impatient, too, though she's had more sense 'bout all of this, I'm a thinkin'. She 'least has enough sense to stay busy."

Marty began to draw her shawl about her for the short walk across the yard. "Been worryin' 'bout Ma, too. Wonder how she's doin'. Haven't seen her fer a while, an' I just know she is missin' Ben somethin' fierce. Wish I could go on over an' see her, but yer pa will never let me—not in this weather."

Ellie looked up from the recipes she was paging through. "S'pose we could go on over an' git Ma an' bring her here," she suggested.

Marty was thrilled with the idea. "We could, couldn't we? Oh, would ya? I mean tomorra, could ya? Ya could leave right after breakfast an' Ma could stay on fer lunch. I'd do up the dishes and the mornin' cleanin' an' ya could—"

"All right," said Ellie with a smile. "Iffen it means thet much to ya, I'll go in the mornin'."

"Thank ya," said Marty.

"I'll talk to Pa as soon as he gets home from town," Ellie promised.

"Thank ya," said Marty again. And she turned with a smile to go see her Kate.

————

Kate was as glad to see Marty as Marty was to get out.

"Oh, I was hopin' fer some distraction!" Kate cried. "I was thinkin' of comin' up to see you, but Clare made me promise not to go out alone with it so slippery underfoot."

Marty smiled, remembering the many times when Clark had warned her of the same thing.

"I was very careful," she said, then confided, "but I've never had a lick of trouble—not with any of the babies thet I carried."

Even before Kate stirred the fire or put on the kettle, she urged Marty to "come see the baby's room."

"It's all done now," she explained as they moved to the door of the bedroom. "Oh, I just love it. Our baby just has no way of knowin' how very special he is. Iffen he knew how much his ma and pa had fussed over 'im . . ." Kate left her sentence dangling and laughed at their foolishness.

They entered the room, and Marty gasped. "Oh, it's lovely."

She crossed to the new crib that Clare had put so many hours on and ran a hand lovingly over the smoothly polished wood.

"He did a fine job on this, Kate," she said and felt that her words were inadequate. Kate must have thought so, too.

"Isn't it beautiful?" she enthused. "I had no idea Clare was so clever with his hands. I've never seen me a nicer baby's bed. An' look—he made a little chest to match it!"

Marty looked about the room—at the frilly curtains, the green walls, the handmade quilts, the pillows, the chest, the carefully chosen pictures, and especially the hand-turned bed—and her eyes shone almost as brightly as did Kate's.

"An' look," said Kate as she pulled open drawer after drawer to reveal tiny baby garments. "We are all ready now. Everythin's here . . . now we just wait."

"Wait," echoed Marty. "Sometimes it seems so long. I hope we can make it . . . both of us."

Kate reached to give her a squeeze, and the two women chuckled as they hugged over the two unborn babies.

"We'll make it," Kate promised. "We'll make it, 'cause it is so much worth waitin' fer. Oh, Mama, it's gonna be so much fun to have a baby of our own. We have been so happy, but this . . . this is gonna be . . . be . . . near to heaven."

Marty smiled. She remembered so well the excitement of waiting for the arrival of her first child. She had anticipated every one of them—that was true—but there was just no excitement like the arrival of the first one. She nodded to Kate, warm memories making her eyes mist over.

"Best we go out there an' have thet tea," she said, " 'fore I git all emotional an' weepy."

Kate led the way back to the kitchen. They lingered over their cups. Marty told Kate about Ellie's proposal to pick up Ma Graham for a day's visit. "It's been so long," she said, her voice full of feeling, "an' I've been so worried 'bout her."

Kate agreed that it would be good for both of them to have a long chat. "But I've been thinkin' thet Ellie needs a break, too," Kate continued. "She has been lookin' rather peaked lately, an' she just seems . . . well . . . different."

"You've noticed it, too, huh?"

Kate nodded in agreement.

"Clark an' me's been talkin' 'bout it," Marty said. "She needs to git out more, thet's what I'm thinkin', but she doesn't really seem to want to, even when she has a chance."

"What chance?" asked Kate.

"Well, I remembered thet the young people were talkin' 'bout a skatin' party, an' I suggested thet Ellie go, but she wanted no part of it."

"But I can understand Ellie not wantin' to go alone."

"Oh, she wouldn't have gone alone. I asked Lane to take her."

"*You asked Lane?*" Kate's shock was evident.

"An' he said he'd be glad to," Marty assured her. "But Ellie said she didn't want to go."

"What else did Ellie say?" Kate asked thoughtfully.

"She said they were all 'kids.' "

"Maybe she just didn't want to go with Lane."

"I don't think so," Marty said slowly. "Ellie seemed to like Lane just fine. They was always laughin' an' talkin' together. Why, he helped her with the dishes, an' she gave him thet favorite dog she fusses over so. It would have been so nice fer Ellie iffen Lane had been round more, with Arnie an' Luke both gone, but he's not been back lately, an' Ellie didn't want to go to the party, an'—"

"Mama," Kate stopped her. "Do you think Ellie an' Lane . . . well, thet they had a sweethearts' quarrel?"

"A sweethearts' quarrel," said Marty in bewilderment. "Land sakes, they ain't sweethearts. They're more like brother an' sister."

Kate looked unconvinced. "Did you ever say that to Ellie?"

"Say what?"

"Thet they were . . . sorta . . . brother an' sister?"

Marty thought back. "Well, somethin' like thet, I suppose," she admitted at length.

"An' what did Ellie say?"

"She said thet . . . she said she didn't want Lane fer a brother," Marty said as she recalled the incident. She hesitated, then began to frown. "Now, why would she say a thing like thet?" she asked Kate.

"It fits, doesn't it?" Kate asked at last. "It sounds to me like Lane an' Ellie had 'em a disagreement."

"I wonder. . . ? I never had me any idea they might have thet kind of interest in each other."

Marty stirred her cup of tea around and around as she thought back over a number of things that had puzzled her. Kate might just be right. Things were beginning to *fit*.

"When I think on it," Marty admitted slowly, "they would be well suited to each other. I couldn't wish anyone finer than Lane fer my Ellie. He's the most sensitive, carin' young man I have ever met."

Marty absentmindedly continued stirring. "I wonder what happened," she mused out loud. "They seemed to be gettin' along so well together. I'm afraid I'm guilty of already seein' Lane as one of my own."

"I don't see thet as makin' a problem," countered Kate.

"Well, somethin' must have happened. I do admit it's had me worryin'. Couldn't figure out fer the life of me what got into the two of 'em. . . . Funny Clark didn't see it. He's usually so perceptive."

"Sometimes it's the most difficult to understand those closest to you," Kate said, and Marty knew she was right.

"Well, now thet we know," Marty determined, straightening up in her chair, "there should be somethin' a body can do 'bout it. Sure wouldn't want to lose Lane as a possible son-in-law." She smiled across at Kate.

"Better go slow, Mama," Kate warned her. "Maybe we are on the wrong track. An' maybe the two of them won't welcome any interference."

"I'll not jump into it," promised Marty. "First, I'll talk it over with Clark an' see iffen he agrees with us. He'll know what should be done—iffen anythin'."

They changed the subject and finished their tea.

"Thank ya, dear," Marty said at the door, giving her daughter-in-law a kiss on the cheek. "I needed that—all of it. Iffen we are right, I feel thet a load's been lifted off me concernin' Ellie. I will admit I was some worried. But I promise," she continued laughingly as she held up her hand, "not to go bargin' in."

Kate laughed with her, and Marty wrapped her shawl once more about her and headed for her own house. The air was crisp and the snow still fell, but Marty felt as though she had been given new courage and purpose to face the many tomorrows ahead.

———

When Marty reached the warmth of her own kitchen, she had further reason to rejoice. Clark had returned from town, and the mail he brought with him contained three letters. Letters from her children! Marty could scarcely believe her good fortune.

Missie wrote that their winter had been mild, and Willie felt it had been the easiest winter yet on the cattle. They had enjoyed the visit of Willie's brother and family. Missie didn't know how her Josiah and Nathan would ever be able to entertain themselves once their cousins had gone. They had all enjoyed one another so much.

The church was continuing to reach out. Two of the regular families had moved away, but Henry had been calling on other ranches in the area and had already recruited one new family to join them. Another family had shown some interest, and they were all praying that they, too, might soon be desiring to share in Sunday worship.

Baby Melissa was growing daily. She was such a contented child, and she already thoroughly believed that her older brothers were the most important people in her world. Everyone loved her, and Missie feared lest the ranch hands would spoil her.

The boys were growing. Nathan had started school as planned and seemed to be a promising student. He was busy trying to teach his young brother, Josiah, to read. Josiah was eager to learn and had managed, under Nathan's tutelage, to recognize half a dozen words. The family laughed about it and tried to dissuade Nathan from further teaching duties.

Missie said that they missed Lane and would be so glad to have him back again. Marty stopped her reading. For the first time since her talk with Kate, Marty realized if Lane and Ellie were truly interested in each other and they were to resolve their differences— whatever they were—Marty would be losing another daughter. It would not be easy, but this time Marty felt she would be prepared. God had helped her to give up Missie and Clae and Luke. Surely He could help her if Ellie should decide to leave them, too. Marty finished Missie's letter and picked up the letter from Clae.

Clae was all excited about the little church where Joe was serving as a part-time pastor. She had never seen her Joe happier than he was now, even though the demands on his time were so great. The people were very kind to all of them, and they felt at home among them. It was the first she had really felt at home since leaving her family behind and traveling east. Clae, at last, felt free to voice her true feelings over the move. At first, she said, she had been so homesick that she had felt she just couldn't bear it, and she had prayed daily for the time to pass quickly so they might go home again. God had now answered her prayer in an unexpected way. He had given them love and friendship and a contentment in His will that she wouldn't have thought possible. She no longer chafed for home—though she still missed them all very much— but she was quite at home where she was, as long as Joe was happy and she had her little family and their new friends.

Esther Sue was getting so grown-up. She loved to help with her baby brother. The baby was a source of joy to each one of them. He looked much like his father, although his coloring was more like his mama.

They were still thinking of accepting a church in the East for a while, although eventually they did plan to come back to the rural area. Joe felt he would be more suitably placed in a farming community than in a city, but he believed he had so much he needed to learn before leaving the area where the seminary was. He could take a pastorate and fit in some night classes for a while and better equip himself for the ministry.

They were all keeping well. It was so good to have a visit with Luke upon his return after Christmas and catch up on all of the news from home. Clae sent her thanks over and over for the parcels Luke had carried back with him from the family. She admitted to shedding a few tears as she unwrapped each one, but they were happy tears, she maintained, and came from a grateful heart that had responded to the love which came with the gifts.

Marty laid aside the letter with mixed emotions. She was so glad Clae and Joe felt at home—and at peace. How good it was to entrust them to the care of the all-knowing and caring Father.

Marty reached for Luke's letter and eagerly tore the envelope open. Luke, too, was full of good reports. He was busily engaged in his studies again. It had been so good to be home. He trusted that all the family was well. He had seen Clae and Joe, and they seemed to be happy in their new work. Joe was fairly bursting with the new knowledge he was absorbing. Especially was he excited about his in-depth study on the deity of Christ—that Christ, as Holy God, could care so much for sinful man was a truth he found staggering.

Luke was back into classes again and was even more sure than before, if possible, that his was a doctor's calling. Such strides were being made in the field of medicine, and he wanted to be right there, a contributing part of it.

The letter was short, as Luke was in a hurry. He had much work to do in preparation for his next day's classes, he stated, but he had wanted to send his greetings home and thank them for their love and support.

Marty drank in the contents of each letter, promising herself that she would read them again before retiring. As she read each page, she passed it on to Ellie, who also pored over each one.

"They all sound fine, don't they, Mama?" Ellie said as she read the last page.

"An' I'm so thankful," Marty responded, with the hint of tears in her eyes. "Nothin' makes a mother happier than to know thet her family is fine."

Ellie rose to go check on her supper, and Marty sighed contentedly as she carefully tucked each letter back into its envelope so Clark might read them as soon as he came in from the barn.

She had spoken the truth. Nothing made a mother happier than to know her children were all happy. Kate and Clare were eagerly waiting for their new baby. Missie was enjoying the visit of family and thrilled with each new accomplishment of her own little ones. Clae and Joe were happy in the work they felt called to do. Luke was thrilled with each new discovery as a physician-in-training. Arnie could hardly wait each night to get home to his Anne. Nandry's family continued to grow and flourish. That left only her Ellie. Ellie's eyes still bore a shadow. She would talk to Ellie tonight, but first she must have a chat with Clark to get his reaction to Kate's theory. Marty did so want her sweet little Ellie to be happy, as well.

EIGHTEEN

A Talk With Ellie

"Clark," Marty said softly and waited until Clark lifted his head from the page he was reading.

He didn't answer but silently looked at her, waiting for her to continue.

"Had me a talk with Kate today," Marty told him.

"Ya said ya did."

"She is so excited 'bout the comin' of thet baby. They have everythin' in readiness now. Don't know how the two of 'em are ever gonna be able to stand the next six weeks or so." Marty chuckled before she went on. "But thet weren't all we talked 'bout. She's been worried 'bout Ellie, too. She has noticed thet Ellie just isn't her usual happy self."

Clark nodded slowly, concern showing in his face.

"Kate prodded some an' got me to thinkin'. Do you think there's any chance thet Ellie is sweet on Lane? I mean thet they might sorta like each other an' have had a fuss 'bout somethin'?"

The corners of Clark's mouth turned down in surprise at the idea. "Never thought of it, but why not?" he finally said. "I mean, Lane is an attractive young man with a real love fer people, an' Ellie is a pretty an' pleasant girl. Why not? Why didn't we think of thet? It's not only possible, but it's most likely." Clark pondered a moment. "Do ya s'pose thet's what she meant by not wantin' Lane fer a *brother*?"

"I wonder iffen it might be," Marty answered him, shaking her head back and forth. "Don't know why I didn't see it afore."

"Guess we were just thinkin' *family* too much where Lane was concerned."

"Guess so. Then d'ya think it might be somethin' like thet troublin' Ellie?"

"Well, they sure could care fer each other, I see thet now. But why there should be any trouble with the carin' I still don't see. Neither of them are selfish or prideful. Don't see why they can't work out their little differences, if differences there be."

"I was wonderin' iffen we should have a chat with Ellie an' see if there's some way we could help 'em sort it out."

"Where is Ellie?"

"She left fer the barn an' thet dog of her'n again."

"Ya mean dog of *his'n.*"

"Yeah, his'n."

"I don't know," Clark wondered aloud, rubbing his chin, "I've never felt it too wise to interfere where heart matters are concerned. Usually it's better to let 'em work it out on their own."

"Thet's 'bout what Kate said." Marty dropped a stitch and continued on with her knitting.

"Hurts me, though," she confided softly. "Ellie's been sufferin', I can tell. Lane don't rightly look so good, either."

"Maybe a body can beat round the bush some an' come up with somethin'."

"Ellie's pretty shrewd. Don't know iffen you'll fool her none."

"Might be easier to talk to Lane."

Marty's knitting needles stopped. "Now, what would ya say? 'Ya carin' fer my daughter an' havin' some kinda fuss? She's eatin' her heart out, an' I wanna know why'?"

"Yer right," said Clark. "Thet wouldn't be so easy, either."

Marty's needles began to slowly click again. She was usually a fast knitter, and the sound gave away the fact that her mind was not on her work. "What do ya think we should do?" she asked at last.

"Wish I knew fer sure. One thing sure is we should pray about it."

At Marty's nod, Clark bowed his head and led them in a fervent prayer for their daughter. And for Lane.

"I'm thinkin' the only way might just be to up and come right straight out with it," Clark observed after he raised his head.

"I think yer right," agreed Marty, and Clark laid his book aside and stood up.

"Guess I'll take me a little walk," he said, "an' see iffen I can discover what is so special 'bout a certain dog."

Marty's eyes looked deeply into Clark's to assure him that she trusted him to do and say the right things where their daughter was concerned, and then her knitting needles began to pick up speed.

───────

Clark walked into the kitchen and pulled on his coat against the cold. He didn't bother to light another lantern. The winter moon shone brightly in the sky, and millions of stars sparkled above him. His way would be well lit to the barn, and once there, Ellie's lantern would light the interior for both of them.

He did not hurry. He needed time to think. He needed time to pray once more. He had no idea how to approach the delicate subject with his daughter. It helped that they had always been able to talk easily to each other. At times like this, Clark was so glad there had been years of establishing a strong connection with each of his children. It was well worth it for a father to take the time, he knew with great certainty.

The snow crunched beneath his foot and crutch, and his breath preceded him in smoky little puffs. He opened the barn door and entered, turning to close it tightly behind him. He wanted to give Ellie the advantage of adjusting to his presence before he turned to look at her. He found her sitting on a pile of straw, gently stroking the dog she called Rex.

Clark cleared his throat and crossed over to lean on a half

partition. For a moment neither of them spoke.

"He's really growin', ain't he?" Clark said at last.

"Sure is," responded Ellie.

"Seems like a nice dog. He learnin' well?"

"He's really quick," said Ellie.

"You've always thought 'im kinda special, ain't ya?"

Ellie agreed that she had. Clark knelt down and stroked the dog with his large work-roughened hand. The dog squirmed with the pleasure of it but did not leave Ellie.

"Seems to me thet's more'n a dog yer holdin'," Clark observed.

Ellie's head came up quickly, but she did not ask her father what he meant.

Clark continued to stroke the dog.

"Seems like it's a dream thet yer holdin', as well," went on Clark, and Ellie's head bowed over the dog again. "A dream . . . an' maybe a love."

Tears came to Ellie's eyes and started to slide down her cheeks. Clark reached out and gently brushed one of them away.

"What is it, little girl?" he asked softly. "Do ya love a man who doesn't return yer love?"

"Oh no. He does," Ellie said quickly. "He . . . he wanted me to have a locket fer Christmas. He would have come courtin'. I know thet, Pa, iffen I would have given 'im any hope at all."

"An' why didn't ya?" asked Clark simply.

"Why?"

"Yeah, why? Didn't ya feel like he's the kinda man ya could love?"

"Oh, I do love 'im, I do," sobbed Ellie.

Clark reached out and drew his daughter into his arms. He let her cry against him, saying nothing, only holding her close and stroking her long golden curls.

When Ellie's sobs appeared to be lessening, he spoke again.

"I'm afraid ya lost me," he said against her hair. "Ya say thet he would have come courtin'—an' ya say thet ya love 'im. Then why are the two of ya so miserable an' there's no courtin' bein' done?"

Ellie pulled back and looked at her father, eyes wide in astonishment.

"I can't," she sobbed again. "Ya know thet. I can't." When Clark did not respond, she said, "Mama needs me."

The words soaked slowly into Clark's consciousness, and he pushed the girl away from him and looked into her eyes. "Whoa, now," he said. "What is this yer tellin' me?"

"Mama needs me," Ellie repeated.

"Sure, Mama needs ya, but she sure ain't expectin' ya to go on bein' her housemaid fer all the years to come."

"But the baby—"

"Mama has had babies afore—an' she's made out just fine, too. Oh, I will admit I was some worried, too—at first—but she's doin' just fine now. Why, yer mama is no softie. She can handle most anythin' thet needs handlin', an' one little baby, more or less, sure ain't gonna bother her none."

"But it's not just thet," said Ellie.

"It's not?"

"No."

"What else, then?" said Clark, fearing that a fresh torrent of tears was on the way.

"Lane is going back west as soon as the LaHayes get back to care fer the farm."

"So?"

"Every time one of us goes far away, it pains Mama. You know how it hurt her when Missie went, and then Clae, and now Luke. It would nigh kill her iffen I went, too."

"I see," said Clark. "Yer thinkin' thet yer mama just wouldn't be able to let ya go, huh?"

Ellie nodded with her head up against him.

"Well, I'm admittin' thet yer mama sure does prefer her young'uns close by. I also happen to know the thing thet Mama wants more'n anythin' in the world is fer her children to be happy.

Now, iffen ya think thet yer happiness lies with a certain young man by the name of Lane, then thet's what Mama wants fer ya, even iffen it takes ya many miles away."

Ellie's eyes still showed doubt. "Oh, Pa," she said, "do ya really think so?"

"I know so," answered Clark. "Fact is, I just came from talkin' with yer mama. She is worried 'bout ya. Has been fer days. We didn't either one of us guess what was wrong, or we woulda straightened ya out long ago. It was Kate thet got suspectin'. Guess we had just thought of Lane as family fer so long thet we never even thought he might not seem like family to you."

Ellie's eyes began to glow again. "Oh, Pa," she said, "I love both you an' Mama so. I'd never want to hurt Mama. Never!"

"And yer mama would never want to stand in the way of yer happiness, either. Now wipe away those tears, and let's go see yer mama."

Ellie did so, the best she could, then bent to stroke the patient Rex once more before hurrying to the barn door. Clark lifted the lantern from its hook and followed her.

Suddenly Ellie stopped. "But, Pa," she said in deep concern, "I already told Lane no."

"I don't think Lane will be givin' up thet easy like," he assured her. "Iffen he does, he's not the man I thought 'im to be."

Some of the fear left Ellie's eyes, and she quickened her steps. Clark had all he could do to keep up with her. As he hung up his coat on the peg in the kitchen, he heard her say, "Oh, Mama," and then what sounded like both laughing and crying.

NINETEEN

Dark Shadows

Someone was knocking on the door, making far more noise than should be necessary. Marty fought for consciousness, at the same time wishing she could remain asleep. Something told her it was not time to get up yet, even though she could not see the clock in the darkness.

Clark had roused and was hurriedly dressing. Marty's mind flashed her a message of "Ben." *This is what happened when Ben . . .* But no, it couldn't be that again. Then why would someone come pounding on their door now? Fear gripped Marty's heart. It must be more bad news.

Clark left the room hurriedly without a word, and Marty heard his footstep on the wooden stairsteps. He had not stopped for boot or crutch and hopped down on one bare foot.

With an effort, Marty threw back the covers and stepped out onto the cold floor. She was glad for the rug nearby that offered some protection from the winter chill. She felt around with one foot for her bed socks and crossed to the closet hook to grab her robe. Voices drifted up to her. Excited voices. It sounded like Clare. Who had awakened Clare, and what might the trouble be?

Marty tried not to hurry down the steps. A fall in the dark certainly would be no aid to whatever the problem was. She held firmly to the rail and felt her way down carefully. Yes, it was Clare's voice. Clare's voice mingled with Clark's, Clare's muffled by horrible sobs. Marty hastened her steps.

When Marty entered the kitchen, she was more bewildered than ever. Clark had lit the kitchen lamp, and in its soft glow, she could see the outline of two men. Her men. Clark was supporting Clare, and Clare was weeping against him uncontrollably. Marty tried to voice a question, but it wouldn't form on her lips.

"It's Kate," said Clark over Clare's head. "She's in terrible pain."

"What's happened?" Marty was able to gasp out the question.

"He doesn't know. It just came on sudden like in the night. I'm gonna go git Doc. Ya think thet ya can—?"

But Clark didn't finish his question before Marty moved to her grown son and turned him toward her.

Clare seemed to get hold of himself. "Oh, Ma," he groaned, "I'm so scared. I've never seen anyone in such pain. We gotta git back there, Ma. We gotta—"

"We will," said Marty. "I'll just pull on some boots an' grab a shawl."

Clare took Marty's hand, and they hurried toward the little log house. He had taken command again now. The rough sobbing had ceased, and he was thinking rationally.

"Maybe the baby is on the way," Marty said as a means of assurance.

"It's too early yet."

"Some of 'em come early."

"Not this early."

"Maybe Kate figured wrong."

Clare made no response, and Marty thought he strongly doubted it.

"Some women do have a great deal of pain when—"

But Clare didn't want to listen. "We don't want the baby comin' now," he said. "It's still too early. It would be dang'rous fer 'im to come now."

Marty turned at the sound of someone hurrying to the barn. Clark was on his way for the doctor. She prayed him Godspeed and continued along the icy path.

"Pa's on his way," she said to Clare. "Won't be long an' the doc'll be here."

They had not yet reached the house when Marty could hear Kate. She felt Clare stiffen beside her. Poor Kate—she had never been a crybaby about discomfort. Truly Clare was right. Something was terribly wrong with her. They hastened into the little house, and Marty kicked her boots into a corner by the door and shed her shawl as she passed by a chair. Already Clare had half run through to the bedroom. A lamp had not even been lit, and Marty fumbled around in the semidarkness to find it and the matches. Kate continued to toss and moan on the bed, and Clare dropped on his knees beside her and tried to soothe her with his words and hands.

"Pa's gone for Doc, sweetheart. It won't be long now. Just hang on. Hang on."

Clare turned back to Marty and his eyes were pleading. *Do somethin', Ma,* they seemed to say. *Do somethin' fer my Kate.*

Marty moved to the bed and gently reached out to the girl, smoothing her matted hair back from her face. "Kate," she said, raising her voice to be heard above Kate's groans, "Kate, can ya hear me, dear?"

Kate responded with a nod of her head and another moan.

"When did this start?"

Kate managed to indicate that it had started about bedtime—a little—and then increased in intensity during the night.

"An' where is the pain?" continued Marty.

Kate laid her hand on her lower abdomen.

Marty placed her hand there, too. She could feel the tightening of Kate's muscles as another groan passed Kate's lips.

As the contraction passed, Marty spoke to Kate, trying to keep her voice light to ease some of the tension in the room.

"Kate," she said, "I do believe thet yer gonna be a mama."

"No!" Kate gasped out. "No! It's too early—too soon. I don't want 'im to come now. He's too little."

"Listen," Marty said sharply. "Listen, Kate. Don't fight it, Kate. Don't struggle against it. Try to relax. Maybe—maybe it will pass— but ya gotta calm yerself. Fer yer sake an' the baby's."

Marty could see Kate's big violet eyes in the dim light given off by the lamp on the dresser. Marty knew she was thinking of her baby. She wanted her baby. She would do anything that she could for his safety.

"I'll try," she whispered. "I'll try."

"Good girl," Marty said, then knelt down beside Clare and began to stroke the girl's cold hand. "Now, Clare, I know thet you've been prayin', but let's pray together."

Clare led them in prayer. "Our God," he said, a catch in his voice, "ya know our concern here. We don't want to see Kate in such pain, an' we don't think it's time fer the little one yet. Help us all to be calm with yer help, Lord. Help Kate at this time to feel yer love—an' our love. God, ya know our desire. We want our son safely delivered. I want my Kate—" Clare's voice truly broke here, and Marty wondered if he would be able to continue, but he quickly recovered. "But, God, in spite of our wants, we gotta say as we been told to say, 'Thy will be done.' An' we mean it, Lord, 'cause we know thet ya love us and ya want our good. Amen."

Kate had lain quietly the entire time Clare was praying. Clare leaned over and kissed her cheek as soon as he had said his "Amen." Kate stirred again, and Marty knew she was fighting to try to relax in spite of her intense pain.

"Clare," Marty said, "make us a good fire in the cook stove, will ya? And put on a couple kettles of water to heat."

Clare went to comply, and Marty moved closer to minister to the girl on the bed. She smoothed back her hair, straightened the crumpled blankets, stroked her flushed cheeks. And all the time she fussed and comforted, she talked quietly to Kate, trying to distract her mind from the pain.

Kate heroically tried—with all her being she tried. Marty could see her brace herself against the pain and then fight with all of her might to relax in spite of it. Clare started a brisk fire and filled the kettles as Marty had told him. He even brought a pan of water so Marty might sponge Kate's face. The hours dragged by. Marty felt the doctor was long overdue and feared lest he had already been called out on some other emergency. Just as she was about to give up, she heard hoofbeats in the yard. She turned to the window and breathed a prayer of thanks as she saw two riders dismount.

Clark was leading both horses toward the barn, and Doc was hurrying toward the little house with his black bag grasped firmly in his hand. Never had any man looked more welcome to Marty than did Doc.

Clare was already at the door, taking Doc's coat and giving him a report. Marty remained in Kate's room until the doctor appeared, and then she left him with the girl and went to the kitchen to wait for Clark.

She busied herself with the coffeepot. She didn't know if there would be anyone who would be wanting coffee, but it gave her something to do. With Kate now in the doctor's hands, Marty had time to think.

What if Kate's baby *was* on the way? Would it be developed enough to be able to survive? What would happen to Clare and Kate if they lost their baby? What would happen to their faith?

Marty reached down and laid a hand on her own stomach. Her baby responded with a strong kick. Marty's eyes filled with tears. "Please, God," she prayed, "don't let anythin' happen to the baby. They could never stand it, Lord. They've been workin' an' dreamin' an' prayin' fer thet little'un fer so long. It would break their hearts to lose it now. Iffen . . . iffen . . ." and Marty placed her hand over her unborn. "Iffen it has to be one of 'em, Lord, then . . . then take mine. I think I could bear it better'n Kate." Even as Marty spoke the words silently, her mind was filled with the knowledge of the great pain that losing her baby—the little unseen someone she had learned to love—would bring her. If only there was some way she could protect Clare and Kate from the awful pain of losing the baby they loved.

Another thought quickly followed, almost taking Marty's breath away. What if something happened to Kate? How would Clare ever be able to stand that? Again Marty prayed. "Not Kate. Please, God, protect Kate . . . fer Clare's sake."

Clark came into the kitchen, rubbing his cold hands together.

"Any word yet?" he asked, his face serious.

"No. Doc is with her now."

"What do you think?" Clark dropped his heavy mittens onto a nearby chair.

"I think thet . . . thet the baby is on the way."

"Can it make it?"

Marty shrugged wearily. "I don't know. It's early . . . too early. But some have. I don't know. I'm afraid, Clark, really afraid."

Clark crossed to her and drew her to him. Their baby protested, and a smile flickered across Clark's face in spite of his anxiety.

"Feisty little rascal, ain't he?" he commented and Marty eased away.

"She," she said in a whisper with a smile and moved to the stove. "Ya want some coffee?"

"Would help to warm me up some, I reckon."

Marty poured two cups. She wasn't sure if she would be able to drink from hers. She had no desire for coffee. She suddenly noticed as she crossed to the table that things were very quiet in the bedroom. It was a relief not to hear Kate tossing and moaning, and Marty hoped that the quiet was a good sign.

Clare entered the room. His eyes looked heavy and his face drawn.

"It's the baby, all right," he said in a tired, resigned voice.

"How is Kate?"

"Doc has given her somethin'. Just to help with the pain. Doc can't find a heartbeat on the little one. 'Fraid thet . . . thet somethin' is wrong."

He lowered himself onto a chair and put his head on his arms on the table. Marty was at a loss. What did one say to an aching son? This was not a childhood disappointment that they were dealing with. This was a life. Two lives. How did one give support at such a time?

Clark reached out and gripped Clare's shoulder with a firm hand. Clare did not move or respond, but Marty knew that he felt the love and support of his father.

When Clare was able to speak, he continued slowly. "Doc says Kate is strong. Her pulse is good an' she is fightin' hard. She should be fine when this is all over."

Marty breathed a thankful prayer.

"How long does Doc think it might be?" asked Clark quietly.

"Can't say."

Marty brought Clare some coffee. To her surprise he drank it, though she wasn't sure he was aware of doing so.

The long night hours slid slowly by. From time to time, members of the family went to the bedroom to check with Doc. About the only assurance he could give them was that Kate seemed to be holding up well.

Dawn came, the air brisk and wind-chilled. Ellie arrived at the little house. Unbelievably, she had slept through the commotion of the night before, her bedroom being at the back of the house. Now she came fearfully, looking for her family and wondering what were the circumstances of an empty house. Her face paled as Clark explained the situation to her, and then she went to work preparing some breakfast in Kate's little kitchen. Marty had not even thought of the need for food.

Clark left to do the chores. Clare moved as if to go with him, but Clark waved him back to his chair. Instead, Clare went to see how his Kate was. He came back to the kitchen with his face even more somber than before.

"Doc doesn't think thet it'll be long now," and he lowered himself to the chair again. Marty wondered if he might be better off choring than sitting there with Kate heavy on his mind.

Ellie served breakfast. No one ate much, but a few of them went through the motions. Marty took a plate of pancakes and some bacon and coffee to the doctor. He eased himself onto a chair by Kate's bed and ate. He knew from long experience that one must eat to maintain strength.

It was nearing eleven o'clock in the morning when the baby girl arrived, tiny and stillborn. There was nothing that anyone could do . . . or say. Clare held his infant daughter in his arms and shook with his sobs. Then he passed her to Marty, who, through her own tears, lovingly bathed the little bit of humanity who was to have brought such happiness into a home. Clare went to the baby's room and found the tiny garments that Kate had requested for their little one to wear. They had been sewn with such love and pride and were to have been worn with such happiness. Now they would represent the love wrapped snugly around the tiny baby as it was committed to the small coffin which Clare and Clark sorrowfully fashioned together.

Kate continued to hold her own. Clare was so thankful that nothing had happened to his wife. With the help of the doctor's medication, she slept through most of the first day and on through the night. The next morning, Clare spoke gently to Kate of their loss. She had been vaguely aware of the fact before she slipped off to sleep. After they had embraced each other and cried together, Clare carried the small casket that held their little daughter into Kate's room, so she might see their child. Clark and Marty went on back to their house and left the two of them alone.

The burial was a quiet family affair. The preacher spoke the familiar words of strength and encouragement to the family members who gathered around the tiny grave.

In the days that followed, Kate regained her strength quickly after her ordeal, though a shadow lingered in her eyes. She clung to Clare in their sorrow. Clark and Marty prayed daily—sometimes hourly—for their children in their pain. Marty wished over and over that she could somehow bear it for them, but she could only be there, suffering with them. Somehow they got through the first difficult days. With time it would get easier, but, oh, it was going to take so much time, and the love-built nursery room was a constant reminder of just how much they had lost. It was hard for Marty to stand the strain of the sorrow, and without meaning to— or even realizing that she was doing so—she began to draw away from the intensity of the pain.

TWENTY

Nandry

Lane came as soon as he heard the news, spending time with Clare and allowing him to talk out his feelings concerning the death of his infant daughter.

Ellie hardly knew how to respond to Lane, now that she'd had her talk with her ma and pa. If she was free to make her own future, as they assured her she was, then she hoped that her pa was right and Lane wouldn't give up easily. But in her heart, Ellie feared—feared that Lane might have taken her previous word as the final answer. What if he did not wish to pursue it further? Ellie would be the loser indeed. Yet could she be bold enough to approach Lane herself? It wasn't at all in keeping with how she had been brought up, and Ellie doubted very much if she could bring herself to do it.

So for now, at least, she kept her conversations with Lane courteous but brief.

Marty now had some very difficult days to live through. Each time her child moved, she remembered that she had fought against this baby. She had not wanted it. Indeed, had she gotten her way, it would not have been . . . at first. Now Marty loved this baby. Whoever it was within her had completely captured her mother love. Still . . . she felt guilty. It was true she hadn't wanted it . . . and yet it was still safe, while the small body of the baby Kate and

Clare had wanted so very much right from the beginning lay in the churchyard under a heap of winter snow. It didn't seem just or fair.

So in the sorrow that Marty shared with her son and daughter-in-law, there was also mixed in a good deal of guilt. Could they see it? Did they, too, feel the circumstances were unjust, that she was unworthy to be bearing another child? True, when Kate had been in pain and her baby in danger, Marty had been willing to exchange her baby's life for the life of Kate's baby if the Lord would have accepted such a bargain. Marty was beginning to understand how very difficult it would have been for her actually to go through with such an agreement. She loved the small life within her more than she had thought possible. Yet poor, poor Kate! She had loved her baby, too. Marty wondered if Kate and Clare would be bitter toward her and the coming baby. She did not want to face them. And in the days following the death of their infant and the gathering for the burial at the church, Marty found little excuses to keep from close contact with the young couple. What could she say? How did they feel about her? About Clare's new little brother or sister soon to make an appearance?

Ellie, fortunately, had been to see Kate daily. She helped her with her housework until Kate was able once again to take over for herself. Even then Ellie went, dropping in for a chat or a cup of tea. Marty knew she must go, as well, but she begged "foul weather" and stayed close to her fire.

———

It was Nandry who unexpectedly brought Marty to her senses. Nandry came to call in spite of the bad weather. She had left all the children at home with Josh. Marty knew, as soon as she saw her daughter drive into the yard, that something deeper than the need for companionship had driven Nandry out alone and on such a day.

Marty was still concerned about Nandry. Something was

bothering the girl—had been ever since they'd come home. Nandry never had said anything about it, but Marty knew it was there. Marty had the feeling it was somehow connected with Clark—Clark and his lost leg. But surely enough time had passed by now for Nandry to get used to the sight and the idea of Clark's need for a crutch.

Marty held the door for Nandry now and lovingly welcomed her in. Her first explanation for the visit sounded like Nandry simply had taken a notion to get out of the house for a few hours. Her small brood was driving her beside herself, she maintained. Marty nodded, remembering well the feeling.

Nandry inquired about Kate, and Marty assured her that from all reports she seemed to be doing fine, that Ellie was presently with her.

Marty busied herself putting on the coffeepot and cutting some slices of Ellie's loaf cake. Nandry talked easily of everyday things. She wanted one of Ellie's recipes for pumpkin bread. Andy had fallen and bitten his tongue. It hadn't been a bad cut, but it had bled profusely, and Mary had screamed in fright, thinking Andrew would surely bleed to death. Baby Jane had fallen down a few steps; she wasn't hurt badly, but it did frighten them all. Tina had come home from school with a gold ribbon as the best speller in the class; Josh was so proud of her. He had never been good at spelling.

Nandry, unusually talkative, continued to chat until Marty poured the coffee and settled down at the table with her. Then, with a quickness Marty found hard to follow, she changed from her current casual subject.

"How's Kate takin' it?"

Marty was taken aback. The fact was she didn't really know how Kate was taking it. Oh, outwardly Kate seemed to be handling it fine, according to Ellie. But Marty had no way of knowing how Kate was feeling deep inside. She couldn't admit that to Nandry, so she replied defensively, "She feels bad, of course."

"I didn't mean thet," responded Nandry. "I mean, is she able to accept it?"

"Accept it?"

Nandry looked at Marty searchingly, her eyes repeating the question.

"Accept it?" said Marty again. "Well, it happened, didn't it? One has to accept it—iffen ya want to or not."

"Ma," said Nandry, "don't beat round the bush. Ya know what I'm meanin'."

"No," said Marty slowly, "I'm 'fraid I don't."

"Does Kate feel God has a right—thet He was fair to do what He done?"

"God?" said Marty in disbelief. Was Nandry actually asking what it seemed like she was asking?

"Ma, we know thet God could have saved thet there baby fer Clare an' Kate iffen He had wanted to—just like He could have saved Pa's leg iffen He had put himself out some."

There. It was out. Pain showed in Nandry's eyes—pain and anger. Marty looked at the girl, shock and fear sweeping through her and making her feel heartsick.

"It's true," continued Nandry, her tone reckless. "It's true, and one might as well say it. No use just pretendin' thet it ain't."

Marty reached out a hand and laid it on Nandry's arm. She'd had no idea there was so much anger and bitterness there.

Nandry shrugged off the hand.

"But . . . but . . . it ain't like thet," began Marty, silently imploring the Lord to give her wisdom.

"It ain't? Well, how is it, then? I s'pose Pa hoppin' round on one leg is just a figment of my 'magination, huh?"

"I didn't mean thet. I mean—well, I mean God didn't just take Pa's leg to be spiteful. He—"

"How d'ya know what He did an' why?"

"At the time," said Marty quietly, "I didn't, an' I fought it, too. I had to come to the place where I could honestly say, 'Thy will be done,' an' God did His will, an' good came of the sorrow."

"Enough good to make up fer a good man losin' his leg?"

Marty hesitated at the words spat out on the table between them. Nandry had always been particularly devoted to Clark in an unusual way. Marty had hoped Nandry had long since properly sorted out the relationship with Clark as her father.

"I think so——" began Marty hesitantly. Then, with more conviction, "I know so. Why, so many things happened to show it so. The little church was started. Dr. de la Rosa went home and made peace with his family. An' the . . . the most important was what happened in the life of Jedd, yer first pa. He——"

But Nandry interrupted, rising from her chair with her eyes sparking angrily. "An' what did *he* ever do to deserve the mercy of God? Him thet run out on us, thet left Ma to die alone while he ran off to chin-wag an' chew tobacca with some old cronies. Are ya tellin' me thet God would favor a man like thet over one who was upright an' carin' an' lived. . . ?" But Nandry could not go on. She was weeping uncontrollably now, her shoulders shaking with every sob.

Marty rose to her feet slowly because of her cumbersome body. She was dumbstruck. What could she ever say to this angry and agonizing girl? How could she make her see that God *is* love? That He gives it freely whether a person "deserves" it or not? How could she ever get her to understand that bitterness and hate against her father were not in keeping with God's plan for her life—could not bring happiness or peace or anything good to anybody? Oh, poor Nandry, to have carried such a terrible burden for such a long, long time!

Marty moved to her and took her into her arms. As Marty raised her eyes, she beheld a stricken Ellie standing in silence at the kitchen door. Marty had not heard her return, and she was sure Nandry was not aware of her presence, either. Ellie stood with a white face and parted lips as though unable to comprehend. Marty wondered how long she had been standing there and how she would respond to what she had heard from the lips of her adopted older sister.

Then Ellie took a deep breath and moved into the room. She took Nandry's hand and gently led her back to her chair. Nandry sat down again, physically and emotionally spent from her outburst. Ellie passed her a hankie and Nandry blew loudly.

Ellie waited for a moment and then spoke quietly. "Nandry," she said, "I think I know how yer feelin'. At first, when I heard 'bout Pa, I wanted to fight it, too. I blamed God . . . a little bit. I blamed God fer spoilin' a good man. You know what I thought? I thought thet I might not be proud to walk down the street in town with Pa anymore. Can you 'magine that? Feelin' ashamed to be seen with a man like Pa simply because he had only one leg?" Ellie shook her head sadly, as if she felt guilty over ever having such a thought. "I always thought my pa 'bout perfect, an' I was 'fraid I wouldn't see 'im as perfect anymore. It would be embarrassin'. People would stare. I looked at the other men around. 'He's not as good as my pa,' I'd think, 'an' he's still got two legs.' I knew it was wrong—I knew it all the time—an' then God started talkin' to me 'bout it. He pointed at my own life. I had pride, I had vanity; I even discovered some deceit. 'See,' said God, 'yer not perfect. Is yer pa ashamed to walk down the street with you? He should be, iffen it's perfection yer wantin'.' I knew God was right. My cripplin' was greater and more deadly than Pa's. Mine was to the spirit; his was only the body. I prayed an' asked God to fergive me an' to help me grow from the experience of Pa losin' his leg, so the price of it might be worth somethin' in my life—both fer my gain an' so thet Pa could remain proud of me.

"Now yer pa, Nandry, had 'im many faults." Ellie's voice was gentle. "What ya have said 'bout 'im is prob'ly right. I don't know, I didn't know 'im. But God must have seen someone worth savin'. An' even iffen there wasn't anything worthy at all, God still loved 'im. An' Pa loved 'im. Loved 'im enough to want to make sure he had thet chance 'fore he died. Pa didn't knowingly give his leg fer yer pa. But I think he would have—iffen he had had some way of knowin', I think he would have. Because our pa knows thet a leg is less important than a soul.

"I think thet Pa would be hurt iffen he knew the loss of his leg somehow brought bitterness to yer soul, Nandry. He wants to strengthen ya an' help ya to grow with every experience of his life, and iffen he doesn't do thet, then it brings him pain and disappointment—far more pain than the loss of thet leg did."

Nandry had been listening silently to Ellie. Marty sat praying— praying that God would give Ellie the right words to minister to the need of the young woman, praying that Nandry would be able to understand and accept the words.

Suddenly Nandry began to weep again, quiet weeping now. Ellie put her arms about her and let her cry. At last Nandry lifted her head.

"Yer right," she said. "An' I've been wrong. All these years I've been wrong. My pa wasn't right in what he did, but that gave me no call to do wrong, too. I'm more guilty than 'im 'cause I know better. I shoulda been prayin' fer 'im all those years. I know Clae was. Used to make me mad at her. 'Let 'im git what he deserves,' I'd think. Thet was wrong—so wrong." And Nandry dropped her face in her hands and cried harder.

"Oh, Ellie," wept Nandry, "can God ever fergive me?"

"Iffen He couldn't," said Ellie, "we'd all be in trouble."

"Ma," wept Nandry, seeming to suddenly realize that Marty still sat nearby, "would ya pray fer me?"

Marty did. Ellie followed with another prayer, and then Nandry cried out her own pleading for forgiveness. After the prayer time, they poured fresh coffee and shared further the truths they had learned.

Finally Nandry looked at the clock and declared that Josh would wonder what had happened to her, and besides, she was anxious to talk with him about what had happened this afternoon and the lifting of her burden.

Ellie put on her coat and went with her to get her team, and Marty stayed at the table rejoicing and doing some serious thinking.

Nandry had been wrong to bundle up all of her years of bitterness. She should have been able to trust God. She had been taught ever since she had been in the Davis home that God is *God* in all circumstances of our lives, and He loves His children. Nothing happens to those He loves that catches Him by surprise. He is always there to see one through the difficulty and to bear each person up on wings of love. Good can follow on the path of sorrow. All things can work for good to those who love Him.

Marty knew it all. She even believed it all. So why was she sitting at her kitchen table when just across the yard was her daughter-in-law who needed her? *I don't know what to say,* pleaded Marty. *I just don't know what to say. I still have my baby. And, God, you know I want my baby. Is that selfish? Can I go to Kate, with me so obviously expecting my child, when she has just lost hers?* Marty wept silent tears before the Lord.

Trust Me came a quiet voice, and Marty wiped her eyes on her apron and rose from her chair. She would take Kate the new shawl she had been knitting. Perhaps something new and bright would be welcomed by her on this dreary winter day.

———

Marty met Ellie at the door. "I'm goin' to see Kate fer a few minutes," she said.

"Oh, good," responded Ellie. "Kate's been so lonesome fer ya. But ya know Kate. She wouldn't think of askin' ya to come out in the cold."

"She's been wantin' me?"

"Every day she mentions ya."

"Why didn't ya say so?"

"Kate asked me not to. She didn't want ya to take any chances on harmin' yer baby. She's countin' on yer little one more'n ever now, Mama."

Marty turned to hurry on out, but she did slow down and carefully place her footsteps on the path. Her eyes stung with her unshed tears. How insensitive she had been.

Kate was at her door to welcome Marty. She must have seen her coming. She ushered her into the small kitchen and steadied her while Marty slipped out of her boots. Marty noticed that Kate was still quite pale.

"How are ya, Mama?" Kate asked anxiously.

Marty felt it was she who should be asking such a question. "I'm fine, dear. An' you?"

Kate smiled. It was a courageous smile for one who had just experienced such sorrow.

"I'm fine, too . . . now. Would ya like a cup of tea?"

"I think not."

"Coffee, then?"

"No. Truth is, we just finished havin' coffee with Nandry."

"*Nandry* was over . . . on such a cold day?"

"Guess she felt she needed it bad enough to come."

"I didn't notice her come in . . . but then, Ellie an' me was talkin' 'bout that time."

Marty took a chair and produced the bright blue shawl. "Brought ya somethin'," she said. "Thought ya might be needin' somethin' new to look at."

Kate smiled. "It's lovely, Mama. I love the color . . . but ya know thet blue is my favorite color, don't ya?"

Yes, Marty had known.

Kate held the shawl, wrapping the long tassels around and around her slim fingers.

"I shoulda been here afore," Marty began slowly, "but . . ."

"It's okay, Mama. Clare an' I both know how much yer hurtin' with us. I was just so 'fraid thet the grievin' might cause harm to thet new brother or sister. Are ya sure yer okay?"

"I'm fine."

"Ya can still feel movement?"

"Oh yes. She's a busy one."

Kate smiled at the "she" and sighed with relief. "I didn't think much 'bout it at the time, but thinkin' back, I realize I hadn't felt any movement fer a few days. I thought maybe my baby was just restin' or thet I was just so used to it I didn't notice or somethin'."

"Ya think thet. . . ?" Marty couldn't voice the question.

Kate answered it anyway. "Doc said our little one died two or three days 'fore . . ."

Her voice trailed off, and Marty hurried to fill the space with words. "I'm so sorry, Kate."

Kate blinked back tears. "I'm sorry, too, Mama. But Doc also said God sometimes uses thet way to care fer a baby thet has some . . . some kind of problem. I thought of Wanda, Mama. I know Wanda loves her Rett and thet she wouldn't give him up fer the world, but I'm . . . I'm not sure I . . . I'm not sure I could take thet, Mama. Iffen our little girl was goin' to be . . . not well . . . not whole . . . then I thank God He took her. Am I a coward to feel thet way?"

"A coward? No, Kate. Certainly not. I . . . I think there are harder things to face in life than . . . than death."

"Clare an' I talked 'bout it. At first it was so hard. We wanted our baby so much, an' then Clare said, 'Let's just count the blessin's outta all this.' At first I couldn't see 'em. Clare had to remind me. 'We still have each other,' he said. 'An' we are both still well an' strong. The doctor says this isn't likely to happen again, so we'll be able to have more babies. We don't have a child who is sickly, either in mind or in body. She will never suffer. She is safe in heaven, without even sufferin' any of the pains of this earth.' So, ya see, we do have lots to be thankful fer."

Marty blinked back tears.

"We've grown through this, Mama. We've grown closer together. I've always loved Clare, but through this . . . I have learned what a wonderful, carin', unselfish, and godly man I am married to. I not only love 'im, but I respect 'im as the spiritual leader of our home."

Marty reached out and took the younger woman's hand.

"An' we've learned more, too, Mama. We've experienced first-hand that all those things we've been taught concernin' God through the years are true. He is there when ya need 'im, helpin' ya through the difficult places, easin' yer hurt. We've felt the prayers of family and friends, too. Never have I felt so . . . so . . . loved and sorta protected as I have in these last difficult days."

Marty fumbled for her handkerchief. Here she had come to minister to Kate, and instead Kate was ministering to her.

"Clare said we might go up fer supper—soon as we are invited," Kate said with an abrupt change of subject. "So how 'bout an invitation? I'm dyin' to step outside even fer a few minutes." She smiled and added, "I could bring somethin' to add to—"

Marty began to laugh through her tears. "Yer invited," she said firmly, "tonight. We'd love to have ya. We've been missin' ya so. It seems like such a long, long time."

"It does to me, too," Kate admitted. "But I'm feelin' a little stronger each day now. I'm even plannin' on going to church again next Sunday—iffen the weather isn't too bad. Doc said I should guard against a chill fer a while. I'm prayin' the weather will be nice."

"I'll join ya in that prayer," promised Marty.

"Oh, Mama," said Kate, "I'm just countin' the days now until yer little one is here. It's gonna be so much fun to have 'im to hold and play with."

"Her," corrected Marty.

"Oh yeah—her. It was *ours* who was to have been the boy. I'm glad thet it wasn't. She was a beautiful little girl, wasn't she? Clare said he learned one thing. With God makin' little girls so cute, it won't matter next time whether God decides to send a boy or a girl."

"Guess it won't matter none to me, either," agreed Marty. "It's just a little game we have always played at our house. Sorta boys against girls. Right now, the girls think they are outnumbered. They're not really—when ya count Nandry an' Clae. They count 'em or don't count 'em as suits their cause." Marty laughed.

"Maybe God would send us one of each iffen we'd ask."

"Whoa, now!" exclaimed Marty, holding up a hand. "I'm thinkin' one will be 'bout all I can handle!"

They laughed together, and Marty rose to go.

"I'm so glad ya came, Mama," said Kate with great feeling. "I've been missin' ya so. Pa has dropped in now an' then, an' thet has been a real help. It helps Clare, too, to have Pa."

Marty gave Kate a warm embrace, and both of them felt between them the struggle of the little one against the confinement.

Kate backed away laughing. "She's alive an' kickin', all right. Little rascal! I can hardly wait to meet her."

Marty could hardly wait, as well. "See ya fer supper. I'll hurry on home an' share the good news with Ellie."

"I'm lookin' forward to it. It'll be so good to be with you all again," Kate stated, then added, "You be careful on those slippery paths, now."

Marty promised and walked carefully toward her home, breathing deeply of the cold, fresh air. She really should make herself go out more often. The air was good for her. She could do with more exercise, too.

Kate needed to get out, as well. Marty prayed the weather would soon warm up so Kate might be able to get out and put some color back into her cheeks. Dear Kate. She was so brave about it all. Marty wondered about the little room. Had they left it the same? She hadn't had the heart to ask. With God's help, they would soon be needing it again.

TWENTY-ONE

Lane Comes for Supper

"Look who I talked into joinin' us fer supper," Clark announced, and Marty looked up expecting to see Clare entering her door. Instead it was Lane who stood silently in the doorway, nervously pulling off his mittens.

"Lane! How nice to see ya!"

Marty felt, more than saw, Ellie's head lift.

"We've been missin' ya," Marty went on. "How're things goin' at the LaHayes'?"

"Fine," answered Lane. "Just fine. Had a letter from the boss yesterday. He says the folks will be home next week. Mr. LaHaye, Willie's pa, has decided to stay on out west. Willie's brother might even go out there an' join 'em iffen he can find a buyer fer his place."

"He wants to sell?" Marty's voice held surprise.

"Guess he kinda likes the West," explained Lane.

"Well, come on in and warm yer hands by the fire," Marty invited. "We're havin' a nice roasted chicken fer supper, an' I think Ellie has got fresh corn bread bakin' to go with it."

As Lane moved into the room, Marty added, "Me, now, I just sit around all day an' watch folks work."

The group laughed comfortably and moved toward the table.

Lane had not dared to look directly at Ellie. He wondered if she would be able to read his thoughts.

He had pondered much how he could support Ellie, as his

wife, if he stayed in the area. True, he could farm. He knew a bit about taking care of farm animals now, but he still knew nothing about planting and raising crops. He could learn, he told himself. He could ask. He would beg for the information—down on his knees if need be—if it meant having Ellie. But then, there was the matter of money. In the West, the prices were still right for the man who was brave enough to want to strike out on his own. In this farming area, all the land had already been taken and farmed. Those who might wish to sell were demanding a high price for their farms. Lane knew; he had already been inquiring. Take Willie's brother, for instance. The price he was looking for was so far from what Lane would ever be able to afford that the banker would likely laugh in his face.

No, there just appeared to be no way. No way at all that Lane could see he could ever make a decent living for Ellie in the area. And Ellie could not hurt her mama by going west. It seemed like a dead end to Lane.

He avoided Ellie's eyes so she could not read the pain in his own. Perhaps it didn't matter that much to Ellie, he reasoned. Perhaps she did not care for him in the way that he cared for her. There were many farm boys around about who would be more than happy to provide Ellie with a home of her own. Lane had seen that fact the night of the social. Ellie would be much better off—happier maybe—with one of them. And, more than anything else in the world, Lane wanted Ellie's happiness.

"I thought when ya said ya'd found someone to share our table," Marty was saying to Clark, "thet ya walked over with Clare an' Kate. They are joinin' us tonight, too."

Clark's eyes lit up. "Wonderful," he said. "Thet must mean Kate is beginnin' to feel better. It'll be great to have some of the family back again."

Ellie moved gracefully about the kitchen, putting the finishing touches to the table and dishing up the inviting food. Lane watched Ellie when he was sure she wouldn't notice. From the kitchen window she took a small violet with soft blossoms of deep purple to place in the center of the table. "Almost matches Kate's beautiful eyes," she said to Marty.

"So the LaHayes might be leavin' us?" Clark was saying, pushing a chair over to Lane. "Never thought they would be thet taken by Willie's West. Does grow on one, though."

Lane thought of the West. He loved it. Grow on one? He couldn't imagine one could live any place in the world that could be any more appealing.

"S'pose yer rather anxious to git back yerself?" Clark was saying.

Lane wished to be truthful, and he hardly knew how to respond to Clark's question. "Guess there are things 'bout here thet grow on one, too" was all he said, glad when Clark did not question him further.

Tramping on the porch announced the coming of Kate and Clare, and Clark moved to the door to welcome them and take their coats. He kissed Kate on the forehead and told her how good it was to have her able to join them.

Clare and Lane shook hands vigorously. Though it had been only a matter of an hour or two since they had been together in the woods, they had fallen into an easy camaraderie that Lane deeply appreciated.

Clark assigned seats around the table, and all of them took their places. Clark took his usual seat at the end of the table, and Marty sat opposite him at the other end. Kate and Clare sat to Clark's left, and Lane and Ellie were left with the places on Clark's right. Lane was very conscious of Ellie's closeness, but he was thankful he would not need to look into her eyes over the table.

The talk was cheery and light. Even Kate joined in with a sparkle in her eyes. Ellie was the only quiet one in the group. She stayed very occupied with making sure the bowls were kept full of food and the bread plate refilled. She fussed pouring coffee and took longer than necessary preparing the dessert. Marty wondered if she had taken time to eat anything.

After the meal was over, Clark threw more logs on the open fire in the living room fireplace and invited the others to sit and enjoy its warmth. Marty began to help with the dishes, but Ellie sent her from the kitchen, saying that Kate needed her in the living room far more than she needed her in the kitchen. Marty was finally convinced and joined the family there.

Lane puttered around, feeling rather self-conscious. He poked at the fire occasionally, adding a comment to the conversation now and then to fulfill his social obligations, and found himself shifting pillows around and around in his chair. With all of his being he ached to be in the kitchen with Ellie, yet he dared not go. He was sure he could not be trusted—he was bound to blunder and make some comment or plea that would let her know how much he cared for her. He mustn't. He knew that he mustn't. To do so would only hurt her more, and Lane could not bring her pain.

If only he could leave, he kept thinking. It was pure agony just sitting there listening to the family talk.

All the while his ears strained toward the kitchen. He heard every sound Ellie was making. He knew just how far she had progressed in the washing and drying of the dishes. There . . . she was placing the clean ones back on the cupboard shelves. Now the cutlery. Then the cups on the hooks. She wiped the table and the cupboard. Her cloth went *swish, swish* as she circled the inside of the dishpan before pouring out the dishwater. Now she was replacing the pan on the hook and hanging up the dish towels— evenly—to dry beside the big black cook stove. There . . . she was done. She would be removing her apron and wiping her hands on the kitchen towel. Would she join them, or would she excuse herself and go to her room?

Ellie entered quietly and took a chair by the fire. She sat looking into the flames, as though looking for a message there.

The evening had not gone well for Ellie. It was the first time she had really seen Lane since . . . since Christmas, except for gatherings such as the church services and the funeral for Kate and Clare's baby. She had wondered just what to say when she did see him. What would *he* say? Would he ask her if she had reconsidered? Pa had said Lane wouldn't give up that easily. Well, it appeared he had. Perhaps he hadn't really cared that much after all. *But he did,* Ellie argued within herself. She was sure of it. Then why did he say nothing . . . do nothing? Was he afraid he would be refused again? Ellie was troubled. It was hardly the place of a girl to . . . No, she wouldn't even think about it.

Ellie tried to join in with the conversation, but she soon knew it was no use. She excused herself and went back to the kitchen. Tears rolled down her cheeks as she fixed a plate of scraps for Rex and quietly let herself out of the house.

Lane stuck it out for a few more minutes. He had been right. Ellie didn't really care that much. He finally thanked his host and hostess for the good meal and told them he really should be heading for home if he was to be of use to the men in the woods the next day. The logging for the winter was almost completed. The sawing and chopping would come next.

Clark and Clare both rose to their feet with the intention of going with Lane for his horse, but he waved them both back to their chairs.

"Be no need," he assured them. "Stay here by the fire and enjoy the good company. Me, I know where ol' Jack is."

He let himself out and walked silently to the barn, his heart heavy. *Next week,* his heart kept saying, *next week and I'll be gone.*

He opened the barn door and was surprised to see the soft glow of the lantern. He wasn't aware that the Davises left a light in the barn at night. That was risky, and no farmer ever—

And then Lane saw Ellie, her head bowed over the nearly grown Rex. She was stroking him gently, and tears glistened on her cheeks.

Lane did not know whether to make his presence known or to

walk home, leaving his horse. At that moment Ellie raised her head. She gasped slightly and rose to her feet.

"I . . . I . . . just came to bring 'im his supper," she explained quickly.

Lane cleared his throat. He didn't know what to say. "He's really growin', ain't he?" he finally stammered.

Ellie brushed self-consciously at her tears. "Sure is." She tried a chuckle, pushing back the tail-wagging Rex.

There was silence.

"Ya goin' home?" Ellie finally asked.

"Yeah. I was. I . . . I . . . thanks fer thet good supper. Sure beats my batchin' meals."

"Yer welcome. Anytime. Guess ya won't need to batch much longer, huh?"

"Guess not." A pause. "Sure beats Cookie's meals, too, though."

They both laughed halfheartedly.

Ellie reached and scooped up the dish in which she had brought Rex's supper. "When will ya be wantin' Rex?" she asked, "or will ya be able to take 'im?"

"Oh, I'll take 'im," Lane hurried to answer. He didn't add that he wasn't sure how he was going to get a dog out west on the train. *There must be some way,* he thought.

"I wasn't sure what a rancher would do with a cattle dog," Ellie said. "Rex is gonna be real good with cattle. He already can bring them in from the pasture. Watches their heels real good, too. He'd be great as a farm dog."

"Wish I could be a farmer," Lane said slowly.

Ellie showed surprise. "Thought ya loved the West an' ranchin' an'—"

"Oh, I do. I do, but I'd . . ." Lane stopped. "Look, Ellie," he said, "we gotta talk an' we can't talk here. Can we go back to the kitchen or . . . or somethin'?"

"We can walk."

"Ya won't be too cold?"

"This is a warm coat."

Ellie put down the dish again and reached for the lantern. Lane thought she was going to take it with her, but instead she carried it to the open door, blew it out, and set it up against the barn.

"Don't want to chance a fire," she explained. "Pa lost a barn once."

They turned toward the lane. Overhead the winter sky was clear. Stars—multitudes of stars—twinkled above them. A pale yellowy moon showed its last quarter. The wind lightly rustled the frosted branches of the trees. They walked in silence.

But the silence didn't last too long.

"I still have thet locket," Lane said.

"Oh?"

"I'd still like ya to have it . . . even though . . . even though . . ." He decided to change his approach. "I said back there thet I'd like to be a farmer. Well, what I meant was thet . . . thet iffen there was any way so's I could stay in the area so thet . . . well, so thet . . . but try as I might, I can't think of any way to come up with the money it would take fer a farm."

"Ya found thet ya like farmin' better than ranchin'?"

Lane wanted to be truthful. "No," he said. "No, I reckon I still like ranchin' the best."

"Then why would ya want to farm?"

"I . . . I thought you would know thet."

Ellie stopped and leaned her arms on the corral fence. Lane stopped beside her.

"Ellie," he said, taking a deep breath. "Ellie, I love ya. I know I have little to offer. Not near what a man should be offerin' a woman. I know ya said thet ya can't go out west 'cause it would break yer mama's heart. I'd stay here an' farm or work in town iffen only there was some way . . . some way to . . . to make a decent livin' fer ya. I've laid awake nights tryin' to sort it all out, but—"

Ellie laid a hand on his arm and Lane stopped in midsentence.

"Lane," she said softly, "ya said ya still have thet locket."

He was puzzled at her interruption but nodded his agreement.

"Do ya have it here?"

Lane lifted a hand to his inside breast pocket.

"Right here," he said.

"I think I'd like it now," whispered Ellie.

Lane pulled forth the locket with trembling hands.

"Would ya fasten it, please?" asked Ellie.

Ellie pulled aside her hair and turned around so Lane could fasten the locket around her neck. His fingers felt clumsy, and he wondered if he'd ever get the tiny clasp fastened. By some miracle he did. Ellie turned back around and, standing on tiptoe, placed a kiss on Lane's cheek. "Thank ya," she whispered.

Lane felt like he was going to come apart—hope and fear colliding in his chest.

"Ellie, please. Don't tease," he pleaded.

"I'm not teasin'."

"But—"

"A moment ago, ya said thet ya loved me."

"I . . . I . . . do—"

"An' I accepted yer gift, given with yer love."

"But the kiss—"

"Lane," interrupted Ellie, "I would never kiss a man I didn't love."

"But what about yer mama? Ya said—"

"I had a talk with my mama . . . after my pa had a talk with me. Both of 'em say I have to make my own life . . . thet they want my happiness wherever it leads me. Iffen it's the West, then—"

But Lane stopped her. "Oh, Ellie," he said, his voice sounding choked. He drew her close to him.

They walked and talked a long time in the crisp moonlight. At last they heard the door slam and voices over the frosty night air, and they knew Clare and Kate were on their way home.

"It must be gittin' late," sighed Ellie.

"Too late fer a chat with yer pa?"

Ellie smiled at him. "Don't s'pose it's *thet* late," she assured him, and they walked hand in hand toward the house.

TWENTY-TWO

Ma Comes Calling

The time for Marty's confinement was drawing near. Thinking about Ma Graham, she was concerned she had not seen her for such a long time. She knew that Ma had her family, but Marty felt maybe Ma needed her, too.

Their previous plans for Ellie to go and pick up Ma for a nice, long visit had not materialized. The unexpected birth and then the loss of Kate's baby had wiped away all thoughts of the visit from their minds. Now Marty was ready to try again. She wasn't sure if it was because she thought Ma needed her or because she knew she needed Ma.

Marty was happy to see Ellie bloom again, now that she and Lane had worked things through. She felt that, if anyone deserved to be happy, it was her Ellie. She even felt a bit of satisfaction that, in the near future, the two sisters might again have each other. But Marty was also aware of just how difficult it was going to be for her to actually give up Ellie as she had done with Missie. She needed to talk to Ma. Ma would understand exactly how she felt.

So Marty laid out her plan before Clark.

"Been thinkin' a lot 'bout Ma Graham," she began. "Wonderin' how she's doin'."

"I been thinkin' on her, too," Clark responded.

"Sure would be good to sorta check on her," continued Marty.

"I'm goin' to town day after tomorra. I can do thet. Thought I should stop by an' see iffen there's any way I could help."

For a moment Marty was silenced.

"Wasn't really thinkin' 'bout what she might be needin' from town or such," she eventually continued. "Thinkin' more along the . . . the *fellowship* lines."

"I see," nodded Clark. "Lou's wife is right there. An' I expect thet the rest of her girls git over to see her, too."

"Sometimes one needs neighbors as well as family," Marty persisted.

"I just don't think it would be wise right now."

"What wouldn't be wise?" asked Marty innocently.

"You makin' a trip out in the cold to go see Ma."

"Did I suggest thet?"

"Not in words, ya didn't, but it's what ya were aimin' at, ain't it?"

"Well, sorta . . . but not exactly. What I was really wonderin' was iffen ya would mind goin' on over an' pickin' up Ma fer a mornin' an' then takin' her on home again."

Clark laughed. "Well, why didn't ya just come out an' say so?"

"I wasn't sure what you'd think of the idea," said Marty truthfully.

"What I think 'bout it an' what I agree to do 'bout it are often two different things," said Clark wryly, "an' well ya know it."

Marty reached a hand to Clark's cheek. "I know," she said, "an' I love ya fer it."

Clark laughed and turned his head so he might kiss her fingers. "I'll see," he said, and Marty knew that was his promise.

"Tomorra?"

"Tomorra."

Marty went to bed happy with the knowledge that on the morrow she would have a visit with her dear friend again.

———

When Clark was hitching the team to the sleigh the next morning to make his promised trip to pick up Ma, Lady began to bark, running down the lane toward an approaching team. It was Lou Graham.

Clark threw a rein around a fence post and walked toward the upcoming sleigh, his crutch thumping on the frozen ground.

Lou was not alone. Carefully tucked in with warm blankets, Ma Graham sat beside him.

After a neighborly "howdy," Lou explained. "Ma's been frettin' 'bout not seein' Marty fer a spell. I was goin' on by to pick up some feed barley at the Spencers', so I brought her along fer a chat while I'm gone."

"Well, I'll be," said Clark. "I was just hitchin' my team to come on over an' git ya, Ma. Marty's been right anxious to see ya."

Clark helped Ma down, and Lou prepared to be on his way again.

"I'll bring Ma on home whenever she an' Marty think they've had 'em enough woman talk," Clark joked.

"Ya mind? Thet sure would help me out some. Then I can go on back by way of town an' git some things I'm needin'."

The team left the yard, and Clark walked to the house with Ma. He would put the horses back in the barn and give them some hay until they were needed to return Ma home.

Marty couldn't believe her eyes when Clark ushered Ma into the kitchen. She knew Clark couldn't possibly have been to the Grahams' and back already.

She laughed when she heard the story and settled Ma down in one of the comfortable kitchen chairs. Ellie put on the coffee and placed the cups on the table. Then she set a plate of sugar cookies beside the cups and excused herself.

"Think I'll just run off down to Kate's fer a bit," she said.

"Not so fast, young lady," Ma said with a knowing smile. "What's this I'm hearin' 'bout you and thet there young, good-lookin' cowboy?"

Ellie blushed.

"It bein' true?" continued Ma.

"It's true—thet is, iffen you've been hearin' what I think ya might have been hearin'."

Ma pulled Ellie close and gave her a big hug. "I'm happy fer ya," she said hoarsely. "I've always saw you young'uns as sorta my own. I wish ya all the happiness, Ellie, an' God bless ya . . . real good."

Ellie thanked her with misty eyes. She and Ma Graham had always had a special relationship, as if Ma was the grandmother she did not have.

Ma turned to Marty. "So how ya been doin'?" she asked simply. "You've had ya quite a winter. I've been thinkin' so much on ya. First, ya had to git over the rather surprisin' news of bein' a mother again. Then ya had the awful hurt to bear with Clare an' Kate. Now this. Must be a little hard to take, on top of everythin' else."

Marty had known Ma would understand. Ma did not believe in talking in circles. She went straight to the heart of the matter.

"Yeah," she answered, carefully choosing her words. "Guess it has been a rather rough winter. My, it was hard to see Clare an' Kate go through thet pain. But I'm so proud of both of 'em, Ma. They have both been so strong through it all. They've showed me a lesson or two."

"I could see when I saw 'em in church thet they hadn't let it bitter 'em. I'm so glad, Marty—so glad. Bitterness is a hard burden to bear. I should know. I've had me my bouts with it."

"You?"

"Sure did. I woulda just gone on an' on a carryin' it, too, iffen ya hadn't come along when ya did an' straightened me out."

"Me?"

"You'll never know just how set I was to sit an' feel sorry fer myself before Christmas there. Oh, I know. I didn't really tell ya all I was feelin', but I was all set fer a good, long bitter spell. I felt it just wasn't fair thet I should lose two good men in a lifetime. *Some women don't even like the one they got,* I reasoned, an' here I was with

two I had loved deeply an' I lost 'em both. Didn't seem fair somehow. Didn't even seem worth fightin' to keep up a good front fer
the kids. Then ya came by an' made me realize it did still matter
to my kids. I started thinkin' on it an' I saw somethin' else, too.
True, some women don't like the man they got. Thet's to their
sorrow. But I had me two good companions. Now, how many
women could be so blessed? An' here I was a fussin' 'bout it."

Marty smiled at Ma's way of thinking it all through.

"So I decided," continued Ma, "thet I just should be thankin'
the Lord fer all the good years 'stead of fussin' 'bout the years to
come."

"An' it helped?"

"Ya bet it helped. Every day I think of somethin' more to be
thankful fer. I have a good family—mine an' Ben's. We raised us
good young'uns. That's truly somethin' to be thankful fer."

Marty agreed wholeheartedly. What a burden it must be to
have children who fought against their parents, against the Lord.

"I have lots of good mem'ries, too, an' a mind still alert enough
to enjoy 'em."

Marty hadn't thought about the "mind" bit, but Ma was right.

"So it's easin' some? The pain, I mean?" Marty asked softly.

"It still hurts. Many times the mem'ries bring a sharp pain with
'em, but each day I tell myself, *This is a new day. It can be just a little
bit easier than yesterday was.*"

Marty rose to get the perking coffee.

"An' how is it fer you?" asked Ma.

Marty suddenly realized that things were just fine for her. Yes,
she had wanted to bring Ma to her house so that she could cleanse
herself of all of the pain of seeing her Clare hurt so deeply. She had
wanted to pour out to Ma that she was going to lose her Ellie, and
she didn't know how she would ever do without her. She had
wanted to feel Ma's sympathetic eyes upon her, to feel Ma squeeze
her hand in encouragement, to see the flicker of pain on Ma's face,
mirroring her own. She didn't want that now. Not any of it. She

didn't deserve it. Every mother had to watch her children suffer at times. Every mother had to someday loosen the strings and let her children go—not just one of them, but all of them, one by one. It was all part of motherhood. One nourished them, raised them, taught them for many years so that they could be free—free to live and love and hurt and grow. That was what motherhood was all about. Marty swallowed away the tears in her throat and smiled at Ma.

"Things are fine," she assured her, "really fine. We've had us a *good* winter. Kate an' Clare came through their sorrow even closer to God an' each other than before. There will be more babies. Nandry turned all her bitterness 'bout her pa an' Clark's accident over to the Lord. Ellie has found the young man she wants to share her life with, an' he will make her a good an' God-fearin' companion. An' me—well, I still have me this here little one to look forward to. Ellie an' me's been hopin' fer a girl, but I wouldn't mind none iffen it was another boy—just like his pa—or one of his older brothers."

Marty had not looked forward to coming back from the West to a church without Pastor Joe. Not only did she miss her son-in-law as family, but she knew she would miss him in the pulpit, as well. The adjustment had not been as difficult as she had feared. The young minister who now was shepherding the local flock was easy to learn to love and respect.

Pastor Brown was his name, though many of the people in the congregation called him Pastor John. He had taken a good deal of ribbing in his growing-up years. "Hey, John Brown," the kids would call, "Is yer body molderin' yet?" Then would follow a chant of "John Brown's Body." John hated the teasing. He had tried unsuccessfully to get his family to call him Jack. Perhaps then the kids would miss the pun in his name. It didn't work. His family never seemed to remember that he preferred Jack, and on the few occasions where they did remember, the kids didn't stop their teasing anyway. John decided to develop the ability to laugh with them. It was difficult at first, but it did help him to develop a delightful sense of humor. One thing John Brown was never guilty of, and that was making fun of another individual. Humor was never intended for this, he maintained. It was to make people laugh *with,* not *at* another.

Pastor Brown seemed to have a true gift of sensitivity in dealing with people. The older members of the congregation marveled at how well he could often right a difficult situation. Even the children in the church respected him. Never could he be accused of intending hurt to another.

Clark looked up in surprise from his harness-mending to see Pastor John approaching him.

"Hello there," he called. "Be right with ya. I'll just hang me this harness back up on the pegs, an' we'll go on in an' see what the womenfolk got to eat fer a bachelor preacher."

Pastor John smiled. "I've already been in the house an' greeted the womenfolk. They've already given me an invite to dinner, so I'm way ahead of you. Smells awfully good in there, too."

"Well, let's go on in an' sit a spell, then," said Clark.

"No, no. You go right on fixing your harness. I'll just sit here on this stool and watch you while I'm talking. Anything I got to say can be said right here."

Clark understood that there was something the young man wished to talk about in private, so he resumed his work on the harness, letting the preacher pick his own time and pace.

"Been a long, mean winter," spoke the parson. "Sure will be glad to see it coming to an end."

"Me too," agreed Clark. "Me too. An' I expect all the animals thet been winterin' through it, both wild an' tame, share our feelin'."

"Reckon they will at that."

"Speakin' of animals, ya got one with ya?"

"I'm riding, all right. Too hard walking in this snow."

"Best bring it on into the barn."

"Not too cold out there in the sun, and I won't be long."

"Still, it can be feedin', though," Clark responded. "Might take us a long time to eat up all those vittles the ladies are a fixin'."

John Brown laughed.

"Go ahead," said Clark. "Bring 'im on in an' put 'im in thet stall right there. I'll throw in a bit more hay." And Clark grabbed his crutch and went to do just that.

The parson brought in his horse and pulled off the saddle.

"Never could stand to see a horse eat with a saddle on his back," he said. "Makes me wonder how I'd enjoy eating if I had to stand there holding my day's work in my arms."

Clark laughed at the comparison. "Never thought on it," he responded.

The horse was tended, and Clark went back to his harness. The pastor pulled the stool closer so they could chat as Clark worked.

They talked of many things. Besides the winter, they discussed the new developments in town, the growth of the church, and the new members in the community. Clark was sure none of these subjects was the one the young preacher had come to talk about.

"Hear tell you're good at solving a man's problems," the pastor said at length.

Clark did not raise his head. "Don't know 'bout thet. I've had me a little practice. Seems I have my share of problems to solve."

The preacher reached down and picked up a long straw, which he proceeded to break into small pieces.

"You got a problem needs carin' fer?" Clark prompted.

"Sure do. And I never had one quite like it before—and I'm not sure just what to be doing with it. I've been praying about it for three days now, and something seemed to tell me to come and see you."

Clark continued to work on the strip of leather before him.

"I'm not promisin' to be able to help ya, but iffen ya want to share it and work at it together, I'm willin' to listen."

The preacher cleared his throat. "It's kind of a touchy thing," he said. "I won't be able to give you too many details because I don't want to break confidence."

Clark nodded to say that he understood.

"It's one of my parishioners," the preacher began. Clark could feel how very hard this was for the young man.

"Rumor has it that he's been seen in town . . . doing . . . ah . . . doing something he shouldn't be doing."

"Rumor?" said Clark, raising an eyebrow.

"Well, a pretty reliable source, really. I say 'rumor' because I haven't talked to the individual involved yet, and a man is innocent until proven guilty, right?"

"Right," said Clark.

"Well, this ah . . . source . . . says he has seen this occur more than once. He's concerned that others have been seeing it, too, and that it will reflect on the whole church."

"I see," said Clark.

"If it is happening, and if he is doing . . . what he shouldn't be doing . . . the man's right, Clark. It could reflect on the whole church. It's wrong . . . and it's against God's commandments . . . and I'm really not sure what to do about it."

"Did yer . . . ah . . . source say what should be done?"

"He wants him thrown out of the church."

"What do you want?"

"What I want is of no importance here, as I see it. What I want to know, Clark, is what does the Lord want?"

Clark laid aside the harness then and looked into Parson John Brown's honest blue eyes. He had just gained new respect for the young man.

"Guess we better take it a step at a time," he said and sank down onto a pile of straw, sticking his one leg out before him.

"First of all, someone . . . meanin' you, I think . . . needs to talk to the man and find out, if ya can, iffen he's really guilty as charged. Iffen he refuses to give ya the truth, then one needs to inquire further from the source an' from others. Iffen one person has seen these . . . these . . ."

"Indiscretions," put in the parson.

"This here indiscretion, then it's very likely thet others have seen it also . . . unless yer source has nothin' to do but sit him around an' spy."

"It's not like that, Clark. He's a good and reliable man, concerned only for the good of the church. He's not a busybody or a tale carrier."

"In that case, one has to pay considerable attention to his testimony."

"That's the way I feel about it. But the man accused should still have an opportunity to speak for himself."

"Agreed," said Clark.

"So I go to see him and hear his story. Now I need to know what to do about it."

"Well, let's say, first off, that he says he's innocent."

"That would be rather hard to believe, but I'd have to take his word unless we had further proof."

"Okay," said Clark, "we are thet far. He is innocent until proven guilty."

"And what if he admits to his guilt?"

"What does the Bible say?"

"You mean about taking the two or three witnesses to show him the error of his way?"

"Iffen he admits to his guilt, I don't reckon he can seriously deny the error of his way, though it's true thet some have tried."

"All right, let's say that he does admit his guilt but he has no intention to stop . . . to stop doing what he has been doing. What then? Does our little church discipline its members?"

"First, I think we need to understand what discipline is all about and why it is sometimes necessary."

"It's not easy to discipline a fellow believer, Clark. Who says that I'm so strong that I'll never fall? I'm not good at setting myself up as judge and jury."

"An' yer not the judge. God's Word is what we judge a man upon. Iffen He says thet it's wrong . . . then we can't make it right."

The young minister nodded his head.

"But should we bring judgment upon him . . . or leave it to God to judge?"

"Iffen ya committed a sin, do ya think you'd need to be making things right?"

"Certainly. I'd be guilty, and as such, I'd need to straighten the thing out with God and make restitution if necessary."

"The Bible teaches thet all the members of the church are of the same body. Iffen any part of my body sins, my whole being is held responsible. Iffen any part of the church body sins, we are all responsible to git thet thing made right. Iffen we, as the rest of the church, accept it as okay an' pass it off, then we, too, are guilty of thet sin."

The young preacher sat deep in thought. "His sin is my sin if I make no attempt to correct it when I know about it," he concluded.

"Somethin' like thet," said Clark. "I never was a theologian, so's I'm not sure how they would explain it."

"Then it's my responsibility to see that it's cared for. Boy, I hate that, Clark. It's not an easy thing to point a finger at another man."

"It's not easy. But it's not as hard as it seems when one realizes the purpose of the finger pointin', as you call it."

Clark shifted his position on the straw and continued. "Church discipline is done fer two reasons . . . to keep the body pure before God and to bring the erring one back to a forgiven and restored relationship with God. Never should it be done fer any other purpose. It's not to punish, or to make someone pay, or to whip someone into reluctant shape, or show the community thet we really are holy and pure. God already knows whether we are or not."

"'To restore them to a right relationship with God,'" mused the young preacher. "Then what about the need to send him from the church?"

"Iffen he makes the thing right before God, there's no need to throw him out. He's still part of the body . . . fergiven just like you an' me's been fergiven."

The preacher smiled. "Boy," he said, "I much prefer that way."

"We all do," said Clark, "only on occasion, it doesn't work like thet. Iffen he won't listen an' won't make it right, then comes the tough part. Then ya have to . . . to excommunicate 'im. Thet's tough, Brother Brown. Thet's really tough."

The parson sat deep in thought.

"Clark, I'm going to ask one more thing of you," he said at last. "I'm going to see this church member tomorrow. Now, I haven't told you his name or anything about him. If he sees his sin tomorrow and asks for God's forgiveness, then you need never know the particulars. If he doesn't, then I'd like you and a couple of the other deacons to go with me next time. If he still doesn't agree to do something about it . . . only then will we bring the matter to the congregation. Now, I'm hoping and praying that all of that won't be necessary, and I'd like to ask you to pray with me that God will work in the heart of the man so that we won't lose a Christian brother. I know it's hard to pray not knowing, but . . ."

"No problem," said Clark. "I've prayed fer many a need not really knowin' just what the need was, an' I certainly know thet ya need God's special wisdom an' guidance as ya speak to the fella."

The preacher nodded his agreement.

"I think thet it might be in order to take time fer some prayer right now," went on Clark.

They knelt together in the straw, earnestly beseeching God for His help and wisdom.

"Thank you," said the young parson, taking Clark's offered hand. "Thank you for the support. I feel like part of the burden has lifted already."

"Yer doin' a fine job, son," Clark said sincerely. "I want ya to know thet we all appreciate ya an' we're prayin' fer ya daily."

The young man smiled and stood up from his cramped position. He put out a hand and helped Clark stand, passing him his crutch. Then they heard Ellie calling them to the dinner table.

"Boy," said the young preacher, "am I hungry! It just comes to my mind that I forgot all about having some breakfast this morning."

"Then I'll expect ya to eat hearty at the dinner table," laughed Clark. "Can't imagine a son of mine ever gittin' himself so busy thet he'd ferget to eat."

TWENTY-THREE

Ellie Makes Plans

The LaHayes arrived home from their trip west more than anxious to share their experiences with the Davises, so they soon came over to visit.

They were full of news of Willie and Missie and their three small children. The baby was a dear, they insisted, and she was already crawling, and Missie was extremely busy trying to keep her out of mischief.

They praised Willie's spread; they praised the little neighborhood church; they praised the school operated by Melinda; they praised the mountains, the hills, and the grazing land.

Iffen they say somethin' good 'bout the wind, thought Marty, *I'm gonna really doubt their sanity.* But the wind was not mentioned.

They had now made up their minds. They were going back. They would put the farm up for sale and leave as soon as possible.

They brought gifts from Missie for each of her family. She even sent a hand-crocheted blanket for her new little brother or sister. Marty ran her fingers over the soft wool and pictured their daughter working over it. Marty could imagine Nathan or Josiah questioning, "What ya makin', Mama" . . . and Missie's answer, "I'm makin' a blanket fer yer new aunt or uncle." How ironic it all was.

"An' ya fell in love with the West, too?" Marty asked Callie.

"I loved it," she responded with no doubt. "It took me a little longer than it took my menfolk, but when I made up my mind, I was really sure."

"Do ya have a place in mind?"

"We looked at a few. The one we liked best already has a small house, a big barn, and a well."

"How far is that from Missie an' Willie?"

" 'Bout a four-hour ride."

Marty had no idea how far that would be in actual miles, but it did seem wiser to measure it in time rather than in distance.

"Plenty close enough to git together often," Callie assured her.

"What 'bout yer pa? Who does he plan to live with?"

"Willie got 'im first, an' Pa loves it there. He already has his own saddle horse—three of 'em, in fact—and he loves to help with the cattle. He'd take a daily shift iffen Willie would let 'im. Willie does humor him and lets him go out some but not on a daily basis. Willie has declared him the best fencer on the place, though. Pa loves the men in the bunkhouse, too, an' would have moved right in with 'em, but Willie an' Missie insisted that he have the small back bedroom in the ranch house. It's quieter back there, Missie says, but Pa ain't askin' fer no quiet. He loves to be right in the thick of things."

"I'm so glad he's happy out there."

"Oh, he's happy, all right. Never seen him so happy since Ma died."

"So he'll stay on with Willie an' Missie?"

"He's promised to come an' be with us some, too. He's rather anxious to help us fix up the new spread."

It all sounded good to Marty. She hoped with all her heart that it would work out well for them.

"Do ya have a buyer fer yer home place yet?" she asked.

"Not yet, but we are sure we will sell with no problem. Spring is the best time to sell—spring or late fall. Ain't too many folk out looking fer farmland with the snow piled up to one's ears."

Marty agreed.

"Will ya stay till it's sold?"

"Don't know fer sure. We're sure in a big hurry to git on back.

Like to git things in order an' a small herd out on the range as soon as the spring grasses start to grow. We've talked to Lane. With a bit of persuasion, I think he would stay fer a while. Maybe care fer things till a buyer comes along. Iffen he agrees, we hope to git on back there as soon as we can."

Marty felt a small stirring in her breast, a stirring of hope. Maybe Ellie wouldn't need to leave her so quickly after all. Marty knew that Ellie and Lane were making plans, but she hadn't asked what the plans were. Ellie would tell her in her own good time.

Marty served coffee and cake to their visitors and listened to the talk circulating around and around her. It was good to share in such enthusiasm—in such dreams—even if they did belong to another.

———

Ellie had sat enraptured, drinking in every piece of news about Lane's West. She wanted to feel a part of it so she might feel at home when she finally arrived. She wanted to know and love it just as Lane did. She felt that something about the bigness of the West would correspond to the bigness of the man.

"Have ya heard," Ellie asked her mother, "they want Lane to stay on an' care fer the farm till it sells in the spring?"

"Is he goin' to?"

"It's sort of an answer to prayer," replied Ellie enthusiastically.

Marty looked up from her mending.

"Lane and me thought he would have to leave soon. Which meant I would need to travel alone later."

"Why later?" asked Marty.

"Oh, Mama, you know very well I wouldn't up an' leave ya before thet new baby comes. An' I don't plan to leave ya right away afterward, either. Not till yer well on yer feet an' I'm sure things are goin' fine."

"That would have been a problem," agreed Marty.

"The biggest problem would have been our weddin'. We

talked of two possibilities . . . an' I didn't care fer either of 'em. We could have been married now an' Lane gone on alone an' me come later. I wouldn't like losin' a husband so soon after I'd gotten one," she said, smiling shyly. "Or," she continued, "we could've waited an' been married when I got out there. I didn't like thet, either, 'cause it would have meant you an' Pa wouldn't have been at my weddin'."

"I wouldn't have liked thet, either," admitted Marty.

"So ya see, this is sorta an answer to prayer," Ellie repeated. "We can git married soon after yer baby is born an' I can stay on here and help ya in the daytime, an' we can live over in the LaHaye house. Callie has already promised us thet we can."

It sounded good to Marty. Ellie would not need to leave for a few months yet. Marty would welcome each additional day.

"Sounds like ya got it all sorted out."

"We been workin' on it."

"So when do ya plan the weddin'?"

"Well, thet there little one is due the end of February, right?"

"According to my calculations."

"So we thought we could be married 'bout the end of March. Thet way ya won't wear yerself all out gittin' right into a weddin' after the baby comes, an' after the weddin' I can still come over days to help ya out."

"Land sakes, girl. You've really spoiled me. Ya think I won't be able to care fer yer pa an' the little one after a month of time?"

"Well, we don't want to rush ya, Mama."

Marty blinked away tears. Ellie was more than considerate as a daughter.

"Look here, dear," she said. "I'm in no hurry to lose ya . . . ya know thet . . . but ya go ahead an' make yer plans just as ya would have 'em to be. Don't stop to fit all of yer life round me. I'm just fine now, an' I'll be just fine after this here little one gits here."

Ellie crossed to put her arms around Marty. "I'll tell Lane thet the end of March is fine, then," she said.

TWENTY-FOUR

Church and Home

Clark was out milking the roan when Pastor John rode up. His smile was broad and his handshake firm as he joined Clark in the barn. "It worked," he beamed. "We don't have to take the next step. And more importantly, we don't need to take away his membership."

Clark responded to his smile with an enthusiasm of his own.

"Just wait till I git done with Roanie here, an' I want to hear all 'bout it," he said. "I'm near done."

The pastor walked about the barn, stopped to pet a cat, and strolled around some more. Clark could tell he was anxious to share his experience. He hurried to finish up with Roanie.

Clark hung his pail, brimming with foaming milk, well out of the reach of the barn cats and pulled a stool over for himself and one for the preacher.

"Sit ya down," he offered, and the parson sat.

"Went to see him as I said I would," Pastor John began. "It was kind of tough, I don't mind telling you that. Didn't know just where or how to start, but we did get to the point. I told it to him just like it had been told to me. Then I said I wanted to hear it from him. Was it true or not true? At first, he was very ambiguous. I thought sure I would get nowhere. I was even expecting him to outright deny it. He was getting a little angry, too, and I thought maybe I had really missed it." The man looked around the barn for a moment.

"Well, I decided that we'd better stop right there," he continued, "before things got out of hand. So I said, 'Mind if we have prayer before we go on with this? I consider you my friend and brother, and I don't want to lose you as either.' He looked surprised but he bowed his head. We prayed together, and pretty soon I could hear his sobs. Clark, he cried like a baby. Don't know of anything that ever was harder for me than that man's sobs."

The young preacher stopped, his face full of emotion. "Finally, we were able to kneel down there together, and he confessed it all to the Lord and promised to make the thing right . . . as right as one can. Some sins one can't erase, Clark, but you know that. I expect that his past might haunt him more than once in the future. He knows it, too. We've got to really pray for him. It's not all over yet. Maybe never will be. That's the trouble with sin. It leaves ugly scars."

Clark nodded in agreement.

"I did leave him feeling forgiven and clean again, though. He said that he was so glad to be rid of the thing that he just couldn't rightly express it. I'm glad I went . . . though it was the hardest thing I've ever had to do."

"I'm glad ya went, too," Clark assured him.

"Well, the next thing for me to do was to go call on . . ." Parson Brown stopped and grinned, "my source."

Clark grinned, too, and nodded again.

"First time I went I didn't find him at home. Next day I got busy again and couldn't. Mrs. Watley had another bad spell, so I spent the day with the family."

"How is she?"

"She's perked up again. Can't believe the stamina of the woman. We've thought so many times that she was going, and she seems to fight it off every time. Well, I finally got back to my 'source' yesterday. I told him just what I've told you. I wasn't sure how he would respond. Thought maybe, in light of things, and fearing a public knowledge about it and all, he might still want to put the fellow out of the church. Well, Clark, when I told him, great big tears started running down his cheeks and he just kept saying, 'Praise the Lord' over and over. 'We've still got our brother,' he said, 'Praise the Lord!'"

Clark was deeply touched, and he could tell Parson John was, too. They sat in silence for a minute, each with his own thoughts. Clark broke the spell.

"So we will be worshipin' with 'im on Sunday." It was a statement, not a question.

"He's part of the body. A worthy part, I'm thinking."

"Like your 'source' says," smiled Clark, "'Praise the Lord.'"

"I'm so glad I came to you, Clark. You steered me in the right direction."

"Now, back up some," interjected Clark. "I don't recall steering you nohow."

"But you—"

"*We* talked 'bout it. We talked together 'bout what the Word says. You knew what it says. You made yer decision. You really knew what to do all along. Iffen ya think back a bit, you'll remember."

The preacher thought back a bit. He grinned. "I still needed you, though," he insisted. "Needed an older, wiser man to think it through with me. But thanks. I see now. You didn't push or steer me. You let me work it through myself—step by step, with the Word to guide me. You could have just out and told me what to do, but you didn't. Thanks, Clark. I think I've learned a bigger lesson this way. Maybe next time I'll be smart enough to go through the Word step by step on my own."

Clark put a hand on the young man's shoulder. "Ain't no harm in sharin' a burden with a brother. I'm here anytime I can be of help. Remember thet."

"I will," said the preacher. "And thank you."

"Now," said Clark, lifting the pail of milk from the hook and reaching for his crutch, "let's go see iffen the coffeepot has any fresh coffee."

―――――――

Another letter came from Luke. As usual, the note was brief since he didn't have much time to write. He told them he was writing at a time he really should be studying. He was thinking a lot about his mother. Was she taking good care of herself and the coming baby? He gave doctorly advice as to what she should be eating, how much exercise she should be getting, and the danger of overdoing. Marty smiled as she read. How strange it was to have her "baby" mothering her. No, not mothering—doctoring. Luke would make a good doctor, as long as he could keep from becoming too personally involved with each of his patients. Marty didn't want to even think of the day when Luke would lose one of those he treated. The day would come. All doctors had to face it. It would be hard for Luke. He was so tender to the pain of others. Marty prayed that he might be able to handle it without too much anguish.

Clae wrote again, too. They had seen Luke briefly. He had come home with them for Sunday dinner following the church service. The kids loved him. Baby Joey had a tooth. He had been miserable cutting it but was his happy self again once the tooth was finally through. Clae hoped they didn't have to go through the same thing with each tooth that he cut.

―――――――

Arnie and Anne came for Sunday dinner. It was the biggest gathering the Davises had had for many Sundays. Kate and Clare came from next door, and Nandry and Josh and the children came, too. It was so good to see Nandry able to laugh and joke with the rest of them. She looked younger and happier than she had in years. Lane came, too, as he did each Sunday. He and Ellie took much teasing, but they didn't seem to mind it. The whole house looked as if it was vibrating with the chatter and laughter. Marty looked about her and quietly thanked God for each one of them. Tina was getting so grown up. She was almost a little lady, and Marty had to realize that it would not be long until her grandchildren, too, would be leaving their nests. *My, there's no other way to say it . . . how time does fly,* she reminded herself with a wry smile.

In spite of the enjoyment of her family, Marty felt especially weary when the day came to an end and the last of the visitors had put on coats and headed for home—the last of the visitors except for Lane. He and Ellie were still talking in the kitchen, their voices low and full of love and hope. Marty turned to Clark and said she thought she would just go on up to bed.

Clark's eyes went to the clock. "A mite early yet, ain't it?" he remarked, slight concern in his voice.

Marty, too, looked at the clock. She couldn't believe the evening was still so young. Had the clock stopped? But no, it was still ticking, and it said only ten minutes to eight. She gave him a tired smile. "Well," she said, "it was a big day. Not used to so many of 'em all at once, I guess. It's been quite a spell since they all been here together."

Clark nodded and rose from his chair. "Yer right," he said. "Yer wise to git off yer feet," and he came over to walk with her up the stairs, giving her aid without seeming to.

Marty readied herself for bed and crawled beneath the warm covers. How good it felt to just stretch out and commit one's weary body to the softness of the bed. *Yer gittin' old,* Marty told herself. *Ya gotta admit it. Yer showin' yer age.* She sincerely hoped she wasn't yet as old as she felt on this night. She was so weary, yet she didn't really feel she was ready to sleep.

When Clark came up to bed much later, Marty was still awake. She had shifted her position often, trying to find a comfortable way to rest. It didn't help much.

Clark stroked her forehead. "Are ya feelin' okay?" he asked. "Ya seem mighty restless."

"Guess I just overtired myself a bit," she responded. "Either thet or I just came to bed too early. Not used to goin' to sleep at eight o'clock."

"It's now ten-thirty," Clark told her.

"Oh," said Marty. There was a moment of silence. "Then I s'pect I'll be able to drop off anytime now."

Marty did eventually manage to fall into a light and fidgety sleep.

———————

It was about two o'clock in the morning when Clark was awakened. He wasn't sure at first what it was that brought him to consciousness, and then he felt Marty stir and heard a slight moan escape her. He could tell she still wasn't fully awake, but he knew she wasn't sleeping soundly, either. He waited for a moment and the sound came again.

"Marty," he said, laying a hand lightly on her arm. "Marty, are ya all right?"

Marty stirred and opened her eyes. Clark could just faintly see her face in the moonlight that streamed in their window.

"Are ya all right?"

"I fergot to pull the blind," Marty mumbled.

"Ferget the blind. Are ya okay?"

Marty shook her head. "I don't know. I . . . I think so. It's just . . . just . . ."

"Just what?" insisted Clark.

"I don't know. Havin' a hard time sleepin'."

"Is it the baby?"

"The baby? The baby's all right."

"Is it time?" persisted Clark, feeling like shaking Marty to bring her to full consciousness.

"Time? Time fer the baby?" Marty's eyes flew wide open. "Clark," she said, excitement in her voice, "maybe thet's it. Maybe it's time fer the baby!"

Clark chuckled in spite of himself. "Did ya—a mother many times over—fergit thet little one is gonna ask to be born eventually?"

Marty responded with a chuckle. "Guess I got kinda used to it . . . just bein' there."

Clark rolled out of bed and lit the lamp. Then he hopped to the window and pulled down the blind. The light being on might concern Kate and Clare if they were to spot it, he reasoned, and this could well be just a false alarm.

Clark crossed back to the bed.

"Now, tell me," he said, "how're ya feelin'?"

"I don't know. I just can't sleep right, an' somethin' seems different . . . I don't know . . ."

"Think back," insisted Clark. "Can't ya remember what it was like with the other ones?"

"Clark," said Marty, sounding a bit annoyed, "any mother will tell ya thet they can all seem different. Just 'cause one bears one baby don't mean thet ya can read all the signs."

"But there must be somethin'—" But Clark's words were cut short by a gasp from Marty.

"What is it?" he asked, his hand reaching out to her.

Marty took the offered hand and squeezed it tightly, but she was unable to answer his question.

Clark was sure he knew the answer. "I'll go git Ellie," he said and hurried to dress.

Ellie was soon there, sleepy eyed and anxious in her warm blue robe.

"Mama," she asked with concern, "Mama, are ya all right?"

Marty settled back against her pillow, preparing herself for the next contraction, and assured her that she was.

Clark leaned over Marty. He was buttoning on a warm wool shirt, the one he always liked to wear when he was going out into the cold. Marty looked puzzled for a moment.

"Where ya goin'?" she asked through some kind of haze that seemed to hang about her.

"Fer the doc," he answered. "An' the sooner the better, I'm thinkin'."

Marty still didn't appear to understand.

"The baby's on the way," explained Ellie patiently as Clark left hurriedly, his crutch thumping on the wooden stairs. "Pa will be back with the doc 'fore we know it. Now, Mama, you've got to think . . . think . . ." Ellie commanded. "Is there anything I should do? I know nothin' 'bout this."

But it looked as though Marty was still thinking about something else.

"The doc," she said slowly and then seemed to fully understand. "Oh, Ellie," she said, "tell Pa not to bother. I don't think there'll be any time fer the doc."

Ellie was terrified. "There's gotta be! Ya just started yer labor an' the doc ain't thet far away. You hang on, now."

Another contraction seized Marty, and she groped for Ellie's hand. Ellie prayed, wondering if Marty was ever going to relax again.

She did, falling exhausted back against her pillows.

"Listen, Mama," Ellie pleaded. "Can ya talk to me?"

Marty nodded her head.

"Can ya think straight?"

"I . . . I think so," panted Marty.

"You've been at birthin's. Now, the doc will be here soon . . . I'm countin' on thet. But, just in case . . . just in case . . . ya gotta tell me what to do."

Marty nodded.

"Okay," she said, her face showing her deep concentration. "Here's what ya do."

Clark had never pushed his horse like he pushed Stomper that night. The moon aided him on occasion, but often he had to travel on his own instinct and that of his horse. The moon seemed to be playing games. It would bob out from a cloud just long enough for Clark to be relieved because of its light, and then it would slip behind a cloud again, leaving Clark totally on his own, traveling a rutted and snow-covered wintry road. Clark, pushing his steed as fast as he dared, learned to pace himself, riding hard by the moonlight and slowing down when he had to feel his way.

It seemed forever before he was pulling up to the doc's hitching rail. Clark prayed that he would be home and not out on some other call. Why was it that youngsters always insisted on arriving in the middle of the night?

Doc was home and quickly answered Clark's persistent knock on the door. He was not long in pulling on his clothes and grabbing his black bag.

"One thing we can be thankful for," he said, throwing the saddle on his mount, "yer wife has never had a speck of trouble with any of her deliveries."

Clark did take some assurance from the doctor's statement, but still he was feverishly anxious to get back home to Marty.

The moon again was uncooperative. Clark's horse was headed home while the doc's horse was leaving a warm stall, so Clark found himself often out in front of the doctor.

That was fine, Clark told himself. His horse knew the road better and it was good that it should lead the way.

Before they had reached the Davis farmyard, the moon had decided to disappear altogether. They were used to it by now and urged their horses on at a fast pace in spite of the darkness.

When they arrived, Doc dismounted and threw Clark the reins to his horse. Without a word, they parted company—Clark going toward the barn, riding his horse and leading the doctor's, and Doc hastening toward the house.

There was a light in the kitchen. Through the window, Doc could see Ellie moving about.

"Good," he said to himself, "she has a fire going and the kettle on."

He entered the house without knocking and threw off his heavy mittens and coat, tossing them on a nearby chair. He was halfway across the kitchen floor before he remembered his hat. He turned to throw it on the top of the pile of outdoor clothing.

"How's yer ma?" asked the doctor before starting upstairs.

"She seems to be fine," answered Ellie. "She's asked me fer some tea."

The doctor slowed midstep. If Marty was asking for tea, there was no need for him to be in such a hurry.

He stepped to the fire to warm his chilled hands.

Ellie went on with her task of pouring hot water into the teapot and setting out a cup.

———

It wasn't long until Clark flung open the door and burst in upon them. His eyes quickly swept across the room. Ellie and the doc were both standing in the kitchen as though nothing of importance was going on in the rest of the house. Clark was perplexed . . . and a little annoyed.

"How is she?" he asked. *Why are they both down here?* he wondered.

Doc turned to him. "She's fine. She just asked Ellie to fix her some tea."

"Tea?" echoed Clark. "At a time like this?"

He started for the stairway, the doc close behind him, and Ellie bringing up the rear with the tea tray in her hands. They entered the room together. Clark was very relieved to see that Marty was no longer tossing. She seemed quite relaxed as she lay against the pillow. *A false alarm!* Clark thought. *The false labor passed already.*

Marty looked up at the three of them. "Yer a little late," she said lightly.

"Late?" Clark responded. "Well, it weren't easy travelin'. The road was rutted, and the moon wouldn't—"

Marty interrupted him. "We won," she said complacently.

"What ya meanin'?" Clark demanded.

"Me an' Ellie. Didn't she tell ya?" and Marty pushed back the covers to reveal a little wrapped bundle on the bed beside her. "It's a girl."

Two pairs of eyes turned to Ellie. Ellie set the tea tray carefully on the bedside table. Her eyes were wide, and she shook her head dumbly. "I . . . I guess I fergot," she stammered, and then she flung herself into Clark's arms and began to weep, trembling until he had to hold her close to keep her from shaking. "Oh, Pa," she sobbed, "I was so scared . . . so scared."

The doctor took over then. Clark was patting Ellie's back and murmuring encouragement to her. After she had cried for a moment, she got herself under control again. Clark talked her into sitting on a chair and having a cup of tea along with her mother. The doctor examined both baby and mother, telling Ellie over and over what a fine job she had done. At last Clark was able to hold his new daughter. She was a little beauty, in his estimation. He smiled as he rocked her in his arms and paid her a multitude of compliments.

"Okay, you two," Clark said, turning to Marty and Ellie. "Iffen yer so smart, I s'pose ya got her named already, too?"

"No," said Marty. "We waited on you fer thet."

"Any of the names thet you've been talkin' of suits me."

"Well, it's sure not gonna be one thet you picked," countered Marty. "Henry or Isaac or Jeremiah."

Clark laughed. "Well, I won't insist."

"I was thinkin'," said Marty thoughtfully, "thet Ellie might wish to name her."

"Me?" said Ellie, both surprise and delight in her voice.

"Kinda thought since ya did so much to git her safely into this world thet ya had more right than anyone."

"I think thet's a great idea," agreed Clark.

"Well, then," said Ellie, "I like Belinda."

"Belinda," Clark and Marty both said at once.

"Belinda May," continued Ellie.

"Belinda May. I like it," said Clark. "Suits her just fine."

"I like it, too," Marty said. "An' now iffen her proud pa would just bring her on over here, I'd kinda like to git another look at our daughter."

Clark reluctantly laid the tiny baby down beside Marty again, then leaned over to kiss them both.

Doc cleared his throat.

"Well, seein' as I won't be needed here anymore tonight, I guess I'll just be headin' on home to my bed. I suspect that everyone in this house has had enough excitement for one night. Bed's a good place for all of you. 'Sides, this here new mama could do with a good rest."

They all agreed. "See ya a little later," Clark promised Marty and turned to usher all of them from her room.

"Yer not gonna head off fer home without a little coffee to warm ya up," he informed the doc.

"I'll make some," volunteered Ellie. "I need to busy myself with somethin' ordinary to unwind before going back to bed anyway."

"Coffee won't be necessary. Ya already got out the teapot an' more hot water a singin' on the stove. I'll just have me a cup of tea."

Ellie took charge in the kitchen. She was glad to be back to doing something so familiar. Looking back over the night hours she had just experienced, she decided that even though she had been frightened almost beyond herself, it had been exciting, too.

To assist in the arrival of a new little life was an experience not given to many. Now that she was sure her mother and sister were just fine, she could relax and maybe even treasure the memory. One thing she was sure of: It was a night she would never forget.

TWENTY-FIVE

Sharing

The next day the household awakened early, in spite of the lack of sleep the night before. There was too much excitement in the air for anyone to be able to sleep very long. Besides, the wee Belinda awoke to insist on an early breakfast, and not being used to the cries of a new baby in the house, the whole family got up with her.

Ellie hurried across the yard over to Kate and Clare's with the good news. The commotion of the night before had failed to waken them. They immediately headed for the big house with Ellie.

Kate was the first to reach Marty's bed. Little Belinda had just finished her nursing, had her diaper changed by her pa, and was snuggled down beside her mother again for a much-deserved nap. It was hard work being born, and she had some resting to do.

Kate stood gazing at the baby, her eyes filled with love and tears.

"She's beautiful, Ma," she whispered. "Just beautiful."

"Ya want to hold her?" asked Marty, seeing the longing in Kate's eyes.

"May I?"

" 'Course."

"But she's sleepin'."

"She's got all day to sleep. 'Sides, she likely won't even waken anyway."

Kate picked the wee baby up carefully. "Oh," she squealed, "she's so tiny." She turned to show the little bundle to Clare. "Look here, Belinda May, this is yer big brother. Yer wonderful big brother. Yer gonna be so proud of 'im."

Clare reached out a big hand to the tiny one. Marty could see tears form in his eyes, but he blinked them away. "Hi there, ya little pun'kin," Clare greeted the baby. "Yer a pretty little thing . . . fer a newborn."

"She's beautiful," argued Kate.

Clare laughed. "Give her a few days . . . but then, my ma always had pretty babies."

At length, the baby had been inspected and fussed over enough for the present. Their attention turned back to Marty.

"An' how are you, Ma?"

"Fine. I feel just fine. But then, I had me such good doctorin'."

All eyes turned back to Ellie.

"I'm proud of ya, little sister," Clare said, tousling her hair. "But why didn't ya come fer some help?"

"There wasn't time. Not even time to think, let alone . . . but Mama was great. I woulda never been able to do it without her careful instructions. I had me no idea—"

"You were wonderful," said Marty, "never flustered or nothin'."

"Till afterward," Ellie said, laughing. "Then I just seemed to fall apart."

They all laughed together.

"Well, at least," added Clark, "ya waited till after it was all over. Ya didn't go collapsin' when yer ma needed ya."

They left the room together. It was agreed that Clare would ride on over and take the news of the safe arrival of Belinda to Arnie and Nandry and Ma Graham. Ellie was going to saddle the other horse and go see Lane. Clark would take the team and go to town to get telegrams off to Missie, Clae, and Luke. Kate volunteered to stay close beside Marty. They all scattered in various directions, anxious to share the good news.

Marty gained her strength back rapidly, in spite of her many visitors. The new baby was a good baby, demanding only a minimum of attention, much to the chagrin of the household. There were many pairs of willing arms that would have been more than happy to hold and fuss over her more, but she was content to be fed and changed and then tucked in once more to her bed for another nap. As the days passed by, she began to spend more time awake. Even then, she did not cry except when she was hungry. She didn't need to. There was usually someone there to hold her anyway. Clark was spending more and more time in the house on the wintry days.

"Little girl," Marty overheard him say to the baby, "I sure am glad ya chose to arrive in the winter when a body can be in, 'stead of at plowin' time." Marty smiled to herself. Never had Clark had more time to enjoy one of his babies.

Daily Marty felt her previous vigor return to her body. She was feeling much more like her old self and gradually took on the household duties. She felt Ellie's questioning eyes on her at times, but as Ellie could see for herself, Marty was happiest when busy. And when Marty assured her she truly had the strength and was not merely pushing herself, Ellie did not protest. Marty told her to spend some time planning for her upcoming wedding. Ellie had been collecting and preparing the things she would need for her own house.

Marty helped with the preparations, too. In the quiet of the long evenings, she pieced quilts and hemmed tea towels. Pillowcases were embroidered and rugs hooked. Marty quite enjoyed being involved and, before long, was nearly as excited as Ellie about the coming event. It didn't make her as sad as it had when she first knew the inevitable was coming and Ellie would be leaving home. Especially with Belinda sleeping contentedly in her bed or rocking in her pa's arms.

A package came from Luke. *To my new little sister,* the note read. *Bet you are really something special. I've been waiting for you for a long, long time. I finally am a big brother. We're going to love one another. I can hardly wait to see you. I'll be home just as soon as I can. In the meantime, take good care of Mother. She's someone pretty special, too. Love, Luke.*

Marty wiped her eyes as she handed the letter to Clark. Then she kissed the tiny Belinda and showed her the packaged gift. "From yer big brother," she said. "Big brother Luke. Ya wanta see what he sent?" The baby did not respond with as much as the flick of a tiny eyelash, so taken was she with sucking her fist, but Marty opened the package anyway. It was a pair of baby shoes. Marty had never seen them so small or so dainty. "Well, look at thet," she said, holding the shoes out to Clark and Ellie. "Did ya ever see anythin' like it?"

Ellie squealed with delight. "Oh, aren't they darlin'?"

Clark grinned and reached out to take one of the bits of leather in his hand.

"Most senseless thing I ever saw," he said. "But yer right—they are 'bout the cutest thing, too."

Clae also sent a letter and a package. Hers was more practical than Luke's had been—and almost as pretty. It was a little hand-sewn gown. Marty knew that Clae had not had time for all of the fancy stitching since receiving the word of the baby's birth. Her note explained it. *I took a chance that it would be a girl,* she said. *It was our turn. If it had been a boy, I'd have sent him something else— though I still hadn't figured out what—because he never would have been comfortable in all this ribbon and lace.*

In a later mail, a parcel came from Missie. Marty lifted out a carefully wrapped pale pink sweater. *I know that I sent something before for the new little sister, but I just couldn't resist doing something special just for her now that we know who she is. I've stayed up nights hurrying to get this done. I hope she gets it before she is already too big for it. It comes with love to Auntie Belinda from her nephews Nathan and Josiah, and her niece Melissa Joy.*

———

Marty was sure she had never seen a girl more excited about her wedding day than Ellie. Eyes glowing and cheeks flushed, she slipped into her wedding gown, her hands fairly trembling. "Oh, Mama," she said, "I can scarce believe thet it is finally happenin'! It seems I've waited so long."

"But it hasn't been long," Marty reminded her. "Not long at all. It's only been a couple of months since ya made yer plans."

"Well, it seems half of forever," insisted Ellie.

"Half of forever," repeated Marty. "Yes, I s'pose so." She gazed at her lovely daughter, wanting to hold this moment in her memory for all time. Ellie's gown, white with tiny blue flowers and ruffles at the neck and sleeves, had been carefully and lovingly sewn by mother and daughter together. *How blue her eyes are,* thought Marty. *Almost exactly the same cornflower blue as those flowers. . . .*

The wedding would be in the little community church, with a dinner following at the Davis farm. Because of the time of year and the fact that none of the entertaining could be located in the yard, only the family and special friends were invited to the dinner. Even so, Marty would be hard put to accommodate them all.

Willie's brother's family, the LaHayes, had already taken the stage to catch the train going west. They seemed almost as excited about the plans for their new home as Ellie was about her wedding day. Enough simple furniture had been left behind for Lane to be comfortable as a bachelor. Lane and Ellie had done some shopping on their own and bought a few more pieces. Ellie had hung curtains and scattered rugs and put her dishes in the cupboards. She was finally convinced that Marty was fully capable of caring for herself and the baby, so Ellie would not need to venture over every day to do the tasks for her. She looked forward to being a housewife rather than a housekeeper.

"Wear a warm coat," Marty reminded her daughter. "Thet sun ain't near as warm as it looks."

Who could worry about a coat on such a day? Ellie's expression said. But later she admitted she was glad she had listened to Marty, for indeed the sun was not as warm as it looked, and a cold wind was blowing. Ellie wondered if her carefully groomed hair would be all windblown on the ride to the church.

Clark guided the team of blacks. They were feeling frisky after the long winter of little use, and it took a good horseman to hold them back. Marty was not worried. She had complete confidence in Clark's ability to manage the horses. She held her wee daughter closely against her, making sure Belinda wasn't wrapped so tightly that she would be short of good air to breathe.

It was good to be out in the open and in the brisk air again. Marty wanted to pretend that she could smell spring coming, but in fact she could not. The air was still heavy with winter. *But it won't be long,* Marty promised herself. *Any day now and we will be feeling it.*

Marty could hear another team close behind them and turned to wave to Clare and Kate. Their horses seemed just as eager as Clark's, and Marty couldn't help but imagine what would result if the two menfolk were just to let them go.

When they pulled in to the churchyard, a crowd had already gathered. Impatient teams were tied up to the hitching rails, stomping and champing at the bits. A few were feeding, but most of them ignored the hay that had been dropped before them. They had been eating all winter. Now they simply wished to put an end to their confinement. Marty was sure she knew just how they felt.

Clark helped her carefully down from the high seat and steadied her on her feet before leaving to tie the horses.

Ellie was already on the ground, smoothing her hair and, for the first time, looking a little nervous.

"Ya look just fine," Marty assured her. "Let's go in so ya can get out of thet coat."

They walked the few steps to the church door and stepped inside. The congregation was already seated. Heads turned. Marty could feel many eyes upon them and sensed many smiles. They all seemed to blur before her. She handed Belinda to Kate, who had also entered, and reached to help Ellie with her coat. The gown was not badly wrinkled from the weight of the coat, but Marty spent some time carefully smoothing out the skirt.

"Is my hair all right?" whispered Ellie.

"Just fine. Just fine," answered Marty and brushed at it a bit just to assure the girl.

"I'm so nervous, Mama. I didn't think I would be, but I am."

"Everyone is," Marty whispered back. "It's just part of the ceremony."

Ellie tried to smile at Marty's little joke, but the smile was wobbly and a little crooked.

"Wish Pa would come," she whispered again.

"He'll be here," Marty assured her.

For the moment, Marty had forgotten all about her small daughter, so absorbed was she in the one who stood before her, fearful yet anxious to become a bride. But when she did remember the baby, she turned to look at Kate holding her. Kate stood silently back a pace, holding the tiny Belinda and unwrapping her many blankets. She was rewarded with a fleeting smile, and she hugged the wee baby close.

"Oh, Ma, it's the first time she has smiled for me," she exulted in a whisper to Marty. For just a moment the two women looked at each other, and a lump caught in Marty's throat. She knew Clare and Kate's baby would have been smiling now. Smiling and recognizing her ma and pa. But Kate's gaze with obvious love and care for the little one held no shadow, though her heart must have still been tender over their loss.

Clark and Clare entered, stamping the slush from their boots and brushing off their coats. They shrugged out of their coats and hung them on pegs by the door. Then Clark turned to Ellie.

"Ready, little girl?" he asked softly. Ellie only nodded.

"We'll let Kate an' Clare find 'em a seat first; then I'll sit yer mother."

Kate and Clare moved forward to a pew near the front that had been saved for family. It was then that Marty noticed Kate still holding Belinda.

Clark drew Marty and Ellie close and, with an arm around each of them, led them in a quiet prayer. They lifted their heads, and Ellie dabbed at her eyes with the handkerchief she carried. Marty wiped her eyes, as well, then leaned to give their next-to-last born, their Elvira Davis, one last kiss. In just a few minutes, she would become Elvira Howard, Mrs. Lane Howard. *But,* thought Marty thankfully, *she will always be my daughter, no matter what her name.*

Clark offered Marty his arm and led her to a seat beside Kate. Marty intended to take Belinda back, but when she saw the way Kate looked at the baby, she let Belinda stay where she was. She looked to the front instead and saw a nervous Lane, his eyes fixed on the back of the church as he waited for his bride. Arnie stood beside him, and the young preacher stood before them with an open book.

Maude Colby, Ellie's friend from town, preceded the bride down the aisle. Ellie followed, walking sedately and purposefully on her father's arm. Marty felt such a pride well up within her. Her girl would make a good wife. And Marty couldn't think of anyone she would rather share Ellie with than Lane. Her eyes filled with tears momentarily, but she quickly wiped them away and flashed Kate a little smile.

After the ceremony and the hearty congratulations of family and friends, the wagons and buggies were loaded once again and the eager horses were allowed to run. Ellie, not in the Davis buggy now, had her proper place, tucked in closely beside Lane.

The dinner was a festive affair. In spite of the lack of room, family and neighbors laughed and chatted and ate until they could eat no more. Gifts were presented to the happy bride and groom, and Ellie exclaimed over everything with a great deal of enthusiasm. Lane gave a little speech.

"I will ever bless the day when my boss had the good sense to order me back east to care fer a farm," Lane said amid laughter. "Tell the truth, I wasn't lookin' forward much to bein' a farmer—never havin' been one. Iffen it hadn't been thet I had met Mr. an' Mrs. Davis . . ." Lane stopped and corrected himself, "Ma an' Pa here . . ." More laughter. "Well, iffen I hadn't met 'em an' looked forward to seein' 'em again, I don't s'pose even the boss coulda made a farmer outta me. Boy, what I woulda missed!" exclaimed Lane, his eyes fastened on a blushing Ellie.

Lane became more serious then. "I've got lots to learn yet in life. Lots to learn in the Christian walk, but I've already learned this. Iffen I let God control things, He sure can do a heap better job of it than I ever could. I just have no way of sayin' how thankful I am fer a girl like Ellie . . . how lucky I am to have her fer a wife. I can't express it nohow . . . but I hope to spend my lifetime a tryin' to show her how I feel."

Marty hoped no one saw her slip from the room. She needed a little time to herself. She was happy for Ellie. She wouldn't change things for the world. She just needed a little time to get used to it, that was all.

TWENTY-SIX

Family Dinner

Marty was having a hard time of it trying to convince daughter Ellie that her mother could truly manage without her.

"I might need ya, dear, I might," Marty assured her. "But it ain't to wash the dishes or to git the meals. I can care fer my own house. I haven't felt better fer months. The baby is no problem, an' yer pa fusses over me more'n ever. So it's not yer hands I'm missin', helpful as they are. It's you. Just you. Yer being here and yer company an' all."

"I miss you, too, Mama," Ellie responded, "though I must admit I'm awfully happy where I am."

Marty touched the girl's hair in silent acknowledgment that she understood and accepted the truth of her daughter's words.

"We'll come whenever ya want us to," Ellie promised.

"Then come join the family fer Sunday dinner."

"I'd like thet. I'll come early and help ya git ready."

Marty laughed. "Haven't ya been listenin' to a thing I've been sayin'?" she said, giving Ellie a playful pat on the bottom. "I'm fine. I can fix a dinner fer my family. Honest!"

"All right," said Ellie. "You fix it, an' we girls will do the cleanin' up. Fair?"

Marty laughed again. "Fair," she said and let it go.

"An' while yer a fixin'," said Ellie as she was about to leave, "how 'bout some lemon pie? Seems I haven't had a good one fer ages. I never did git the hang of makin' lemon pie."

"Okay," Marty cheerfully agreed, "lemon pie it is. An', Ellie . . ."

Ellie hesitated, her hand on the door.

"Thanks fer stoppin' by," Marty went on. "I needed a little chat. I've been missin' ya."

"I've missed ya, too," said Ellie, "an' Kate an' Pa an' even Belinda. She's growin' already, Ma. Just look at her."

Marty turned to look at the baby lying contentedly in the crib in the corner of the kitchen. She was playing with her hands and crooning to herself.

"She is, isn't she? She's already got her pa all twisted round those little fingers, I'm a thinkin'."

"Thet weren't a big job," answered Ellie. "He was a pushover the day she arrived."

Marty smiled.

"See ya both on Sunday, then."

Ellie nodded and left the kitchen.

Marty crossed to the window and watched Ellie walk out to the barn, where Clark would hitch up the team to her wagon. Marty went back to the baby, who was dropping off to sleep. "Little girl," she whispered, stroking the soft cheek with one finger, "ya have no idea what a big achin' void yer helpin' to fill."

Sunday came and with it the family. They all followed Clark and Marty's team home from church, making quite a procession. Marty smiled to herself as she thought of the sight they must be making.

The women and children were let off at the house, and the men went on down to the barn to unhitch the animals.

Soon everyone was inside, joshing and joking good-naturedly as they flocked through the kitchen. Marty shooed anyone who wasn't fixing the meal out to other places in the house. The menfolk settled themselves around the fire in the family living room.

The children gathered in the upstairs hall with toys Marty and Clark had fashioned and acquired over the years. All except Tina. She insisted she was now one of the ladies and asked to help set the table. And of course Baby Belinda was too little for the children's play and lay contentedly in her pa's lap in the big, much-used rocker, obviously enjoying the motion of the chair and the solid arms around her.

Arnie cocked an eyebrow at his pa. "Been noticin' yer not as good 'bout sharin' as ya used to be," he remarked.

"Meanin'?" said Clark, frowning slightly.

"Ever'time I see ya, yer a hoggin' thet girl. She belongs to all of us, ya know."

There was laughter around the circle, and Clark reluctantly passed the small baby to Arnie.

He didn't get to keep her for long. From there she went to Josh and then to Clare, and finally Lane even got a chance to hold her. She turned on the charm for each one of them.

"I can see it all now," said Arnie. "Pa's gonna be awful busy guardin' the gate when this one grows up. Boy, ain't she somethin'?"

They all agreed, and Clark looked as if he would pop some buttons.

"Look at thet smile," said Clare. "Ever see so much sweetness in such a little mite?"

The group of men had turned their full attention on the baby, admiring and commenting on every little thing she did. Belinda cooed and squirmed and smiled at all her admirers.

It was not long until they were called to the table. They all took their places rather noisily, but complete silence reigned as Clark led them in a fervent prayer of gratitude to God. In the midst of the prayer, Marty heard a contented gurgle, and when she raised her head she saw that Clark was still holding the baby.

"My goodness," she said to him after the chorus of *amens*, "how ya plannin' on eatin' with the young'un in yer arms?"

"It's a leg I'm missin'—I got me two hands," Clark noted with a grin.

"Well, ya need 'em both fer eatin'." Marty laughed. "My lands, she's gonna be so spoilt she won't be fittin' to live with." Marty got up from her place and took the baby girl.

"I'll hold her," volunteered Arnie quickly.

"She don't need to be held. She'll be perfectly content here in her bed." And Marty bent to lay the baby down.

"Don't seem fair somehow," put in Clare. "All the rest of the family is round the table."

"An' she will be, too—give her time."

"Aw, Grandma," coaxed Tina. "She'll miss what's goin' on."

"I don't think she's gonna miss it thet much," said Marty. "None of the rest of ya ever got so much holdin'."

"That's different," Arnie continued. "There was more babies than big folk then. Now it's been turned round. Lots of people here to hold a young'un now."

Marty looked around the table. "Yeah, lots of big folks, and lookin' round this table, I s'pect thet it could very soon be turned the other way again."

They must have caught her meaning, and Marty noticed a couple at the table exchanging glances and looking a bit sheepish.

"Anybody got anythin' to tell us?" she asked, a twinkle in her eye.

Arnie swallowed hard and looked at Anne. "Well," he said, "we hadn't planned on an announcement just yet, but yeah . . . I reckon we do."

There was laughter and congratulations for the blushing new-lyweds. Marty could feel their joy, but then she thought of poor Kate and a pain went through her. Kate was slowly pushing back her chair and rising to her feet. Marty felt her throat constrict. Poor Kate. It was just too much for her. Too soon. First Belinda and now this. But Kate was not rushing from the room. Instead, she was standing with a hand on Clare's shoulder and a smile on her face. "I'm glad 'bout Arnie and Anne's announcement," she said in a clear, soft voice, "glad fer them and glad because . . . well, I just think it's important fer every child to have a little cousin 'bout his own age."

"Are ya sayin'—?" began Ellie, but Kate stopped her with, "Sure am! Just 'bout the same time as Anne. Doctor just told me fer sure yesterday."

Marty couldn't help the happy tears. She was going to be a grandma again—twice over.

TWENTY-SEVEN

Surprise

Ellie knew Lane really didn't have a whole lot that needed to be done around the farm. The animals had all been either sold or shipped off to the new ranch in the West. There were no fences to fix, no wood to cut, no harness to mend. At first he had enjoyed it since it meant he had lots of time to spend with her, but after a few days of drinking coffee and watching her work around the kitchen, she could tell he was beginning to grow restless. She didn't blame him at all. She was used to being busier herself, and now and then she, too, felt time hanging a bit heavy on her hands. At least she had baking to do, clothes to wash, a house to keep clean, and many little tasks about the home. She tried to think of some ideas for Lane to fill his hours, but nothing presented itself. It was hard for him to just sit around waiting for the farm to sell, she could tell.

"Lane," she ventured one day, "I been thinkin'. We're only a couple of miles outta town. Ya think it would matter any to the LaHayes iffen ya were to take a town job?"

Lane's expression indicated he wondered why he hadn't thought of it. "Don't rightly know what I'm fittin' to do in a town," he said reflectively, "but it sure is worth a try. Would ya mind?"

Ellie smiled to assure him. "I know thet it's hard fer ya not to be busy. An' I don't blame ya one bit. Fact is, I don't think I'd care much to be married to a lazy man. Why don't ya go on in an' make a few inquiries? Ain't a thing more in the world fer ya to do round here."

Lane saddled his horse, kissed his wife good-bye, and rode from the yard.

————

At first it appeared there would be no work for Lane in the small town. The bank needed another man and the town's one tailor said he could sure use some help, but Lane did not have the required experience for either job. He was about to give up and head for home again when the man from the general store waved him down.

"Hear tell yer lookin' fer work."

"Sure am. Willin' to try most anythin'. Ya need a man?"

"Not me, no. I got all the help I need, but I hear thet Matt over to the livery is down sick an' poor ol' Tom is 'bout wearin' hisself out tryin' to keep up with things. Ya might wander on over there an' see iffen he's found somebody yet."

Lane thanked him and turned his horse to the livery stable. Funny that he hadn't thought to try it first off, since he sure knew about horses.

The man was right. Old Tom did want another man, and Lane started in right away on his *town* job.

The chance to work not only helped put Lane in a much better frame of mind concerning himself, but it enabled him and Ellie to begin to tuck away a little money week by week, as well. They both felt good about it, and when Lane would ride in at night, tired from lifting feed sacks and grooming horses, Ellie was there waiting for him with a warm fire and fresh-baked bread. Their marriage prospered under such an arrangement.

————

One day as Ellie matched socks from the day's washing and waited for Lane to return for supper, she heard Rex barking. The sound of his bark told Ellie that someone had arrived. It wasn't Lane, she knew, and it wasn't one of her family. Rex barked as though the visitor was a stranger.

She hurried to the window and saw a tall man in a long, dark coat tying his horse to the hitching rail. Ellie had never seen the man before. "Maybe it's a buyer fer the farm," she mused and hoped with all her heart that it might be so.

She answered the knock and greeted the man cordially.

"I understand Lane Howard lives here."

"Thet's right," said Ellie. "I'm Mrs. Howard."

"Is Mr. Howard in?"

"Not at the moment. He works in town, but I'm expectin' 'im home 'fore long."

"Mind if I wait for him?" the man asked, and Ellie wasn't sure for a moment if she minded or not.

"I'll just wait out here if it's all right."

"Ya needn't do thet!" exclaimed Ellie, chiding herself for hesitating. "Ya can come on in an' have a cup of coffee while ya wait."

The man did not refuse and followed Ellie into the small kitchen. Ellie pushed the coffeepot she had in readiness for Lane's supper onto the heat and nodded at a chair.

"Just sit ya down," she offered. "He should be home most any minute."

She looked at the man. His clothes were different from what the farmers round about wore, she noticed. And he didn't really dress like the men from town, either. He must be from the city, she concluded. If he came about the farm, he must be coming on behalf of someone else. He didn't look like a farmer.

She decided to ask, but before she could speak, the man spoke to her.

"Nice farm here," he commented. "Well kept."

"First-rate," agreed Ellie, ready to give an honest sales pitch. "There's been lots of time an' money put in on it. It's in real good shape."

"Didn't see much stock about."

"Stock's all been sold right now. But it has good pastureland an' plenty of barn room. Barns fer cows, with good milk stalls, lots of pigpens, a real fine horse barn thet holds eight head, big chicken coop, five granaries . . . or is it six? . . . no, five, I think. Even got a root cellar an' a real good well."

The man looked just a shade puzzled, but Ellie hurried on. "Lots of good crop land, too. Had a first-rate stand of barley last year, and the lower field had a hay crop like I've never seen afore . . . an' thet field out back, the one ya can't see too well from the road—" Ellie caught herself. " 'Course ya can't see any of the fields too well just by ridin' on by 'cause of the snow, but it'll soon be ready fer workin'. Folks hereabouts say they expect an early spring this year. Some of the farmers are already gittin' their seed ready to plant."

"Interesting," the man said, but he really didn't look much interested.

"There's a good garden plot, too," Ellie continued, since it was at least something to talk about. She reached for a cup to fill with coffee for the stranger. "Even got a few fruit trees. Pa says thet apples would do real good here, but no one's gotten round to plantin' 'em yet."

"You just buy the farm recently?" asked the man as Ellie returned to the stove.

Ellie stopped in midstride. "Us?" she said. "Oh no, it's still fer sale," she hurried to explain. "We're just livin' here till it sells. The LaHayes already moved on out west an' left us to care fer the place till someone buys it. We're goin' west, too, as soon—" Ellie stopped herself. Now, that didn't sound good. The man might think something was wrong with the farm with everyone moving away.

"Not thet we wouldn't like to buy the farm ourselves, but my husband really prefers ranchin'. An' 'sides, we don't have the money thet it takes to buy a farm. Takes a heap of money to git started farmin' nowadays." That didn't sound good, either. Might scare a body off.

"One soon is able to make it back, though, on a good farm—an' this is a good farm," she hurried on, but then she decided she'd said enough. Whatever the man was here for, she didn't want something she said to give the wrong impression.

The man said nothing, and Ellie placed a steaming cup of coffee in front of him.

She checked the biscuits in the oven and stirred the vegetables. They were ready. She hoped that Lane wouldn't be too late.

The silence now hung heavy between them. The man didn't seem too inclined toward conversation. In fact, he seemed rather impatient and kept drumming his fingers on the table, an irritating thing to Ellie. At last Ellie heard Rex bark again, and this time she could tell it was Lane who was approaching. She heaved a big sigh of relief and glanced across at the close-lipped stranger.

"Thet's my husband now," she said. "He'll be in as soon as he cares fer the horse."

The man grunted his approval. Ellie was about to start dishing up the supper but changed her mind. She'd better hold off for a few minutes while the man had his talk with Lane about the farm. Somehow, Ellie didn't expect the stranger to accept an invitation to join them at the table.

Lane came in with a puzzled look on his face.

"Lane, this is . . . is . . . I'm sorry, sir. I didn't even ask yer name."

"Peters," said the man, extending his hand to Lane and rising to his feet.

"My husband," finished Ellie lamely.

"Mr. Peters," said Lane, shaking the hand. "I believe I had the pleasure of rentin' ya a horse a little earlier."

Mr. Peters seemed taken aback. "To be sure," he said, looking more closely at Lane. "If I'd known whom I was talking to, I could have saved myself this trip. I was told that you lived on the farm."

"We do," said Lane good-naturedly, "but there's nothin' to do hereabouts right now. All the stock's been sold. We have one horse an' one dog. Don't keep a man very busy. We are just here till—"

Mr. Peters stopped him with an impatient gesture. "Your wife explained," he said hurriedly.

"Please," said Lane, "sit yerself back down an' tell me how I can help ya."

He's here 'bout the farm, Ellie started to say, but she decided she wasn't sure about that anymore.

"The matter is a private one," said Mr. Peters, pulling forth a small case that Ellie had not noticed when he had arrived.

Lane looked surprised.

"Well, I guess we are 'bout as private as we can git," he responded.

Mr. Peters cast a glance toward Ellie.

"Nothin' is so private as to exclude my wife, sir," Lane said firmly.

Mr. Peters said nothing but opened up his case and spread some papers out before him.

He pulled a small pair of spectacles from his pocket and balanced them on the end of his nose. Then he cleared his throat and said, "I understand that you are Lane Howard."

"Thet's correct."

"Who is your father, Mr. Howard?"

"Well, I . . . I don't have a father. Thet is, he died when I was five years old."

"And his name?"

"His name? His name was . . . ah . . . Will. They called him Will. His real name was William. William Clayton Howard."

"And your mother? Where is she?"

"She died only one week after. She'd been hurt in the same storm."

"And her name?"

"Rebecca. Rebecca Marie."

"Who raised you?" asked the man.

"An aunt. A maiden aunt. Her name was Aunt Maggie. Ah . . . Margery. Margery Thom."

"Is she living?"

"No, sir. I heard 'bout four or five years ago thet she had passed on."

"So you weren't with her when she died?"

"No. I left when I was fourteen."

"Why?"

"Why? 'Cause I wanted to. I didn't feel thet I should stay."

"Were you told to leave?"

Lane looked a bit annoyed. " 'Course not."

"What were the circumstances?"

"The what?"

"The circumstances. Why did you go if you weren't told to leave?"

"My aunt married. She was older. Had never married before. People round town said it was gonna be hard fer her to adjust to bein' married. They also said it would be even harder with me there to . . . to . . ."

"Folks said that?"

"Well, they didn't say it right to me. They didn't know when I overheard 'em. But I did."

Ellie felt rather unsettled. Why in the world all the strange questions? Why should this man come in from nowhere and begin to ask her husband things concerning his past? Things he had shared only with her.

"What about the man? Your aunt's new husband?" the questioner went on.

"What 'bout 'im? He was a businessman in the town. Well established. He was an undertaker."

"Were you afraid of him?"

"Afraid? No. He had never been anythin' but kind to me."

"Did he have a family?"

"No. He had never married before, either."

"But you didn't think you wanted to live with him—or with your aunt—after she married him?"

"It wasn't like thet. I hated to leave. I cried all the way to the train station, iffen ya must know. It was just thet I loved Aunt Maggie. She had been so kind to me, an' I wanted her to be happy in her new marriage."

Ellie thought she heard the stranger mutter something about busybody tongues, but she wasn't sure.

"Did you keep in touch?" he went on.

"Till she died, I did. My last letter was returned to me marked 'Deceased.'"

"I see," said the man, adjusting his odd glasses.

"I'm sorry, sir, but I really don't understand what this is all 'bout," said Lane. "Now, I got nothin' in my past I want to hide, but it does seem a bit unusual thet a total stranger would walk into my house and put so many private questions to me."

"I understand how you must feel," said the man, removing his glasses just a moment before they surely would have fallen. "But one cannot be too careful, and I do need to be entirely sure that you are the Lane Howard I am looking for."

"Lookin' fer?" puzzled Lane, and Ellie moved a step closer and put her hand on the back of his neck.

"You didn't mention the name of the man your aunt married," said the persistent man at the table, placing his glasses back on his nose once more.

"It was Myers. Conwyn Myers."

"Did you keep in touch with Mr. Myers at all?"

"Not really. My aunt often wrote of him, and I sent my greetings through my letters to her."

"I see," said the man. Then, "One more thing, Mr. Howard. What is your full name?"

"It's William. William Lane Howard. William from my pa. They called me by Lane so thet it wouldn't be confusin'."

"Well," said the man, shuffling through his papers, "everything seems to match."

"Match to what?" asked Lane. "I do wish, sir, thet you'd be so kind as to explain yer presence an' questions."

"Yes," said the man, "I do believe that I am free to do so."

Ellie and Lane exchanged glances.

"I am Stavely Peters," said the man, emphasizing each of his words carefully. "Stavely Peters, attorney-at-law. I am here representing the estate of the late Conwyn Myers. Mr. Myers was a well-respected and good businessman. He left everything in very good order . . . and . . . he left everything to you."

Lane slowly rose to his feet, shaking his head in bewilderment.

"He left it all to you, Mr. Howard. You were the closest of kin that he had, and he also knew just how special you were to his wife, Margery."

"But I . . . I . . ." Lane stood there with Ellie clinging to his arm. "I'm much obliged . . . to be sure," Lane stumbled over the words, "but . . . but beggin' yer pardon, what would I do with a funeral parlor?"

"He sold the funeral parlor. Sold the house, too. Said that by the sound of your letters, you loved the West and would never want to leave it."

"Oh, he's right. I don't," Lane assured the man.

"Everything that he leaves you is in cash. I have the note right here. All that needs to be done is for you to sign a few papers and then for us to visit your bank together."

"My bank," laughed Lane. "I've never had me the need fer a bank in all my life."

"Well, I'd advise you to become established with one now," said the lawyer. "It's a bit too much money to tuck in the toe of your boot." This was the closest to humor that the man had come.

"Yes, sir," promised Lane. "I certainly will, sir. Right away in the mornin'."

"I stopped by the bank on my way here and made arrangements to have it taken care of tonight. They are most anxious to have your account, I might add, Mr. Howard, and will be more than accommodating, I am sure. I am anxious to have the matter settled and to be on my way back to the city. I will confess that it has taken me much longer than I had hoped to locate you and get the estate finalized."

"I'll git my horse right away," Lane said, looking like he didn't know what had hit him.

He turned to Ellie. "Will ya be okay till I git back?" he asked her.

She clung to him for a moment. "I will iffen I don't burst," she whispered. "Oh, Lane, can ya believe it?"

Lane put her from him gently and gave her a big grin. He reached for his coat.

"I'll hurry," he promised. "I'll hurry as fast as I can. Then we'll talk all 'bout it when I git home."

He kissed her and hurried after the city lawyer.

Ellie turned back to the stove to cover the pots. Who could tell when—or if—they ever would get around to eating their meal?

TWENTY-EIGHT

Plans

"What are we ever goin' to *do* with it all?" Ellie asked when Lane returned and showed her the figure on the bank paper in his hand.

To Ellie it had seemed to take forever for Lane to return to the farm, but, in truth, the transaction had taken place very quickly. The lawyer had been right. The town banker was most anxious to be of every assistance in order to be assured of handling Lane's account. Both banker and lawyer were in a hurry to get the matter finalized.

Lane could not believe his eyes when he was shown the amount of the bank note. There it was. The large sum of money was placed securely in the bank under his name.

"I been thinkin' an' thinkin' all the way home," Lane answered Ellie's question. "There's just no end to what we can do."

"I'll git my own sewin' machine," Ellie began enthusiastically.

"Ya can have two of 'em iffen ya want to," promised Lane, and Ellie laughed.

"An' I'm gonna git those new shoes I saw in Harder's window."

"New shoes? Thet's nothin'. Won't even make a dent in the money."

"Oh, Lane. I can't believe it. I just can't believe it!"

"Nor can I. It all seems like some strange dream."

Lane pulled Ellie down on his lap and pressed his face against her fragrant hair. "The best part of the dream," he said, "is thet now I can give ya the things I wanted to . . . the things ya deserve. I was so scared thet I'd never—"

"Did I ask fer things?" Ellie scolded gently, running her fingers through his hair. "All I really wanted was you, an' ya know it."

Lane pulled her close and kissed her firmly. "I know it," he whispered. "I know it, an' thet's what makes our love so special."

"Oh, Lane, there's so much we could plan, so much to talk about—but we'd better eat this food, don't ya think?" Ellie reminded him, pulling herself free. "Even iffen we don't feel like it, we'd better eat. Thet is, if it's still fit to eat."

They began to eat their overcooked meal, but neither of them really tasted it. There was too much to think about . . . to dream of. It seemed the possibilities were endless. They talked and laughed as they ate and as Ellie cleared the table. They talked as they washed and dried the dishes together and on into the evening until bedtime. There was just so much to discuss with this un-expected turn of events.

"Ya know one thing thet I'd like to do?" asked Ellie as they lay snuggled together under the warm quilts of their bed.

"What?"

"I'd like to git an organ fer the church. Just a little organ—but a nice organ. Do ya think we could?"

"Why not? I think it's a great idea. I've been thinkin' 'bout what we could do special like fer the church—both this church an' our little church out west. Hadn't thought me of an organ, but thet sounds like a first-rate idea."

"Let's, then!" exclaimed Ellie.

Lane kissed her on the ear.

"Ya know what I was thinkin'?" he asked her.

"What?"

"We have the money to buy the farm."

"What farm?"

"*This* farm."

"Us? Why?"

"Why? Then ya won't need to leave. You'll be here, near yer ma, just like ya wanted an'—"

"But, Lane," Ellie protested, "ya don't want to farm. Ya want to ranch."

"I know, but I wouldn't mind. I'll—"

"No, ya won't. I'd never let ya. Never, Lane."

"But—"

"Listen! Mama is all prepared to let me go. It'll be hard fer her, sure, but she'll make it. She wouldn't want us to change our plans just fer her. She would be unhappy iffen she thought I was unhappy, an' I could never be happy iffen I wasn't sure thet *you* were happy—don't ya see?"

"But I could be happy, as long as I was makin' you happy."

"I wouldn't let ya do it. You've always wanted to ranch. Now ya can have a ranch of yer own. Not just a little spread to git by on, but a real ranch—one ya can be proud of. An' someday . . . someday maybe you'll even be as blessed as Willie an' have some sons to take it over after ya."

Ellie felt Lane pull her closer and kiss her hair. Then she could feel the tears on his cheeks in the darkness.

Everyone rejoiced with Lane and Ellie over their good fortune. Ellie began in earnest to prepare for their move. She was more anxious than ever now. She couldn't wait to see Lane's West, to share in purchasing a ranch and establishing a home—their home. She couldn't wait to see Missie and to once again be near to her older sister. Though they were born to different mothers, their Ma Marty had been truly a mother to them both, and they felt very close in heart, though the miles now separated them. Daily Ellie prayed that the farm might hurry and sell so they could be on their way. April passed and May came. With the warmer winds, the snow had disappeared, even in the shadowed places. Ellie fancied that soon she would be smelling spring flowers, and then the farm would sell, she was sure.

Lane continued to work in town. He still needed the activity, he said. And he and Ellie secretly slipped the extra money into the Sunday collection plate for the use of the young preacher. He needed it worse than they did, they were sure. The organ had been ordered, and there was great anticipation over its arrival. Lane and Ellie had also laid aside, in the preacher's care and keeping, a sizable amount to be spent in the years ahead as the church saw the need.

Ellie was restless each day as she waited for Lane to come home. Signs had been posted in the town that if anyone was interested in the LaHaye farm, they were to go to the local livery and talk to Lane Howard. There had been a few inquiries but none of a serious nature.

Then one day Lane came home long before his usual time.

"Yer early," said Ellie, a question in her statement as he poked his head in the door.

"Aren't ya glad to see me?" he teased.

"'Course, but supper isn't ready."

He pulled her to him and kissed her. "Fergit supper," he said. "I have some news."

"Good news?" she inquired.

"I think so."

"Then share it."

"I quit my job."

Ellie looked puzzled. "Ya quit yer job! Thet's fine. I'm not complainin' none . . . but . . . why is it such good news?"

"'Cause . . . I quit my job so I'd have time to git ready to go on home."

"Home?"

"We're free to go now. A man bought the LaHaye farm today."

Ellie threw herself into his arms. "Oh, Lane!" she squealed. "Lane, thet's wonderful!"

He picked her up and swung her around the room. "Thet's

what I think!" he shouted back at her. "Finally—we are really on our way."

Marty and Clark both knew how eager Lane and Ellie were to be off to start their own home. So they rejoiced with the couple and welcomed the news of the farm's sale. It was a happy time and a sad time, and the Davis tribe gathered together to celebrate the occasion and to prepare for another good-bye. There was much excited talk around the table. Lane had already made arrangements for their train tickets. There wasn't much packing left to be done. Ellie had already carefully boxed everything she could spare, and Lane had crated it for shipment. In just a few short days they would be on their way.

Ellie was disappointed that she wouldn't be able to see Clae and Luke before she left.

"Who knows how long it will be 'fore I see 'em again?" she mourned, and tears filled her eyes that just moments before had been full of anticipation.

"Maybe Luke can pay us a visit when he finishes his trainin'," Lane said in a comforting tone.

Ellie agreed wholeheartedly, but Marty inwardly stated, *Not on your life. Don't want* Luke *staying out there, too.*

Marty remembered back to another girl, just as eager to set out for the West. She'd had to let that daughter—her Missie—go, too.

Belinda cried. Ten people stood to go to her, but Marty waved them all back to their chairs.

"I'll go," she said. "She might be wantin' to eat."

Belinda was not hungry. Only bored. Bored and in need of a dry diaper. She hated to be wet and would not bear it for long.

Marty changed her, glad for the excuse to leave the family gathering for a few minutes. She held the wee baby close and laid her cheek against the soft little head. "I'm so glad thet God was wise enough to send ya to me," she whispered. "Only *He* knew how much I would be needin' ya."

The baby grasped a tendril of her mother's hair and tried to pull it to her mouth.

"Quit it, ya hear?" reproached Marty softly. "You'll have yer fingers all tangled with it. There are better things to be eatin', I'm thinkin'."

The baby gurgled and changed her grip to the collar of Marty's dress. Marty kissed her. It seemed like only yesterday she had held the tiny Ellie in her arms, and here Ellie was on the verge of leaving.

Again Marty studied Belinda. "Well, I still have you," she whispered. "An' no matter how quickly time seems to fly, it will be some time 'fore *you* will be goin'. An' 'fore we know it, Luke will be home, too. Oh, not home to stay. Don't s'pose he'll ever be home to stay again. Not really. But at least he'll be close enough to drop in now an' then, I'm prayin'. Close enough thet I can see fer myself just how he's doin'."

She kissed the baby again and settled her on a hip for the walk downstairs. She was ready to rejoin the others now.

———

On the day of Ellie and Lane's departure, they gathered at the stage station as they had done in the past.

Marty managed her emotions that day very well, she thought. In fact, she managed to hide her tears and even celebrate the occasion with Ellie.

"It's a long, long ride," she warned Ellie. "I thought me at times it would never end. Ya do eventually git there, but by then you'll have had yer fill of train travel fer a while." Ellie only smiled.

"Have ya got the package fer Missie?" Marty asked for the fifth time.

"Right here, Mama. Right here with the other things. I will see thet she gits it just as soon as we arrive."

"Ya sure ya got everythin' ya need?" This was Clark.

"Oh, Pa," laughed Ellie, "they have shops out there, too."

It was not long until their baggage was being loaded. The crated Rex complained some at his close quarters, but Lane rubbed his ear and assured him that he would be taken for a walk at every chance they got.

Ellie, who was holding Belinda until the last possible moment, bent her head to kiss the wee girl. "Know what I'm gonna miss the most?" she whispered. "Watchin' ya grow up." Then the tears were falling freely, and Marty reached out to draw Ellie and Belinda close.

The driver was soon climbing aboard and lifting the reins of the teams. The livery man held the horses' heads and tried to quiet them, but they had been trained to run and were eager to be off.

There were hurried last-minute hugs and kisses, and then Ellie and Lane were climbing into the stage. It wheeled off in a swirl of dust. Marty pulled out her handkerchief to wave the dust from her face and dry her eyes.

They all turned back to their teams; no need to linger longer. Ellie was gone now. She was on her way to her dreams, and the rest of them were left behind to carry on dreams of their own.

On the way home from town, Marty raised her head and took a careful look at the world about her.

"I like it here, don't you?" she asked Clark.

"Sure do," he answered comfortably and seemed to feel that his simple words said it all.

"I don't really think I'm hankerin' fer the West, do you?"

"Nope."

They rode on in silence for a while.

"We still have Nandry an' Clare an' Arnie here. An' Luke will be back, too. An' maybe someday even Clae an' Joe will be back."

"Yeah," said Clark, "maybe so."

"Thet's more'n half of 'em," continued Marty. "Thet's pretty good, huh?"

"Thet's real good—an' ya even fergot one."

Marty looked puzzled for a moment and then remembered the bundle of joy in her arms.

"Well, I did at thet. No offense, Belinda," she said, lifting the small baby and kissing her cheek.

"I guess Belinda will fergive ya—this once," teased Clark.

Marty fell silent again. She breathed deeply of the warming air. She loved the spring. There was always something so promising about it.

"Just think, Clark. 'Fore we know it, we'll have two new grandchildren, too."

Clark grinned.

"Best part of it is," went on Marty, "they'll be right here where we can enjoy 'em."

Clark agreed.

Marty looked about her. There was a nice green haze on the pastures. Leaves were beginning to open on the trees near the road. The blue sky looked as though it was willing strength to the green things to hurry and break free and come forth.

"Almost gardenin' time," mused Marty.

"Yup," said Clark, taking a deep breath.

"Ya gonna help me this year?" It was said with teasing, and they both knew she was referring back many years when he had helped a very young Marty with her first attempt at a garden.

"Will ya let me?" he teased back.

"Iffen yer good."

They both laughed.

"My, Clark," she said after a few moments had passed, "but don't thet first garden of mine seem like a long time ago?"

He looked at her, his eyes searching deep into hers. Then he reached over and took her free hand in his.

"Does it?" he asked. "Seems to me thet it weren't all thet far from yesterday."

TWENTY-NINE

The Legacy

Baby Belinda had been fed for the night. Marty and Clark lay with her between them, spending some time admiring the perfection of the tiny baby before they would tuck her into her own bed for the night. She hadn't fallen asleep yet and lay studying the faces she had learned to love. One of her hands firmly clasped a finger on her father's hand. The other tiny baby fist was knotted in the front of Marty's gown. And so she held them both. Not just with childish fingers, Marty thought, but with cords of love.

As Marty gazed at the baby lying between them, she thought again of Ellie. So much had happened to Ellie in such a short time.

"It's really somethin', ain't it?" she murmured. "I still find it hard to believe. It sounds like somethin' you'd read in a fairy tale or somethin'. Who would have thought any of ours would be left a legacy?"

"An' one of such size, too," agreed Clark. "Oh, true, Lane ain't startin' off a millionaire, but he sure has 'im a better start than a lot of young men."

"I trust 'im with it, though," said Marty. "It won't go to his head none. He'll be responsible and givin', and he'll put the money to good use."

"I been thinkin' a lot on legacies lately," Clark said, brushing one of Belinda's curls between his fingers.

"Like what?"

"Well, the kinds of legacies one can leave behind."

"Kinds?"

"Well, there's the money kind. Everyone is familiar with thet. Not thet we all git one, mind ya—but at least ya hear of one now an' then, like happened with Lane."

Marty nodded in agreement.

"But there's other kinds, too."

Marty waited for him to go on. Belinda let go of her grasp on the gown and waved a hand that hit Marty lightly on the chin. Marty caught the small fist and put it to her lips.

"Take this here little one now—we gotta plan what we're gonna be leavin' her with. An' I'm not talkin' money in the bank. I'm talkin' character—faith . . . love fer others . . . an unselfish spirit . . . independence . . . maturity."

Marty knew where Clark's thoughts were leading them. She nodded silently.

"We've got a big job ahead of us, Marty. It'll be fun—but there will be work and care there, too."

"I was thinkin' the other day," admitted Marty, "here I go again! The diapers, the fevers, the teeth, the potty trainin'. Oh, Clark. There's so much ahead of us."

"Then it will be school, an' teachin' chores, an' friendships, an' 'fore we know it—beaus!" said Clark.

"It's kinda scary," Marty whispered.

"Scary?" laughed Clark. "Maybe. It'd be even more scary iffen we didn't have some pretty good examples before us."

"Examples?"

"Our other kids. Not a rotten apple in the bunch."

Marty smiled, thinking of each one of their family.

"Sometimes I feel so proud of 'em," she admitted.

"Me too," he agreed with her. "Me too."

"Like Kate an' Clare. I was so afraid. So afraid they wouldn't be able to handle losin' thet baby. They wanted it so much, Clark. So very much. Yet not a trace of bitterness. They truly took it like real . . . real mature Christians. They even seemed to grow sweeter an' . . . an' wiser. I was so proud of 'em.

"An' Ellie," Marty went on. "The way she just stepped in an' took over when Nandry was havin' her hard time an' showed her where she was wrong without pointin' fingers or causin' hurt. Ya shoulda heard her, Clark. You'd have been so pleased.

"An' Nandry, too. I had me no idea she was carryin' all thet load of bitterness from the time she was a little girl. An' yet, when she saw her wrong, she . . . she just asked the Lord fer His fergiveness."

Clark swung his daughter up into the air and then laid her on his chest. "Yep, little one, yer gonna have to learn 'bout fergiveness, too." Belinda just stuck her thumb in her mouth and laid her head down against her pa.

"Then there's Arnie," Marty continued. "At his age, an' already a deacon in the church, an' a good one, too. An' Clae an' Joe servin' in a church, an' Missie an' Willie startin' a church out there in their own home, an' our Luke studyin' to be a doctor.

"Ya know," she said thoughtfully and with a smile, "yer right, Clark. There ain't a rotten apple in the whole bunch."

"*Luke*. I'm thinkin' we chose his name well."

"Meanin'?"

"Luke. Luke the physician."

"Never thought on thet before. Guess we did name 'im well, didn't we?"

Belinda lifted her head and reached for Clark's nose with her wet little hand. He chuckled and adjusted her to better see her in the light.

"I'm afraid yer goin' to spoil her with all yer fussin'," scolded Marty.

"Spoil her?"

"She gits held an' rocked an' cuddled so much she'll git to think thet it's all thet her pa's got to do."

"I did it with all the others, too, an' you yerself just agreed there ain't a bad one in the whole bunch," Clark reminded her.

Marty smiled. It was true. He had given a lot of love and attention to each one of the babies.

Clark turned serious. "What did we do right, Marty?"

"Is it important?"

"I think so. We've got Belinda here. We can't afford to go wrong on this one, Marty." Clark kissed his baby on her forehead.

Marty thought in silence for a moment. "Fact is," she finally said, "I don't rightly know what we did right. We made mistakes— I know I did. Lots of 'em. God knows we tried to do what was right. Maybe thet's what He honored—our tryin'."

"Lots of parents try . . . an' fail," Clark reminded her.

It was a sobering thought and one that Marty knew was true.

"We need faith, Clark," she said softly. "We need to really hang on in faith. God didn't fail us before—we need to trust 'im with Belinda, too."

"Trust 'im," echoed Clark. "Trust God—an' work an' spank an' train an' pray like we had it all to do on our own."

"Guess it all has somethin' to do with thet legacy ya were talkin' 'bout. So much depends upon what we leave our children—not to 'em, but within 'em."

"Wish it was as simple as passin' on the family heirlooms."

"Meanin'?"

"Ya don't just pass on faith. Ya have to pass on a desire fer 'em to find a faith of their own. Ya have to show 'em daily in the way ya live thet what ya have is worth livin' an' fightin' an' workin' fer. A secondhand faith is no good to anyone. It has to be a faith of their own."

"Thet's the secret," Marty agreed with feeling. "A faith of their own. I am so thankful to God thet each one of our children made their own decision to let God be in charge in their life."

"An' it doesn't stop there—it goes on an' on. They teach an' train our grandchildren, an' with God's help, they can teach our great-grandchildren. It can go on an' on, an' never end till Jesus comes back," added Clark.

Marty smiled. "It's a mighty big thought," she said. She reached out a hand to touch the head of the baby Clark was holding. Their baby. "An' to think it all starts with a little bundle thet God himself dares to trust us with."

"No," said Clark, and his words were carefully weighed. "It starts long 'fore thet. It starts with a Father who loved us enough to send His Son. It starts with a man an' a woman determined to follow His ways. It starts when two people are willin' to give a child back to the Lord. It starts with all thet—but there never needs to be an end to it. It's the kind of legacy thet truly lasts."

Be the first to know

Want to be the first to know
what's new from
your favorite authors?

Want to know all about
exciting new writers?

Sign up for BethanyHouse newsletters at
www.bethanynewsletters.com
and you'll get regular updates via e-mail.
You can sign up for as many authors or
categories as you want so you get only
the information you really want.

Sign up today